Praise for The Best Girls Series

"If you enjoy a rollicking good romance story, you'll love Best Dating Rules as much as I did."
          Carol Marrs Phipps, Author
          The Heart of the Staff Series

"The line between smut and puritanism has rarely been tweaked so enchantingly, with just the right amount of yearning and heat applied in all the right places that makes the Best Girls books suitable for young-hearted romantics of any age."
          Jan Hawke, Author
          Milele Safari: An Eternal Journey

"Dearen elicits laughter, gasps and even tears. The emotion which she imbues to her characters is enchanting."
          Scotty Shepherd

Books by Tamie Dearen

Sweet Romance

The Best Girls Series:
The Best is Yet to Come
Her Best Match
Best Dating Rules
Best Foot Forward
Best Laid Plans
Best Intentions

Sweet Romance

A Rose in Bloom

Christian Romance

Noelle's Golden Christmas
Haley's Hangdog Holiday

The Alora Series
YA/Fantasy

Alora: The Wander-Jewel
Alora: The Portal
Alora: The Maladorn Scroll

Best Foot Forward

Toni Dean

The characters and events portrayed in this book are fictitious. Any similarity to real persons, living or dead is coincidental and not intended by the author. To the extent any real names of individuals, locations, businesses or organizations are included in the book, they are used fictitiously and not intended to be taken otherwise.

by Tamie Dearen

All rights reserved. Except as permitted under the U.S. Copyright Act of 1976, no part of this publication may be reproduced, distributed, or transmitted in any form or by any means now known or hereafter invented, or stored in a database or retrieval system, without the prior written permission of the author.

Copyright © 2014 Tamie Dearen

ISBN-13: 978-1975846282
ISBN-10: 1975846281

Best Foot Forward
The Best Girls Series
Book Three

By
Tamie Dearen

Acknowledgements

Undying thanks to all my early readers: Nancy, Heidi, Avery, Alyssa, Holli, Wesley, Scotty, and Janna. Your encouragement kept me going, and some of you even took the time to mark mistakes for me. Thanks for being patient with my writing obsession. And most of all, I need to thank my sweet husband, Bruce, who calls himself a writer's widow. He inspired me with romance, acted as primary reader and consultant, and battled jealousy as I spent endless hours, late into the night, in an intimate affair… with my computer.

Special Thanks

Writing can be lonely, but great supporters make it all worthwhile. Some supporters went out of their way to help spread the news about *The Best Girls Series*. A special thanks goes out to all of these great people who helped make this happen: Ramona Moore, Scotty Shepherd, Wesley Daniels, Donna Read Peace, Ashley Longoria, Katy Kornegay, Marsha Herron, Callie Ann Haas, Ellen Berggren, Donna Burkett, and Emily Seawright. You rock!

Chapter One

HORATIO WAS IN LOVE WITH GRACE MARSHALL. And he was determined to marry her. She was perfect in almost every way. She was beautiful, with shoulder-length thick, wavy brown hair and huge hazel eyes that twinkled when she laughed... which was almost all the time. She was always in a good mood. No matter what the weather was like, no matter what anyone did, no matter what anyone said, she always laughed. Nothing seemed to bring her down. When she walked into a room, it was like the sun had appeared from behind the clouds. She was almost perfect, except for her being a little too tall.

But Horatio knew her height wouldn't be a problem for long. He was growing fast, and his big brother was really tall. Horatio was already the tallest kid in Ms. Marshall's first grade class—well, almost the tallest. Madison and Ariel were taller than him, but they didn't count since they were girls. And Ms. Marshall liked Horatio a lot. She had told him how special he was, and she always got excited when he drew her a new picture. And when he got his new shoes, she'd really liked them. He couldn't wait to show her his loose tooth.

"Look, Ms. Marshall! Look! Do you see?" He opened his mouth wide and twisted the tooth to demonstrate how wiggly it was.

"Oh!" cried Grace at the sight of the bloody tooth. She turned her head and swallowed at the queasy feeling that surged in her stomach. "That's really great, Horatio," she said, hoping her face wasn't as green as she felt. She'd always had a problem with blood, but she'd hidden the malady from everyone she knew. Even her own family had no idea how nauseous she became at the sight of a single drop of the red oozing liquid. She certainly couldn't reveal any sign of that particular weakness around her first graders. They'd be certain to plague her with cuts, scratches, and bloody noses at every opportunity.

"I get to put it under my pillow, and I get money for it," said Horatio. "I'll buy you something with my money. What would you like?"

"Horatio, that's so sweet. But I don't want you to spend your money on me. You should buy something for yourself or for someone in your family."

"But I want to buy you something." His lower lip began to tremble.

"The best present you could get me would be another one of your pictures," she said, giving his hand a squeeze.

"Ms. Marshall," said another little boy standing close by. "I have a loose tooth, too. You wanna see?"

"No thank you, Jeffrey. I need all of you to go get your backpacks right now. It's almost time to go." Grace surveyed her noisy class—five girls and thirteen rambunctious boys. She'd only made it through one week, and she could tell this would be a long school year. Now it was Friday night, and she ought to be looking forward to an evening of fun. But tonight would be anything but pleasant. Ever since the week before when Brad mentioned the idea of love and marriage, she'd known she had to break off their relationship. It was wrong for her to keep stringing him along as if her feelings were as serious as his. She had to do the right thing.

*****

Brad had a sick feeling in his gut, and he didn't think he'd caught the stomach virus he'd diagnosed at least forty times in the hospital emergency room earlier in the day. No, this uneasy mood started after his earlier phone conversation with Grace. It was Friday night and he was waiting for her to show up at his apartment, fighting against a sense of impending doom. She'd been acting strangely for the past week, ever since they'd had an almost-define-the-relationship talk and he'd used that four-letter L-word.

He'd dated a lot of girls, but Grace was special. He still remembered the first time he laid eyes on her on a hiking trail with her three tall-and-lanky sisters and two girlfriends towering over her five-foot-two frame. She was tiny, but her personality was huge. She was the boss, and she knew it. She was cute and fun with boundless energy and a contagious enthusiasm for life. He fell for her the first time she winked at him with her gorgeous hazel eyes. And somehow he knew he had to tread carefully to keep her.

In fact her sister, Olivia, had pulled him aside one night at the weekly Marshall family Sunday dinner to warn him he would face a challenge if he didn't want to be thrown out in the cold. Evidently, Grace had a track record of dating one guy for a short time before dumping him and moving on to another. Olivia offered no explanation other than possibly a short attention span.

But Brad was determined not to become another statistic in Grace's dating life. He went to a lot of trouble to treat her the way he thought she deserved to be treated. He was very careful not to pressure her physically, although she was really hard to resist with such an amazing body. It was all he could do to keep his hands from straying below her neck, but something had told him *that* would be a death sentence.

The doorbell rang and his heart skipped a beat. Maybe it was all in his head. Maybe everything would be fine. Maybe he wasn't going to have his heart cut out and handed to him on a platter. But when he grabbed the knob to open the door, a chill ran right up his arm and into his spine. He shivered as the door opened and Grace swept into the room.

Grace had always enjoyed being in charge. She never let her small stature hold her back from wielding her influence, and she wielded it with an iron fist. She lorded her way over her three younger sisters and even her older brother. When she was on a rampage she always got her way. She learned a long time ago how to control her life.

She reached the apex of her height in sixth grade, gradually progressing from being the tallest in her class to the shortest as everyone outgrew her. She also matured at an early age, but her ample endowment had caused more heartache than happiness. She quickly realized all the attention that came from the opposite sex was for one reason only—physical attraction. While her relatively flat-chested sisters bemoaned their lack of curves, she became adept at fighting off the multitude of guys who always seemed to assume since she was well endowed, she was also easy.

So Grace developed a system—a routine—one that allowed her to date without having her heart broken. She wasn't naïve. She knew exactly why a guy wanted to take her on a date. She would string him along, enjoy his company, tease and flirt, but never let her heart become involved. But when she thwarted any attempt at physical intimacy, he would always drop her like a burning coal. Sometimes a guy became insistent, trying to progress beyond her comfort zone, and she simply gave him the boot. She always ended her relationships before anyone became too emotionally involved. No tears were shed. No pain was felt. And Grace could move happily on to the next shallow relationship. It was all about having fun and not getting hurt. She usually ended her relationships after one or two months—three at the most. It was her modus operandi, and it had always worked in the past.

But Brad was different from other guys she'd dated. Perhaps it was because, at thirty years of age, he was six years her senior. But whatever the reason, he hadn't pushed her sexual boundaries. He took her out and entertained her and spent time with her and made her laugh for two months. And not one time had he ever attempted to do more than kiss her. But *man-oh-man* did he ever kiss her. His kisses made her toes curl and clouded her normally clear judgment. She knew if they continued to date, she'd soon be willing to abandon her physical boundaries with Brad.

Grace knew she had to break up with Brad, especially after what he revealed the week before. She couldn't get it out of her mind.

They were watching a baseball game at Brad's apartment, one of her favorite pastimes. Even though her small stature and cute features made her seem like a prissy girl, Grace loved sports of every kind. She liked baseball, basketball, hockey, football, soccer... You name it—she liked it. His roommate, Josh, joined them since he was currently mooning over a girl who wouldn't give him the time of day.

Her eyes kept darting away from the game to look at Brad. He was, in her opinion, the most attractive guy she'd ever met, with six feet of lean muscle. He wore his dark-brown hair closely cropped and sported a goatee, a look Grace absolutely adored. His eyes were blue, light crystal blue, like looking into water. Like her, he was an outdoor and sports fanatic. He was extremely bright, having done his emergency room residency at one of the most prestigious programs in the country. But he recognized her intelligence, never talking down to her even though she was a first grade teacher. She'd never had as much fun with anyone in her life as she'd had with Brad.

The trouble started when Josh was called into work at the hospital, leaving the two of them alone. When Brad reached his hand out to tenderly cup her cheek, gazing at her with his eyelids halfway closed, she felt her heart begin to race. With no more than the lightest brush of his lips across hers, she felt a fire kindling inside her.

"Grace... You're so beautiful." His voice was low and gravelly, and she could hear him breathing fast and heavy. She wanted to let herself go and be fully engulfed in his touch, his caress, his whisper. But she knew this was the dangerous time, when she could easily disregard her own boundaries. She didn't want to do something she would regret later.

He planted light kisses all along her jaw and she lifted her chin to allow him access. His fingers trailed up and down her neck, sending millions of sparks through her nerves until she was squirming in her seat. He moved his mouth back to hers and teased her lips until she pushed her mouth against him, yearning for full contact. But he held back, playing with her lower lip until she moaned into his mouth. At the sound he groaned back and his kiss became more urgent. Harder. Seeking. His tongue slipped between her lips and slid against hers.

Abruptly he pushed himself away and fell back against the couch. "Grace, I can't keep doing this."

She groaned at the loss of his touch and at the breakup she knew was coming. This was it—it was about to be over. She'd had this moment many times before with other guys, but somehow she knew it would be worse to lose Brad.

"I understand," she whispered, surprised at the ache she already felt. "I'm just not willing to give you what you want."

"No, I don't want you to... I mean... I can wait."

"Wait?" Her heart began to beat erratically. "But—"

"I mean it, Grace. I can wait."

She coughed out a bitter laugh. "You'll have to wait a long time. I'm waiting until after I'm married."

"Okay." He reached out and took her hand, pulling it toward his lips.

She wrenched it out of his grasp before he could kiss it. "Okay?" Her voice was shrill. "What do you mean by 'okay'?"

"I'm saying I'll wait until we're married. I love you, Grace. I can wait."

Grace's jaw opened and closed like a guppy. Her mouth was so dry her words cracked in her throat. "I need to go." She leapt toward the door.

"Grace—wait!" He was following her outside. "You can't walk home at night alone. Let me walk with you. We can talk on the way."

"No... I don't want to talk." Her voice was shaking, as were her hands. Her entire nervous system had gone haywire.

"Okay. I won't talk. I'm sorry I said that. I thought I'd waited long enough to tell you, but I won't say it again. Please? Okay? Just forget I said it."

She didn't answer. She couldn't answer. She had no idea what to say—this was not a part of the routine. How dare he knock her off the driver's seat! How in the world was she going to regain control?

True to his word, he didn't speak to her on the twenty-minute walk. When she reached her door she tried to escape inside, but he pulled her against him and held her tight. It felt so good to be in his arms it hurt. He smoothed her hair and kissed the top of her head.

"Grace... Don't freak out on me. Nothing has changed. We're still good together."

When she tore herself from his arms, it felt like she'd ripped off a Band-Aid. She fought back her tears as she rushed through the door to the safety of her home.

But now she had a plan, and it had to work. He wasn't going to break up with her for withholding physical gratification—he'd already made that clear. So she had to force his hand. She had to entice him into crossing the line so she'd have a good reason to end the relationship. And she was dressed for it tonight. Her short tight skirt showed off her smooth tanned legs that looked longer with four-inch heels. Her tight sweater dipped low, exposing as much cleavage as she'd show in a bikini. She even applied a bit of shimmery lotion to her chest to help draw his attention downward. Once he started to kiss her and she encouraged him a little, he wouldn't be able to turn down the invitation.

Perhaps it was mean to trick Brad, but it was the only way to break up without hurting his feelings. She didn't want to tell him she was never going to fall in love with him. And perhaps that wasn't even true. If she were older and ready to settle down, he'd be the kind of guy she would choose. But she'd always kept her heart carefully guarded, so there was no way that could happen right now. She'd made the mistake of letting him get too close—she should never have let it go on so long. No, she'd thought about it, and this was the only way.

Brad swallowed hard as he took in Grace's appearance. She hadn't returned his phone calls all week, and he feared she wanted to break off the relationship after his slip-up. Why had he told her he loved her? He should have known she wasn't ready. Eight weeks of careful work to build up her trust, down the drain with three little words.

But maybe he'd been wrong. She was dressed in the most provocative outfit he'd ever seen. And the gaze she turned on him was so hungry he felt as if she wanted him for dessert. As if to confirm his thoughts, her tongue swiped slowly across her lower lip. His eyes dropped down where her chest was heaving enticingly with each rapid breath. With great difficulty he forced his eyes back to her face.

"I've missed you Brad," she said in a raspy voice as she advanced toward his position, cowering against the front door.

He clasped his hands behind his back. "I've missed you too, Grace. I was worried when you didn't answer my calls."

She wrapped her arms around his neck, pulling his face down to hers. He didn't resist as she offered her lips to him, kissing him with a passion he couldn't help but answer. His arms slipped around her back, and he squeezed as if he could hold her there forever.

"Hi guys!" said Josh, stepping into the living room. "Hope I'm not interrupting anything." He flopped onto the couch and propped his feet on the footstool.

Grace swirled to face him, tugging her short skirt down as two bright red spots appeared on her cheeks.

Josh raised his eyebrows and grinned. "Wow, Grace. You look... Uhmm... You look like you weren't planning on me being here."

"Don't you have someplace to go?" Brad growled between his teeth.

"Not really," said Josh, picking up the television remote. "I thought I'd just watch a movie or something."

Brad was trying to decide how to dispose of Josh's body when he busted out laughing and stood up. "I'm just kidding. I'm going to have dinner with Spencer and Emily. Don't do anything I wouldn't do," he warned as he slipped past them out the front door, his laughter trailing behind him.

Brad let out the breath he'd been holding when the door closed behind Josh. His eyes sought out Grace's, and he saw a fire burning behind her hazel orbs. Her smile was seductive as she pulled him by the hand, backing toward the couch. Seductive? Since when did Grace do anything seductive? Warning bells went off in his head.

Grace felt his hand stiffen in hers. She must be moving too fast—he was getting suspicious. "I've had such a hard week," she said. "Would you mind rubbing my shoulders?"

His expression was so sympathetic she felt a pang of guilt. "Of course not. I'll massage your shoulders for you."

He urged her to sit on the footstool while he sat behind her. His large strong hands began to knead her muscles. She almost melted as the tension she wasn't even aware of began to leave her body.

She thought about the close call at the front door. It was a good thing Josh had appeared when he did. Her scheme to make Brad lose control had made *her* lose control instead. She would have to be more careful. She needed to keep her mind distracted, separated from the sensations that always overwhelmed her when Brad kissed her. She'd thought if she initiated the kissing, if she was the one in control, she'd be able to control her emotions as well. But it hadn't quite worked according to her plan. She had to be more careful.

"Mmmm, that's nice," she murmured as she scooted back onto the couch beside him, snuggling under his arm. She heaved a big sigh, designed to draw his eyes toward her low neckline. She reached her hand to stroke his face and let her fingers drop to amble across his muscular chest. His hand reached out to stroke her cheek, causing her thoughts to jumble in her head.

He bent his face to capture her lips in a tender kiss, sweet and chaste, full of promise. With only the slightest pressure of his mouth on hers, her heart began to thud and warmth spread throughout her entire body. When he withdrew his mouth, she whimpered and tried to follow him, her parched lips seeking the satisfaction only he could give.

He chuckled. "It makes me feel a little better you seem to want it as much as I do." He stretched his arms above his head and stood up. "What do you want to do tonight? Do you feel like going out? Would you like to watch the game down at O'Malley's?"

Grace felt her breath coming faster and faster until her head was swimming. It hadn't worked. He didn't take the bait. How was she going to break it off now?

"Grace? What's wrong?"

She stood up and backed toward the door with one hand in front of her to ward him off. She didn't know what she was going to do, but she knew she couldn't stay.

"What's wrong? Where are you going?"

She shook her head and continued her backward trek until she found the door with her foot. He continued to advance, but she slipped out the door and shut it behind her, holding it tightly.

The door jerked out of her hands. "Grace, what are you trying to do? You can't lock me inside my apartment. I don't understand what happened. What's wrong? Talk to me!" He gripped her shoulders and held her motionless. She stared at him, unseeing.

"Grace, I'm not letting you go until you tell me what's wrong."

"I... It's... There's someone else..." Tears welled in her eyes and rolled down her wooden cheeks. It was almost true. She planned to date someone else—she simply hadn't met him yet.

"What? What are you saying?"

"There's someone else... Another guy... I can't see you anymore." She looked up though watery eyes and saw his face splinter.

"I don't believe it! You're lying, aren't you? What's his name?"

Grace panicked. Why did she lie? Why did she say there was another guy? She scrambled to cover. "Horatio... His name is Horatio."

"How could you do this? What did I do wrong?" His voice cracked and he turned his head away, but she saw the wetness on his face.

"I'm sorry," she choked out.

"Why Grace?" Brad fell back against the door and slid slowly to the ground. "We were so good together." Grace saw him bury his face in his hands before she turned to walk away.

Chapter Two

GRACE HAD NEVER FELT MORE MISERABLE in her life. She was angry with herself for hurting Brad. She still couldn't get the image of his stricken face out of her mind. She'd meant to break off the relationship without hurting him any more than necessary, but her plan had failed. When he didn't react as she'd predicted, she improvised. Her lie had injured him severely, but it was too late for the truth now. She ought to feel a sense of relief she was free from her weighty relationship with Brad. She couldn't understand why her heart was so heavy, unless it was a sense of guilt.

Perhaps she simply needed more time—it had only been one weekend since the fateful breakup. The sight of her puffy swollen eyes in the mirror almost made another barrage of tears come. But it was Monday, and she had to go to the school and be cheery for all of those six-year-olds who were counting on her. After splashing cold water on her face and applying a generous portion of concealer, she forced herself to head to work and put up a brave front.

The day dragged on. Her pulse was rapid as she checked her cell phone for messages, but there was still no word from Brad. Not that she wanted him to contact her. She wanted a clean break—they both needed to move on. Even though she'd done a poor job of breaking up, it was probably the best thing for Brad. He could find someone else—someone who would be thrilled if he professed his love for her. He deserved that. She was so humiliated. She could never tell a soul what she had done and prayed Brad hadn't told anyone either. She was meeting Josh after work, hoping to hear news of Brad. Josh might already hate her if Brad had told him the truth. So be it. Right now, she hated herself.

Josh hadn't told Brad he was meeting Grace for dinner. He knew about the breakup, but Brad wouldn't give any details. And now his roommate was avoiding him and all of his other friends except for the necessary interactions at the hospital. He recognized the signs of heartbreak since he'd been living with it for several months. He owed it to Brad to see if he could help.

"Hey Grace. You look great," he said with a bright forced smile, thinking she looked rather rough.

"Thanks Josh, but I know better." She rubbed the bridge of her nose. "Tell me the truth... How's he doing?"

"He's... He's surviving. What happened? You two looked like things were going just fine when I left the other day. In fact, it looked like things were more than fine." He chuckled a bit.

He saw her face flush as she kept her eyes glued to the table. "Uhmm... What did he tell you?"

Josh tilted his head and studied her. She was definitely hiding something. "All he said was you were a... Let's see... What was that word he used? Oh yeah... He said you were a *psycho*." He saw her flinch, but she didn't protest. "What exactly did you do?" he asked as he reached for a slice of pizza and attacked it with zeal.

Her face turned several shades of pink and red. "I broke up with him so I could date someone else."

"Really? Who is this guy?"

"His name is Horatio. But I don't want to talk about him. I want to talk about Brad. Is he... Is he okay? I know he's mad, but..." Her voice cracked and her hand swiped quickly at her face.

"He's hurt and upset, Grace. How did you think he would be?" He failed to keep the annoyance from his voice, but he regretted his harsh tone when he heard a sob.

"I know. It's totally my f-fault. I just s-sort of went crazy."

"So let me get this straight," he said between bites. "You had a hot make-out session and then went crazy and broke up with him so you could date someone else? Is that right? So I don't understand... If you want to date someone else, why do you care what Brad thinks anymore?"

"I don't know. It sounds w-worse when you s-say it that way. We needed to break up, but I didn't want to h-hurt him."

"I thought you and Brad really liked each other. Why did you start dating someone else?"

Grace shrugged. "He was getting too serious."

The conversation felt a bit surreal to Josh—as if he ought to be hearing these words from a guy instead. "What exactly is 'too serious'? What do you mean by that?"

"He said he loved me."

Now Josh felt defensive. He'd told Charlie the same thing. A guy shouldn't be penalized for speaking about love if it was true. "What's wrong with that? Why wouldn't you want him to love you?"

"But I don't feel the same way."

"*Yet*," he corrected. "You don't feel the same way *yet*. Why won't you give him a chance? What's this Horatio guy got that Brad doesn't have?" Josh snagged another slice of pizza.

"Horatio doesn't want to get married."

"Brad was pressuring you to get married?"

"Well, no... But... But he... But I didn't want a serious relationship. So I had to end it while I could, before anyone got hurt."

"You mean, before *you* got hurt? Because Brad already got hurt, didn't he?"

"It's for the best. If I had let it go on any longer, it would have hurt him even more. He deserves someone who can love him back."

"But you'd rather have this Horatio guy? How well do you know him?"

"Well enough." Josh saw Grace's chin jut out.

"Look, I'm just going to go out on a limb here and say you look almost as miserable as Brad. I wonder if it's possible you like Brad more than you're admitting."

"I'm not in love with Brad!" Grace's face was flushed, and she wadded up the napkin in her hand.

Josh sat back and folded his arms, studying her flushed face. "Okay, if you say so. However, I would like to point out I only suggested you *liked* him. So it seems the person whom you're trying to convince you're not in *love* with Brad... is *you*."

17

Her eyes grew wide and her breathing was so rapid he thought she might hyperventilate. "I... I don't..."

"I think you should call him or text him. I think you guys need to talk."

Grace shook her head rapidly as she grabbed her glass and gulped her water.

He continued, "I think you could work it out if you would just sit down and talk. And you need to dump this Horatio guy, and figure out how you feel about Brad."

"I... I don't think..."

"Just admit it. You made a mistake, didn't you? You regret breaking up?"

Her eyes closed as huge crocodile tears slid down her face, and she nodded her head.

"Just talk to him."

"I don't even understand how I feel. How can I explain it to him? And anyway, it's too late. He won't want to talk to me now. And he's better off without me."

"He deserves to make that call himself. Just try. If he refuses to talk to you, then at least you can say you tried," Josh said around a mouthful of pizza. "Call him. Or better yet, come up to the hospital tomorrow morning and talk to him in person. We're both on duty starting at six."

"I... I don't know... What if he won't talk to me?"

"If it doesn't go well, I'll call you and we'll figure out the next step."

"No, don't bother calling. If it doesn't go well, I'll take it as a sign I was right and we should break up."

"Whatever. I'm sure by tomorrow night everything will be fine. Are you going to eat that pizza?" Josh asked, indicting the slice on her plate. When she turned up her nose he snatched it from her plate with enthusiasm. He'd done a great job of counseling Grace. Maybe he should have been a psychiatrist. No—it was way too stressful. He'd better stick with emergency medicine.

Brad checked his cell phone again on his way to work Tuesday morning—still no word from Grace. Well, good riddance to her. She'd dumped him and he hadn't done anything to deserve it. He wasn't even sure Horatio existed. He suspected the whole breakup occurred because he'd confessed his love for her. Why couldn't she be like every other girl he knew? Most girls would be thrilled to hear those three coveted words from their boyfriends, wouldn't they? Usually, the guys were the ones with commitment issues. He wasn't planning to go begging for her to come back to him. If she wanted him, she knew where to find him. And even as angry as he was, he'd take her back in a second. He couldn't stop thinking about her.

"Hey Dr. Gates? Why so glum?"

Brad turned to the source of the voice. Dr. Kara Dickson, one of the fourth year residents in the emergency medicine residency, was sending him one of her hundred watt smiles. Could people tell he was upset? He'd thought he'd hidden it fairly well. The last thing he wanted was to be depressed and grumpy the way Josh had been acting over Charlie.

He plastered a smile on his face. "It's six a.m. and I'm not much of a morning person. But I'm okay. How're you, Dr. Dickson?"

"Great actually. It seems like all I've been doing lately is studying for my board exams. But I've got tickets for the Yankees game Friday night. You want to go?"

"Uhmm... Well I—"

"Oh! I forgot. You're dating that little brunette girl, right? How old is she? She looks like she's still in high school."

Brad felt his face getting hot. "She's twenty-four years old, Kara."

"I'm just teasing you," she chuckled. "I'm thirty-two—practically an old hag. So I'm jealous of those cute-young-things."

He laughed at her self-deprecating humor. She was anything but an old hag, and she knew it. She was only an inch shorter than him at five foot eleven, with long thick blond hair and the face of a model. He gave her the expected response. "I don't think you look anything like a hag, Kara. And since I'm thirty, I don't think you're that old either."

"Ah, but I'm older than you. So if you ever break it off with that cute-young-thing and want to date an *older* woman, let me know."

"I'll keep that in mind," he said, maintaining his fake smile with great difficulty.

*****

Kara saw the flowers walking in the hospital door and the shapely legs beneath them. The bouquet covered the face, but she knew the girl carrying it must be small. She walked toward the flowers.

"What a beautiful bouquet. Can I help you?"

"Uhmm... Yes... I'm looking for Dr. Gates. Do you know where I can find him?"

When she peered around the flowers, Kara recognized the girl Brad was dating. She noted with considerable irritation she felt like Conan the Barbarian with this petite girl around. "He's in with an accident patient right now. But I can give him the flowers for you."

The girl shifted her feet as her eyes darted around the room. She rose onto her tiptoes as if she could see over Kara's shoulder. "Oh... Well maybe I could wait for a while before I have to leave for school."

"What grade are you in," Kara asked, unable to resist a little dig.

A cherry red blush bloomed on her cheeks. "I'm a teacher—I teach first grade."

"That's nice," Kara replied, looking down her nose. "But I really don't think Dr. Gates will be free anytime soon. He could be in there for a couple of hours."

"Oh, I... I really wanted to see him. I wanted to give him these in person."

"Why are you giving him flowers? Isn't it usually the other way around? I didn't know Brad liked flowers."

"He doesn't... I mean... Would you mind giving them to him and this card, too? It's really important. Maybe I should wait for a while in case he comes out."

"Don't worry. I'll make sure he gets them. And what's your name?"

"I'm Grace. And what's your name?"

"I'm... I'm Leanne," said Kara. Why did she give her middle name? And why was she lying to Brad's girlfriend about his whereabouts? She knew the answer—because this little pipsqueak of a first grade teacher didn't deserve Dr. Brad Gates. She wasn't smart enough. She wasn't sophisticated enough. She wasn't even big enough. And if Kara had her way, Brad would soon see she was the only woman who would ever be able to satisfy him in every way. She'd even gotten tickets to a baseball game in spite of the fact she hated sports. That only proved she was willing to sacrifice to make him happy.

"Okay. Thanks, Leanne. Don't forget to give him the card, too. It won't make any sense without the card." Tears glimmered in her eyes as she handed over the vase and the envelope. She glanced toward the inner-sanctum doors one last time before she relinquished her grasp on the objects.

"I won't forget. Have a good day."

After assuring herself Grace had departed, Kara quickly opened the card. She almost cried out with glee when she read the note. They had obviously had a fight and broken up. This was the best opportunity she could ever have.

Dear Brad,
The white chrysanthemums stand for truth—I'm sorry I lied to you. The daffodils express respect—I respect you. I should have respected you before. I should never have judged you to be like all the other guys I knew. The purple hyacinths mean I'm sorry and I'm asking for forgiveness. I know I don't deserve it, but I am asking for another chance. If you think there is even the smallest chance you could forgive me and we could try again, I'll do whatever it takes to be worthy of your trust. I'm really confused, and I'm just asking for an opportunity to talk to you.
Yours and yours alone,
Grace

"Nice flowers, Kara," said Brad as he emerged from the double doors. "Who are they from?"

Kara slid the card into her pocket. Wow, that had been close. "Oh, just this guy I'm really trying to get rid of. He's been hassling me for months. I think he found out about those baseball tickets and he's hoping to rope me into taking him. Are you sure you can't go with me? Just to keep him from bugging me?"

Brad hesitated. "I don't know. I probably wouldn't be very good company."

"It doesn't matter. Really. I just need to be able to tell him I'm going with someone else. It's not like we'd be on a real date or anything. Surely your girlfriend won't mind you helping out a colleague in need. Or is she the jealous type?"

His brows furrowed. "No she probably wouldn't care at all. Just a minute." He pulled out his cell phone and checked his messages. Then his mouth firmed into a straight line. "You know—why not? I love the Yankees."

*****

"No, I haven't heard from Grace, and I don't expect to hear from her, either." Brad slammed the refrigerator door hard enough to rattle the bottles inside. This was ridiculous—he never lost his temper.

"Sorry. I just thought maybe she might have called you today or come by," said Josh. "I didn't mean to upset you."

"I'm not upset. I just answered your question. I didn't hear from her and I don't care." Brad stared at the apple he held in his hand, thinking he wasn't the least bit hungry. Had he even eaten lunch?

"Right. You don't care. That's why you almost broke the refrigerator when I asked you about it." Josh held up defensive palms at Brad's answering glare. "Look. I know what it feels like to be rejected. I'm not trying to give you a hard time."

"I don't want to talk about it."

Josh said, "I wasn't trying to make you talk about it. I just thought... Did you check your messages? Are you sure she didn't call you?"

"I checked, okay? She hasn't called. She hasn't texted." He didn't mention he'd checked his phone at least twice an hour for the past four days.

"Maybe she's afraid," Josh suggested. "Maybe you should—"

"I'm *not* calling her. You want to know what happened? I'll tell you. She ditched me and told me she's dating someone else. It's *over*." Brad put the apple back inside the refrigerator and carefully closed the door. He wouldn't let Grace change him into an angry sullen man. He couldn't control her, but he could control himself.

He made his visage pleasant, or at least he tried. Josh's reaction indicated his smile might have appeared a little menacing. "Actually, I'm going out with Dr. Dickson on Friday."

Josh's mouth fell open. "You're going out with someone else? You're already giving up on Grace?"

"I'm not giving up on Grace. She gave up on *me*. She gave up on *us*. And yes, I'm going to a baseball game with Kara. Why not? Grace is dating someone else. Should I just mope around forever over a lost cause like you do?" He regretted the words the second they left his mouth as Josh flinched and dropped his eyes. This was all Grace's fault—he would never purposely hurt his best friend's feelings. He scrambled to think of a way to retract his words.

Josh's voice was low and full of hurt. "If you love someone, you don't quit the first time things get rough. And anyway, maybe I think Charlie's worth the wait and worth the work." He spun around and moved toward the door.

"Wait Josh! I'm sorry—"

Josh never broke his stride, throwing out one last hostile accusation as he left the apartment, "Maybe the truth is you don't really love her." The door clicked closed behind him and silence filled the apartment like a heavy fog.

Desperate to escape the oppressive quiet, Brad turned on the television and sat before it, flipping aimlessly between channels as the minutes dragged by. He was startled at a loud knocking.

"Ben," he said, opening the door to reveal a swarthy man with close-cut dark hair and beard. "What are you doing here?"

"What? No 'Hi brother! Great to see you!' or 'Come inside. What a great surprise!'?"

Brad chuckled, "Come on in, Brother. As a matter of fact, I'm really glad to see you."

Ben strode inside, suitcase in hand. "I hope you don't mind if I stay a few days, little brother."

"I'm four years older than you, little brother."

"Yes, but I'm referring to your stunted growth. But don't feel bad about yourself just because you're only six feet tall." Although he only topped him by an inch, Ben never let him forget about his superior stature. He folded his lengthy frame into a chair and let his bag fall on the floor beside him. "And you have that short little girlfriend to help you feel taller, right?"

Brad swallowed with difficulty. He didn't feel like having this discussion with his unsympathetic brother who had a habit of yanking his chain at every opportunity. He'd already blown up while discussing Grace with Josh. Perhaps he could change the subject. "Actually, I'm not with Grace anymore. But that leaves me with some free time to entertain my wayward brother. How long are you here for, and what would you like to do?"

"You're not with Grace? She's the only one of your girlfriends I ever liked. How'd you blow it with her?"

"You only liked her because she laughed at your stupid jokes."

"I liked her because she was the only girl with the intelligence to recognize and appreciate my humor and great wit."

"That's only because your intellect is on a level with her first grade students."

Ben gave a belly laugh. "That might be why she was attracted to you. That and the fact you're so short."

"I ought to pin you to the floor for that. But we already know who'd win that battle."

"Only because you're fatter than I am. It's a middle-weight fighting a heavy-weight."

"I'm not fatter, I'm fitter. This is solid muscle."

"Ha! I'd take you on if you hadn't already torn my rotator cuff. That's actually why I'm in town—I'm having a surgery consult." Ben moved his shoulder, wincing.

"Are you kidding me?" Brad said. "Who's your surgeon?"

"Dr. Blankenstein or Blankenship or something like that." He fumbled in his pocket, pulled out an appointment card and handed it to Brad.

"Dr. Blankenship. David Blankenship. I know him—he's a good guy. Oh man, I'm sorry you've got to have surgery on your shoulder. Did that happen when we were playing around last month?"

"No, you didn't actually do it. I was wrestling this other guy, kind of on a dare—a former football player. He beat me six out of six times. I guess I should have stopped after the fifth time, but I really don't like losing." He laughed again. "But never mind that. Why did Grace break up with you?"

"Maybe I broke up with her? Why do you assume she broke up with me?"

Ben leaned back and propped his feet on the footstool, crossing his arms. He appraised his brother from head to toe. "Nope, I don't buy it. Grace way out-classed your ugly butt. You wouldn't break it off with her unless you were stupid. Hmmm... On the other hand, you can be pretty stupid sometimes. Maybe you did break up with her."

Brad had an urge to wipe the smirk off Ben's face. He forced his fists to unclench and stretched his stiff neck from side to side. Maybe he could divert the conversation before he tore his brother's other shoulder. "Speaking of ugly butts, you never told me how long you're going to be here."

"I'm planning to stay through the weekend if that's okay. I'm doing some business stuff in addition to the surgery consult."

"How is your new business going? Tell me again what you're doing?"

"I'm creating printed books based on people's Facebook entries. They just upload their favorite posts and pictures into the pre-made format, and I print the book for them."

"I can't believe it. My brother, who *never* reads, has a business printing books." Brad chuckled, "Aren't you kind of a hypocrite?"

"They're *picture* books!" Ben narrowed his eyes and furrowed his brows, pretending anger. But he couldn't suppress a laugh. "I think it's apropos I'm making money off of people who are foolish enough to waste their time buying and reading books. Someone is going to take advantage of these people—it might as well be me."

Brad shook his head. "Sometimes I can't believe we had the same parents. Maybe your father was the exterminator. Didn't he have eyes like yours?"

"Very funny. That might explain why Mom always liked me better than you. But maybe we should both be worried—Dad didn't care much for either one of us."

"Ha! That's true. Have you had dinner? We could go grab a bite somewhere. I'm suddenly starved."

"No, I haven't eaten." Ben stood and started toward the door. "Now, I think you were telling me why Grace broke up with you."

"No, I wasn't," Brad growled, falling in step beside his brother, aware his appetite had fled to once again be replaced by a sour stomach.

"Seriously, it's really over? I thought for sure you were going to marry her. I've never seen you so stupid over a girl. I mean, I've seen you stupid plenty of times. But not over a girl—not until Grace."

"Look. There's nothing to tell. We broke up. It's over. I don't even care about her anymore."

"Really?" Ben tilted his head with a wry smile. "Then it's okay with you if I ask Grace out? OW! I think you broke a rib. If I have to have another surgery, you're paying for it."

*****

Grace's heart skipped a beat as her cell phone rang. But a quick glance showed the call was from her future sister-in-law, Emily. She debated whether to answer the call. She might accidentally miss Brad's call if it came while she was talking to Emily.

"Hi Emily. Uhmm, I can't talk long. I'm kind of expecting a call."

"Okay. This won't take long, anyway. Spencer and I just wanted to see what y'all were doing Friday night?"

"Y'all?"

Emily laughed. "Don't make fun of my Texas accent. I meant to say *you*—both of you. You and Brad. Do y'all have plans? Because we were thinking of making fajitas and playing cards while the boys watch the baseball game." She chuckled, "Who am I kidding? I mean, while all three of you watch the baseball game. You're just as bad as they are."

"Uhmm... Can I get back to you on that? I mean... I'd have to talk to Brad first." She felt her eyes starting to water. She had to get off the phone before Emily noticed anything amiss. "Oh, I think that's the other line. I'll get back to you soon, okay?"

She disconnected the call and searched her pocket for a tissue that wasn't totally drenched. She wadded up a handful of wet

Kleenex and stuffed them in the now-empty box and stumbled toward the trashcan.

She jumped at the voice behind her. "Okay Sister—spill it," ordered Olivia. "You've been emptying tissue boxes for days, and I know you don't have a cold."

"It's nothing—just hormones." Grace's phone coughed out a message indication. She hurried to open the message, only to find a communication from Emily about their Friday night plans. Her shoulders slumped along with her spirit as she slinked back to the couch.

"You know we're synced, so don't give me that hormone excuse. What's up? You've been acting weird since Saturday."

"Please, I don't want to..." Her words stopped as her phone rang. Her heart began to race as she checked the caller ID. It was Josh. A nauseous feeling welled up in her stomach. Josh had said he would call if things didn't go well. This must mean Brad had rejected her offer. She silenced the phone and swallowed the bile that rose in her throat, failing to stop a fresh flood of tears.

Olivia was beside her in a second, hugging her sopping face in her arms. "Grace, what happened? Did someone hurt you? I'll kill them for you. I can do it—I'm bigger than you are."

At that proclamation, Grace let out a muffled chuckle. She sniffed and wiped her face on her sleeve for lack of a dry tissue. "It's just... Don't tell anyone, okay? Please? Not even Hannah or Claire or Spencer?"

"Okay, I promise. Our sisters are both out for the evening anyway."

"I... We... Brad and I broke up."

"What happened, Grace? I really thought you were perfect for each other."

"I don't want to talk about it. It's all for the best. You know me—I don't date anyone for very long."

"Yeah, but you don't usually cry when you break up with your boyfriends. What's the deal? Are you in love with Brad?"

"Of course I'm not in love with him!" Grace bit back with vehemence. "I'm the one who broke it off."

"Okay, okay. Whatever you say. I wasn't trying to be offensive, you know."

Grace cringed, "I'm sorry, Sister. I didn't mean to take it out on you."

"But something is different with Brad. Right?"

"But I'm not in love with him." Grace's chest tightened until she couldn't breathe. She couldn't be in love with Brad. They'd only been dating for a couple of months. In fact, she'd broken up with Brad for declaring he was in love with her. The whole idea was ridiculous. She was only feeling guilty because she'd hurt his feelings. And lonely because she missed his company. And depressed because he'd rejected her apology. And despondent because she had so many regrets. That's all it was—she couldn't be in love with him.

"Whatever. I guess it doesn't matter since you two have broken up, unless you think there's a chance you might get back together." Olivia narrowed her eyes at Grace. "Is that why you keep checking your phone? Are you hoping to hear from him?"

Grace fumbled the phone in her fingers, almost dropping it on the floor. "No... I'm expecting a call from a parent. You know... Problems in the home." She realized she'd been lying a lot recently. She hoped she could keep all of her stories straight.

Olivia nodded understanding as she embraced her sister again. "You know what you need? Chocolate therapy."

Grace sniffed. "I'm listening..."

"I'll go buy a pint of Ben and Jerry's Chocolate Therapy ice cream."

"Are you going to eat with me?"

"Absolutely."

"Better make it two."

Chapter Three

Brad was pretending to listen to Ben's diatribe about marketing strategies when his cell phone rang. He snatched the phone to his ear, answering in an anxious voice, "Hello?"

"Hey Brad," said Spencer.

Brad's voice fell with his heart. "Oh, it's you. Hi Spencer."

"You sure know how to make a guy feel wanted," chuckled Spencer. "Who were you expecting?"

"Nobody," Brad lied, attempting to lighten his tone. "What's up?"

"Emily and I were planning to invite you and Grace to come over and watch the baseball game Friday night. Do you have other plans? She hasn't gotten back with us yet."

"I won't be able to come over to watch the Yankees with you Friday night, because I'm actually going to be at the game."

"Awesome—I'm so jealous. I'll just tell Emily you and Grace are going to be at the game."

"Grace isn't going with me to the game. We broke up." The words squeezed through his tightened lips.

"You broke up? Are you kidding me? You and Grace? I mean... I'm sorry, Brad. What happened?"

"I'd rather not talk about it. I'm sure Grace will still want to come over and watch the game with you."

"But surely it's just a temporary thing. You guys were great together. Maybe you waited too long to give her a ring. You know I almost made that mistake with Emily."

"No, we only dated two months." Brad attempted to keep the sour note from his voice. "And trust me, she didn't want a ring from me."

Ben held up his hand. "Tell Spencer I'm available Friday night."

Brad glared at his brother as he debated passing on his request to Spencer. He didn't want Ben spending the evening with Grace. But Spencer had heard Ben speaking. "Who's that?"

Brad's breath whistled through clenched teeth. "My brother, Ben, is here. He's inviting himself to your house Friday night, but don't feel obligated. I'm sure you have other friends—"

"Ben!" Spencer's enthusiastic voice responded. "Sure, we'd love to have your brother over if he's not going to the game with you. He kept Emily rolling with his stories the last time we got together."

"But it might make Grace feel awkward," Brad objected, knowing his excuse was lame.

"No, she *loves* Ben... I mean... She likes him... I mean... And anyway, she hasn't responded to Emily's text, so she might not be coming."

Brad felt his blood pounding in his temples. Why had he accepted Kara's invitation to the baseball game? He glowered at Ben, whose smile looked exactly like The Joker in *Batman*.

*****

Emily felt her throat constricting. "What do you mean? Grace and Brad can't break up."

Spencer pulled her into his arms and kissed her hair. "I'm sorry to be the one to tell you, but they already did. Brad said they broke up last Friday."

"Why?" she croaked out. "Why would he break up with her?"

"He didn't say what happened. But knowing Grace, I'd bet she was the one who broke it off. He just said they weren't together anymore, and he's going to the Yankees game without her."

"Why do you think it was Grace who broke up?"

Spencer scrunched up his shoulders. "She always does that. I don't think she's ever dated a guy longer than two or three months."

"What can we do? I really thought Grace and Brad might be getting married not long after we do." Emily couldn't help the smile that appeared on her face as she glanced at the engagement ring gracing her finger. She'd only been wearing it for two weeks, and she still hadn't gotten over her excitement.

A deep furrow appeared on Spencer's face. "Nothing—there's nothing we can do except be there for Grace and Brad. It's not our place to interfere."

Emily pulled her lips into a tight line. She certainly didn't agree with Spencer, but she didn't want to start a fight. "Don't you think Grace would be interfering if you and I broke up?"

"Yes, I know she'd be interfering—she and Olivia and Hannah and Claire would all interfere. They've been interfering ever since they were born, but that doesn't mean it's a good idea. Believe me. I know what it's like to live with four meddling sisters."

"You know you love your sisters."

"Of course I love them, but that doesn't mean they don't drive me crazy."

"You're not willing to help Grace in her time of need?"

"I'm willing to give her all the help she needs... but only if she asks for it. So we need to stay clear and let them work it out themselves. If it doesn't work out, it wasn't meant to be. And you'd better not get involved, okay?"

Emily chewed on the inside of her cheek as she contemplated Spencer's words. As long as she didn't make any promises, she could still find some way to help. Olivia would know what to do. "What about Friday night?" she asked.

"Well it turns out Ben is in town, so I invited him over. Do you think that's okay?"

"Sure—he's a lot of fun. But is Grace coming? She never replied to my text message. At least now I understand why."

"I'm hoping she'll come for dinner since it's just going to be Ben and us," said Spencer. "I don't think Ben would give her a hard time."

"Well I hope she comes. I bet she's depressed," she said, thinking this was the perfect opportunity to sort out this mess before it got any worse. Surely it wasn't too late to salvage their relationship.

"Emily..."

"Huh?"

"I can see the wheels turning in your head. You wouldn't be planning to interfere would you? Not after we just agreed we shouldn't?"

"No Spencer. I promise I won't go against our agreement." It was certainly fortunate she'd never actually agreed.

*****

Grace had avoided Josh's phone calls for two days—she simply couldn't bear to hear about Brad's rejection of her peace offering. She could call Brad herself, but she didn't want to hear the pain and animosity she knew would be in his voice, especially since she was totally to blame. But she believed everything happened for a reason. So if Brad wouldn't accept her apology, it must mean they weren't supposed to be together. Right?

Why did this breakup hurt so much more than the others? She knew the answer—she had broken her own dating rules and allowed herself to become attached to Brad. Well, she wouldn't let that happen again. She was a pro at emotional detachment in dating. She'd done it before, and she could do it again. She was strong. She wouldn't allow herself to be controlled by her feelings.

Her brother's fiancée, Emily, had been controlled by her emotions. She'd gone crazy when she thought she'd lost Spencer, and her impulsive actions had almost been disastrous. Granted, everything worked out in the end, but Grace was determined to remain in control of her emotions and her actions. She wouldn't repeat Emily's mistakes.

She took a deep breath and steadied her nerves before calling Josh. "Hi Josh," she spoke with a light, airy voice. "I'm sorry I've missed your calls—I've been really busy."

"Too busy to try and save your relationship with Brad?" She didn't miss his accusing tone.

"Look Josh. I did try. He turned me down, just like I predicted. So I have to get on with my life."

"When did you try? He told me on Tuesday he hadn't heard from you at all."

"Then he's lying to you. I totally apologized and really put myself out there, asking for another chance. But he never even responded."

"Are you telling me he didn't speak to you? He just stood there and looked at you?"

"Well... No... I never actually spoke to him."

"Grace—"

"But I tried! I went there Tuesday morning, just like I promised. But I didn't get to see him. I had to leave my card and flowers with one of the nurses—her name was Leanne."

"In the ER?"

"Yes. But I didn't see you either." A nagging doubt invaded her mind. "Are you sure he was on duty Tuesday morning?"

"We were both there, but I don't think he ever got your flowers and card. At least I never saw them, and he didn't tell me about them."

Grace had a sinking feeling. If he'd never received her card, he didn't even know she'd apologized. He'd had almost three more days thinking she was dating someone else. To her distress, she felt tears stinging her eyes. How could she possibly have any tears left after crying every day for almost a week? A sob escaped her lips—so much for controlling her emotions.

"Please Grace, don't cry. I'll figure it out. Maybe it's lying around in the ER office somewhere. Which nurse did you say took your stuff?"

"She said her name was Leanne. She was tall and pretty with long blond hair."

"Okay. I'll see what I can do. Or you could just call him on the cell phone," he suggested.

Grace's heart pounded and her eyes were suddenly dry. "Okay. I'll call him. I'll call him as soon as we hang up."

"Good. You can do this, Grace. I'm pulling for you. I'll hang up now and let you call him."

The phone trembled in her fingers as she punched Brad's speed dial for the first time since Friday night. She hadn't even thought about what she would say to him when he answered. She would just throw herself on his mercy.

She heard his voice in her ear, "You have reached Dr. Brad Gates. I am currently unavailable. If this is an emergency, please call—"

Grace disconnected. What could she possibly say in a message? She had to talk to him directly.

Brad allowed an expletive to slip between his lips as he stared at the small green symbol on his cell phone. Grace had called. Finally. After almost a week of waiting, she'd called him and hadn't even left a message. At this point, could she possibly say anything he would want to hear? Would she tell him she'd already broken up with her new guy? Would she say the other boyfriend had never existed and admit she'd lied? Or maybe she was still with her mystery man, but she'd finally felt some compassion for Brad over her method of breaking up. No, he couldn't imagine any words that would ease the ache in his heart. He'd really thought he was in love with Grace, but she wasn't the girl he thought she was.

His phone vibrated before he could put it away. He froze—Grace was calling again. Should he answer? Maybe she was truly sorry for her crazy actions. Maybe it was just a fluke. Maybe they could try again—a fresh start.

"Dr. Gates!" called a nurse. "They need you. Car accident—two just arrived. One is critical."

He sighed as he turned off his phone. "I'm coming."

Grace hung up when Brad's cell went to voice mail again. Immediately, her phone rang and she answered, pressing her hand to her stomach, "Hello?"

"Hi Grace. It's Emily."

She blinked against sudden tears. "Hi Emily."

"Are you okay? You sound upset."

"No, I'm fine. I was... I was watching a sad show on TV."

"Oh really? What are you watching?"

Scrambling once again to cover a lie, Grace answered with the first thing that came to mind., "Big Bang Theory."

"Big Bang Theory? And it was sad?"

"Well... Yes I always feel sorry for Sheldon because no one understands him."

"Okay… I would never have thought of that. You certainly are sensitive. Uhmm, are you coming over on Friday night."

Grace hesitated. "Emily, I have to tell you something."

"Listen Grace, we know about the breakup. Brad told Spencer about it. But Brad's not coming Friday night, and we still want you to come."

"What did Brad tell Spencer?" Grace hoped Emily couldn't detect the slight tremor in her voice.

"Nothing, really. He didn't give any details. Do you want to talk about it? Spencer claims you probably broke up with Brad because you don't do long relationships. Is that true?"

"Yes, it's true. I don't do long, and I don't do serious. I broke it off, and it's for the best."

"But I really thought you guys were in love, like Spencer and me."

"Oh no, I'm not in love with Brad. It's only been two months—it's way too soon. And would I break up with him if I were in love with him?" Silence greeted her on the other end of the phone. "Emily? Are you there?"

"Uhmm, yeah. It's just that... Oh never mind."

"No. What? What were you going to say?"

"Well, I don't want you to get mad, but Josh just called me."

Grace felt a sudden urge to buy a gun. She spoke in a terse voice, "What did he tell you?"

"Don't be upset with him—I already knew y'all had broken up. Josh just thought you might need a little encouragement to call Brad and fix things up. And he told me about Horatio."

Grace groaned. "Josh is worse than my sisters at keeping secrets."

"So did you call Brad? Are y'all going to talk?"

"I called," Grace admitted, "but he didn't answer."

"So you really do love Brad? And you want to get back together? Because I'll do anything to help. You know that—"

"No—I'm not in love with Brad. I just... I feel bad for hurting him."

"Okay, if you say so." Emily sounded unconvinced.

"Really," Grace insisted. "And like Josh said, I'm dating Horatio now."

"Are you bringing him over on Friday night?"

"No. He uhmm... He has to work."

"Where does he work?"

"He works..." Why did she keep backing herself into corners with these lies? "He waits tables at a restaurant—at Per Se."

"Isn't that a really expensive place?"

"Yeah, it's really pricey. Too bad we can't go there and meet him, but we can't afford it."

"Oh, I bet Steven would take us. That would be fun—so we could all meet him."

Grace felt beads of perspiration on her forehead. She'd forgotten about Emily's generous and wealthy stepfather and his penchant for taking all their friends to expensive restaurants. "But he only works part time, because he's in school."

"What's he studying?"

"Uhmm... Meteorology."

"Okay, well I guess we'll meet him eventually. Right? Unless you get back together with Brad," said Emily.

"I'm afraid that's not going to happen. I don't think Brad even wants to talk to me." Grace's tongue felt thick as she spoke the words. It was as if saying it made it true.

"So about tomorrow night... Are you still coming over to Spencer's to watch the baseball game? I forgot to tell you, Ben's going to be there. You don't mind, do you? We asked you first, so we could tell him not to come."

"Brad's brother, Ben?"

"Uh-huh."

"No, I don't mind him being there. He's fun."

"Maybe he'll cheer you up a little."

"Maybe. I mean... Not that I need cheering up. I'm fine—really."

"Okay, we'll see you tomorrow night. But call me if you want to talk," said Emily.

A voice behind Grace caused her to jump as she ended her phone call. "You look to me like you could use cheering up," said Olivia. "Who was that on the phone? I'm guessing it wasn't Brad, and you two haven't patched things up."

"It was Emily calling about tomorrow night. I'm going to watch the baseball game with her and Spencer. And Ben is going to be there—Brad's brother. You could come if you want."

Olivia scrunched up her nose. "No thanks. I'll pass on a night of watching guys scratch and spit while occasionally throwing a ball."

"I can't believe you don't like baseball. It's very un-American of you."

"Please don't tell anyone I'm a communist because I hate watching baseball. It's just so boring. On the other hand, seeing Ben might almost make up for it. He's pretty cute, although he is a bit arrogant."

"I don't really feel like going," said Grace.

"So you do need cheering up. Do you want ice cream again?"

"Ughh! No, my stomach is too upset."

"Shopping therapy?"

"No, I'm kind of short on funds right now."

"Beauty therapy?"

Grace chuckled, "I could certainly use some of that. I know I look a mess right now."

"We could do manicures and pedicures."

"I've got a better idea," said Grace as her spirits lifted. "Let's color my hair."

"Really? What's wrong with your hair color?"

"I just think a change would lift my spirits. The other day I saw a really pretty girl with blond hair. I think I'd look good with blond hair instead of brown."

"You shouldn't try to look like someone else."

"I could never look like her—she was even taller than you are. Come on, I need this. It'll be a fresh start."

Olivia groaned. "Fine, I'll help. But I'm doing it under duress." She stood and offered Grace a hand up. "Come on, Sister—let's get some hair color and turn you into a blond bombshell."

Laughter exploded from the front door as it opened. "Hey Grace. Hey Olivia," said Hannah as she bounced into the room. "Claire and I just rented *Holiday*. Want to watch with us?"

"Olivia's going to color my hair," said Grace.

"I can help," said Claire. "I helped Jessica put highlights in her hair last month. I know all about hair color."

"We can do your hair while we watch the movie upstairs," said Hannah. "And you can tell us about breaking up with Brad."

"How do you know about it?" asked Grace, with an accusing glance toward Olivia.

"I didn't say a word," Olivia declared, lifting her chin.

"Spencer told me," said Hannah. "We had lunch at Papa's Place today."

"Why wouldn't you tell us, anyway? You always tell us when you break up," Claire asked.

"I think this time is different," said Hannah. "I think Grace is in love with Brad."

"No I'm not!" said Grace. "I'm the one who broke it off."

Claire squinted at Grace. "Why did you break up with Brad? He seemed perfect for you."

"Because... Because he got fresh with me," said Grace.

Hannah shook her head, making her auburn curls bounce. "Nope, I'm not buying it. Brad would never do that."

"How do you know?" asked Grace, as she felt the heat seeping into her face. She bent over to retie her tennis shoe, allowing time for her blush to fade while her face was averted.

"He's just not the type," said Hannah.

"I agree," Olivia said. "Brad would never do that. Maybe you got fresh with Brad."

Grace began, "Olivia! I can't believe—"

"I'm just kidding! I know you didn't do that. But I don't think you're telling us the truth. I think Hannah may be right, and you're actually in love with him." Olivia shared a smirk with the other two sisters.

"I think I would know if I was in love with him. And why would I break up with him if that were true?" Grace couldn't keep the shrill note out of her voice as she felt her stomach tighten. Why did people keep accusing her of being in love with Brad? It couldn't possibly be true. She was always careful to guard her heart and keep her emotional distance when she dated.

"That's a really good question," said Claire. "In fact, that's the question I asked you. Why did you break up with him?"

"I... There's another guy. His name is Horatio." Grace was wondering if she could keep this subterfuge going long enough to have an imaginary breakup with her imaginary guy before anyone insisted on meeting him.

Hannah crossed her arms over her chest, "You gave up Brad for another guy?"

"Why is that so hard to believe?" asked Grace.

Hannah's eyebrows flew up, "Are you kidding me? Brad is the sweetest guy you've ever dated, and he treats you like a queen. And I've seen him in a swimsuit."

"I have to agree," said Olivia. "It's hard to believe you met a guy that was better than Brad."

Grace opened her mouth to argue when her cell phone rang. The caller ID flashed Brad's name, and her heart began to pound. She turned her back to her sisters and answered in a soft voice, "Hello?"

"Hello Grace. I'm returning your phone call." Brad's voice was flat and emotionless.

Grace glanced over her shoulder at her sisters who were eavesdropping shamelessly. She took a few steps toward the kitchen, and they followed, ignoring her glares.

"I... I wanted to tell you... I wanted to apologize..." She heard dead silence on the other end of the phone. "Uhmm, Brad?"

"Yes, I'm here. What are you apologizing for? Are you sorry you broke up with me? Or are you sorry for how you broke up with me? Are you sorry you're dating someone else? Or are you sorry you ever started dating me?"

"I'm s-sorry that... Did you get my card? Or the flowers?"

"No Grace, I didn't get a card or flowers. But if you want to be absolved of guilt, I forgive you."

"I didn't mean to hurt you."

"Grace, hurt doesn't even begin to describe it, but this really isn't making it better. Why did you call me?"

"Josh told me I should call. He said..."

"Look Grace, I don't really care what Josh said. You told me you're dating another guy. Is that really true?"

Grace grappled with her conscience. Should she confirm the fabrication by lying again? If she told the truth and admitted there was no other guy, how would she explain the lie to Brad or her nosy, actively-listening sisters? "I... No... I mean... Yes, but... Listen Brad, could we maybe just get together and talk?"

"No Grace, I'm not the kind of guy who *gets together* with someone else's girlfriend. Maybe after you break up with Horatio or the next guy or the next guy, if I'm still around, we'll talk then."

And then Grace knew it was truly over. When had her goal changed from breaking up with Brad to getting him back? Why did she feel like a hole had been ripped in her chest? She tried to think of something appropriate to say—something she could say without breaking down and sobbing. "Brad..."

"Sorry Grace, I have to go." The line went dead—as dead as her heart.

Olivia watched and listened as the drama unfolded over the phone. She couldn't hear exactly what Brad was saying, but she caught the gist of it. Grace obviously regretted breaking up, but she'd realized it too late. She must have sent a card and flowers to say she was sorry, but he hadn't accepted her apology. When the phone slipped from her fingers and Grace dissolved into tears, all three sisters moved to embrace her and cry with her.

"We won't ask you any more questions," sniffed Olivia. "Let's just go color your hair."

"You'll look so good when we're finished with you," Claire declared. "That stupid guy will wish he'd accepted your apology when he sees how hot you are. Just you wait and see!"

Olivia wasn't quite as confident as her youngest sister about changing Grace's hair color, since she'd never done it before. But what could go wrong?

Chapter Four

"It's not that bad," said Olivia as the four of them studied Grace's hair in the bathroom mirror. Grace had the wide eyes and white face of a person in shock.

"It's orange," said Grace. "I look like a carrot."

"It looks better orange than it did when it was green," said Hannah. "And the highlights aren't orange. They look kind of blond."

"Yeah. Maybe I should put some more highlights in."

"No, Claire," Olivia said. "The highlights are already sort of crispy. I think her hair might just break off if we do anything else to it."

"I look like a crispy carrot."

"It really doesn't look that bad," said Olivia. "It's just a little red, like Hannah's."

Grace's eyes moved to Hannah's shiny auburn locks. "I'm short Olivia, but I'm not blind. My hair doesn't look like Hannah's. "I look like a Bozo, or Ronald McDonald's little sister!"

Olivia cringed at the truth in Grace's words. What could she say to be encouraging?

"It's my fault," said Grace. "I talked you into doing it. I just thought I would feel better if I had a change, but this wasn't quite what I pictured."

"Maybe if you went to a beauty shop, they could fix it," said Claire.

"It's almost midnight," said Hannah. "Do you think they have an emergency clinic somewhere?"

"I'll just wear a scarf. It doesn't matter anyway." She slunk out of the bathroom and fell face down onto the bed, speaking into the comforter. "It's a good thing I don't really want Brad back, because I think my chances just went from slim to none."

Claire and Hannah turned questioning faces to Olivia. "Come on," she whispered. "She needs us now more than ever." The sisters piled around her on the bed.

"What exactly were you apologizing to Brad for?" asked Claire.

Olivia frowned, "Claire, I promised her we wouldn't ask any questions."

"Yeah, but I didn't promise, and I want to know," said Claire. "I thought she'd be in a good mood after we did her hair, and she'd want to talk about it. But there's no chance of that now, so I'm just going to beg until she gives in."

"There's nothing to tell," said Grace as she rolled to face the ceiling. "I broke up with him and told him about Horatio."

"But you changed your mind, right?" said Hannah. "Isn't that why you wanted to talk to him?"

"It's a moot point," said Grace. "He doesn't want to talk to me."

Hannah said, "With your new hair, you could talk to him and he won't even know it's you."

Grace looked like she might burst into tears, but instead she started chuckling. "Maybe I could go to the emergency room and tell him I stuck my finger in a light socket."

Olivia tried to suppress a laugh, but when Claire snorted, they all lost it. They laughed until they had tears running down their faces. Olivia caught her breath and said, "For Halloween, you and Brad could go as Pebbles and Bam Bam."

Grace said, "I was thinking I looked like one of those troll dolls."

Claire snorted again, and when they broke up laughing there was a knock on the door.

"What's going on in here?" asked their mother, Connie, as she stuck her head in the room. "Why are you all up so late on a Thursday night?" Then her eyes fell on Grace. "Good Lord! What happened to your hair?"

The girls laughed so hard they couldn't catch their breath, until Connie stood before them with her hands on her hips. Grace sat up on the bed and fingered her hair gingerly. "I was supposed to get a blond bombshell look, but I accidentally got the Agent Orange bombshell look."

"Oh Grace." Connie's face was aghast. "Why would you do that to your beautiful hair?"

Olivia said, "It's no worse than when she tried to give herself a haircut."

"You're right," Connie agreed. "It's only just gotten back down to her shoulders after that fiasco."

"Remember the time she had orange streaks all over from that self-tanning spray?" said Claire. "At least this time it's only her hair that's orange."

"Yeah, and I still remember when she tried that straightener that got so hot it singed part of her hair off," said Hannah.

"That was right before she gave herself the bad haircut," said Olivia.

"That's enough," chuckled Grace. "At least this time all of you get to share the blame with me. You all helped."

Olivia said, "Only because we felt so sorry for you because you broke up with Brad and now you regret it."

"You broke up with Brad?" asked Connie. "Why would you do that? He was—"

"Please Mom, I've already figured out it wasn't my brightest move."

"She's dating some guy named Horatio," said Hannah. "He's not as cute as Brad."

"How do you know he's not as cute as Brad?" said Grace. "You've never seen him."

Hannah grinned. "But I've seen Brad. If you don't want him, I'll take him. He's adorable."

"I have to admit I really liked Brad," Connie said as her eyebrows knitted together. "He's the nicest boy you've ever dated."

Olivia could tell Grace's emotions were teetering on the edge. "I'm sure everything will work out fine, Grace. You do crazy stuff all the time, but you always land on your feet. And we all love you."

She gave her a hug and Claire wrapped her arm around the other shoulder. "We love you, orange hair and all."

Connie grimaced. "I'm sure we'll get used to your new look."

*****

Brad was in a foul mood when he came home from his shift in the ER. He'd let his temper get the better of him when he'd returned Grace's call. She'd held out an olive branch, and he'd burned it. At the time it had felt good—to hurt her like she'd hurt him. But now he regretted his harsh attitude. He'd cut her off, and he might not get another opportunity.

"Did Grace call you?" Josh had found him in the kitchen.

"Yes Josh. She called at your request, as I understand it. And I'll thank you to stay out of it." Brad grabbed a water bottle and retreated from his roommate, joining his brother on the couch.

Undeterred, Josh followed him and settled into a chair. "Did you talk to her? Did she tell you about the flowers and the card?"

"It's really none of your business," Brad retorted.

"Grace sent you flowers?" Ben asked. "So you're back together?"

"No, we're not together. She's dating someone else." The words tasted bitter in Brad's mouth.

Ben said, "Then why did she send flowers?"

"I don't even know for sure if she sent them. She claims she did, but who knows? As long as she's dating someone else, it doesn't really matter."

"She brought flowers and a card Tuesday morning," Josh said. "But she had to leave them with some nurse. It's not her fault they got lost at the hospital."

"If she really brought them," Brad muttered. He thought it was quite possible she'd made up the story.

"So you're done with Grace? You're not even willing to talk to her? You don't ever want to date her again?" Ben's voice sounded a little too eager when he asked the questions. Once again Brad lamented the fact Ben would spend Friday evening with Grace.

"Didn't you hear me? She's dating someone else."

"Who is this other guy?" Ben asked.

Josh jumped in. "His name's Horatio, but I'm sure she's not serious about this new guy."

"Horatio, huh?" Ben smirked. "I bet I could get her to drop Horatio and go out with me."

Brad felt steam building inside his head. "You leave her alone."

"Look, you don't seem to feel you're capable of winning her back from this Horatio guy, or else you just don't want to bother trying. But if you don't want her anymore, why shouldn't I ask her out?"

"Out of respect for me—that's why. You're my brother!"

"I know I'm your brother. I'm doing this for you."

"How would it benefit me if you dated my girlfriend?"

"Grace isn't your girlfriend anymore—you won't even talk to her. But at least if she's with me you might get to see her on occasion. And if we got married someday, your nieces and nephews would probably look a lot like your kids would have looked if you'd married her. Wouldn't that be nice for you?"

Brad was ninety percent sure Ben was simply egging him on, as was his nature, although his face never hinted he was teasing. But that ten percent uncertainty made his blood boil. "You don't have my permission to date Grace."

Josh said, "I'm not sure you can have it both ways." Brad turned to sear him with his harsh gaze. If his impenitent grin was any indication, Josh was enjoying Brad's discomfort. "I'm just saying you can't date Kara and claim Grace as your girlfriend."

"I'm not dating Kara—I'm just going to a baseball game with her."

Josh shrugged. "I'm not sure Kara sees it that way, according to what she told me today."

Ben added, "And I'm not sure that's how Grace will see it, either."

"Grace doesn't know I'm going to the baseball game with Kara, and she doesn't need to know. It's not a date—I'm certainly not planning to kiss her."

"According to the rules, it's a date because she bought your ticket," said Josh.

"What rules?" asked Ben.

Josh explained, "It's the Best Dating Rules—Emily and Charlie Best's rules. But the Marshall Sisters have adopted the rules, so they apply in this case."

"I'm going to pay her back for the ticket," said Brad. "So it's not a date."

Ben said, "Still, I think it's only fair I should get a shot at Grace, so—"

Brad lunged up from the couch before he lost all control. He stood glaring at his brother with clenched fists. "If you make a move on Grace, I'll rip your other shoulder out of its socket." Ben's only response was a slow smile. Brad stomped into his room and slammed his door. For the first time, he understood why Cain killed Able.

*****

Horatio loved Ms. Marshall's new hair—she looked just like his favorite singer. "Ms. Marshall, I got you something, just like I promised." He stood as close as he could get, pushing Jeffrey out of the way.

"Oh Horatio, I told you not to spend your money on me. I'm not allowed to accept gifts from my students."

"But you took the cookies my mom sent."

"Yes, but that was a gift from your mother," she explained.

He had to get her to take his present—then they would be engaged. "It's from my mom, but I picked it out."

"Are you sure you didn't spend your tooth money on this present?"

"No ma'am. My mom bought it for you."

She opened the little box and her mouth formed an 'O' at the beautiful diamond ring. "Your mom bought this for me?" she asked, narrowing her eyes. "It seems like an unusual gift from a mother."

Grace picked up the ring and examined it. The lightweight plastic ring with the gold-colored split band looked amazingly real at first glance. She peeked at Horatio's anxious face as he watched her reaction. She knew this present hadn't come from his mother, but she couldn't very well accuse him of lying.

"Tell your mother I said, 'Thank you very much.' It's a beautiful ring. I can't wear it at school because it might make the other children feel jealous, but I'll wear it home. Okay?"

"Okay!" he said, grinning from ear to ear.

This was not the first time one of her students had been infatuated with her, but it was the first time it had happened this early in the school year. She would have to be gentle in her discouragement so as not to hurt his feelings.

"Now, would you like to make me really happy?"

"Yes ma'am!"

"Let me see how still and quiet you can sit for reading time, because that's my favorite time."

"Yes ma'am. I can be really still, like not moving at all. And I won't make any noise at all. I'll even hold my breath."

"No, don't hold your breath; you might pass out."

"Really?" Horatio's exultant expression demonstrated his delight at this possibility.

"No, you won't actually pass out from holding your breath, but you don't need to be that quiet. Now go sit down so we can get started with reading time."

She leaned over to reach for her book, and a lock of fried orange hair fell across her face. She chuckled as she tucked the stiff strand behind her ear. At least she had one admirer who wasn't turned off by her new clown coif. She had high hopes her hair stylist would work a miracle at her emergency appointment after work.

*****

"Well... Say something... What do you suggest? I'll pay whatever it takes to fix it. Really, money is no object," Grace rambled on to the girl who'd stood staring at her hair with wide unblinking eyes since she removed her scarf.

"Uhmm... Let me ask the other colorists." Soon there were six stylists, including the owner, gawking in abject horror.

The owner said, "We could maybe shave your head. The shop has some nice wigs."

"Shave it?" squeaked Grace. "Isn't there anything else you can do? Can't we just color it brown again?"

"What do you think, Carlos? You're the expert."

Carlos tapped his finger on his chin, "I'd say give her a pixie cut and a brown temporary rinse to tone it down a little. That's the best you can do. You can't use any more bleach on that hair." He reached out to crackle a strand between his fingers. "I'm not even going to ask what you did to cause this, but please don't ever do it again."

Grace was surprised she didn't have the urge to cry. After her week of stressing about Brad, this seemed like a walk in the park. She smiled at Carlos, "I guess I'm getting a pixie cut. No worries—I'll never do it again."

She wished she could go back in time and make a different decision about her hair. But she wished even more she could turn back the days and reverse the decision to breakup with Brad. What should she have done when he declared his love and intent to marry her? All she knew was her decisions had resulted in heartache. She'd had no idea how much she would miss him. After all, they'd only been dating for two months. But there was nothing she could do about it now—he'd made it clear there was no going back, no second chances. At least her hair would grow back some day.

*****

Ben was really enjoying his visit to New York. Nothing gave him more pleasure than teasing his brother, and Brad had really set himself up this time. He was looking forward to an evening with Emily and Spencer and, of course, Grace. He ought to be able to gain enough fuel in one night to irritate his brother for a week or two. And if he managed to spur him into fighting for Grace, that would be even better. He hadn't been exaggerating when he'd claimed Grace was the only one of Brad's girlfriends he liked. He had no intention of allowing Brad to throw away the best thing he'd ever had.

"So where's Grace?" Ben asked. "She's not coming to dinner?"

Emily said, "She called to say she'd be late. She said something about having a hair appointment."

"Well these fajitas are great—she's really missing out," said Ben.

"She'll be here in time for the baseball game," said Spencer. "She never misses a game."

Ben said, "So before she gets here, we should discuss how we're going to get her back together with Brad."

"Great," said Emily. "Do you have some good ideas?"

"Wait—that's none of our business," said Spencer, as he glowered at Emily.

"Of course it's our business," said Ben. "I'm Brad's brother. You're Grace's brother. It's our job to make sure our siblings don't screw up their lives."

"I agree," said Emily. "Grace is miserable. How's Brad doing?"

"He's even grouchier than usual," said Ben. "Grace kept him a lot more even-keeled. He has obsessive and perfectionist tendencies."

"I'm sure they'll get back together without our help," said Spencer.

"Did he tell you he's going to the baseball game with another woman? She's one of the doctors he works with."

Spencer scrunched his eyes to narrow slits. "No, he didn't say he was going with a girl. They just broke up; I'm surprised he's already dating someone else."

Ben said, "Isn't Grace dating some guy named Horatio?"

"That's right," said Emily. "I found out he's a waiter at Per Se and getting a degree in Meteorology. I'm sure he's a nice guy, but I really wanted her to be with Brad. I think he's good for her, and she's good for him."

"I have to admit, she hasn't been quite as crazy since she started dating Brad," said Spencer.

A knock at the door alerted them to Grace's arrival. "I'll get it," said Ben. "You two just need to remember my ultimate goal is get them back together, no matter what I say to Grace." He opened the door with a flourish. "Come in, Grace. We've been waiting..." His voice trailed off when he caught sight of the girl at the door. "Grace? Is that you?" This girl didn't look like Grace, at least not the Grace he remembered. She was petite like Grace, but she had really short hair and it was... He wasn't sure what color to call it. It was kind of a rusty brown.

"It's me," said Grace as she swept into the room. "I know... The hair is horrible. But believe me, it's a lot better now than it was this morning."

Ben glanced at Emily and Spencer who were gaping in silence. They weren't going to be any help at all. He scrambled to say something reassuring to Grace, "It's cute Grace. I just didn't recognize you."

Grace turned toward him and a laugh burst out. "Ben, that's actually pretty good. I mean, I know you're lying, of course. But you're pretty good at it. Have you taken some acting lessons?"

He smiled at her good humor. "No, but I worked for a while at a used car lot."

"Ah ha! That explains it," she said, flashing her cute grin. "You don't have to be nice. It was a terrible accident, and I've been told I'm lucky to have any hair at all."

"You know, Grace. It's growing on me. I think I actually like it." This time he meant the words he said. She was just so good-natured about everything she couldn't help but look appealing. He was more determined than ever she was the right girl for Brad. His uptight brother had really started enjoying life when he was dating Grace.

"Ben, you're probably the only man on the planet who would say that right now."

Spencer said, "The haircut is cute, Gracie. It's just the color that's kind of weird. But it's probably not the worst you've ever looked. I remember one time when you got such a bad sunburn you were peeling like a lizard. And then one time you put some kind of temporary pink color on your hair, but it took like six weeks to fade."

"Oh, I'd forgotten about that. And I think I swore never to color my hair again. Oops," she chuckled.

"Since I've gotten over the shock, I think I might like it," said Emily. "What did Horatio say?"

"Uhmm... I think he's fine with it," said Grace.

Emily's voice shrieked, "Grace! What is that ring on your finger?"

Ben followed Emily's gaze to Grace's hand. There was a large diamond ring—at least a carat and a half, maybe two carats.

Grace pulled the ring off and stuck it in her pocket. "It's nothing, really. It doesn't mean anything."

"Did Horatio give it to you?" Emily asked. "I thought you just started dating."

Grace hesitated, glancing at Ben. "We're not serious. It's not an engagement ring."

"That looked like a honker of a diamond," said Ben.

"His mother bought it," Grace said, as if that explained everything.

"He sounds like a real winner." Ben relished the way Grace blushed at his sarcastic response. "I can certainly see why you would want to date Harry Toe instead of Brad."

"Horatio," she corrected.

"Horatio," he repeated. "How long have you two been dating? I'm surprised you'd actually date someone else behind Brad's back."

"I didn't," said Grace. "We haven't actually gone out yet, not according to the rules."

"I'm sorry, Grace. But if he gave you a ring, that counts as paying for something," Emily said.

"No," said Ben. "I guess that technically means Grace went on a date with Horatio's mother."

"Please, can we not talk about it?"

Ben softened at her pleading eyes. "Fine. I won't tease you anymore. At least for a while." He winked at her.

"Are you hungry, Gracie? I made fajitas, and the game's about to start. Just grab a plate." Spencer turned on the television.

*****

Brad was rather astonished to find their tickets were behind home plate in Yankee Stadium, but he was still determined to pay for his ticket. His feelings were hurt, but in his heart he knew he still loved Grace. He wasn't about to have an "official date" with Kara on his record. It might interfere with his plan to get Grace back. And that was definitely his plan. Only one week since their breakup, and he'd hardly gone an hour without thinking about her. He'd even dreamed about her. Josh was right—he'd made a mistake when he considered giving up on the relationship simply because Grace had gotten cold feet. He was going to win her back, even if he had to eat humble pie to do it.

"So how much do I owe you for the ticket?" he asked Kara.

"I got them for a bargain price—a friend of my father has season tickets."

"How much?" he insisted.

"Only five hundred."

"Five hundred dollars? Each?"

"Yeah, but you don't owe me anything. I wasn't expecting you to pay. I'm just glad to have your company."

"No, I'm paying for my ticket."

"Whatever makes you happy." Kara grasped his arm and pushed herself against him as she leaned in to whisper in his ear. "This is so much fun."

Brad carefully disentangled his arm from her grasp. "Dr. Dickson, I hope I haven't misled you in any way. This is not a date."

She shrunk away. "I know. I'm just excited about seeing the game. I didn't mean to offend you." She offered him a trembling smile.

He groaned inwardly. "I'm not offended. But I have a girlfriend, and I want to make sure this stays on a 'friends' basis."

"You have a girlfriend? I thought..."

Brad caught the surprise in her tone. "You thought what?"

"I... I thought you said something about breaking up with her. I'm almost sure you said something about it."

His jaw tightened. "I never said anything about breaking up."

"So you're... you're still with her?"

"Yes, I'm still with Grace. And what business is it of yours?" The words came out with more force than intended, and he saw her cringe. She blinked rapidly as if fighting tears. "I'm sorry. If you're upset with me, we don't have to stay for the game. We can end the date now, and you don't owe me anything."

Brad breathed out slowly, trying to control his temper. "No, it's fine. But we were very clear when we made this date... I mean, when we made this *arrangement* we were only going together as colleagues. You told me you wanted me to go with you so some other guy would back off. Was that a lie?"

"No, but I thought when things changed between you and that Grace girl—"

"Who told you things had changed between us? I never said anything of the sort."

"Uhmm, I don't know. I guess it was maybe Dr. Branson who told me you two had had a fight. And then I just assumed..."

"Josh told you that?" Brad felt his blood boiling. He'd been feeling bad about his prickly attitude with his roommate, but not now. Josh had no business airing his private business with anyone, especially not Kara Dickson.

"Oh please don't be upset with him! Dr. Branson is my attending. If you say anything to him, he'll take it out on me and put me on the worst schedule."

"Dr. Branson is a professional, and he would never do that."

"Please! Oh please don't tell him! Maybe I was wrong—maybe someone else told me."

"Actually no one else knew about it." Brad felt like all of his muscles were wound up tight, ready to break.

"So you did have a fight, then?"

"No! Well, yes, but we're still together."

"But you can't blame me for hoping. I know I'd never stand a chance if the two of you were still together, but I thought maybe—" Good grief. Was she actually batting her eyelashes?

"Kara, I was very clear this was not a romantic relationship. Look, let's just forget this and enjoy the game."

"Maybe we'll get lucky and the Yankees will win."

"What, you don't expect them to win?" Brad squinted. "I thought you told me you loved baseball?"

"I do. I love baseball." Her expression was as fervent as her voice. "I love the Yankees. And the Mets, too."

"Well, don't say that too loud around here. Most Yankees fans hate the Mets."

"Who do you like?" Kara asked.

"I like the Yankees and the Giants and the Knicks. I'd like to get really good seats to see the Knicks play sometime."

"Maybe I could get some tickets, and we could go together. I really like the Knicks, too."

Brad couldn't help but feel he was being played. Grace's enthusiasm about sports was one of her most unusual and attractive traits in his eyes. He found it difficult to believe Kara Dickson was being honest with him, but he knew a way to find out.

"Did you watch the Knicks game last week?" he asked, wondering if she would know the Knicks were a basketball team and the season hadn't started.

"I missed the game—I had to work." Her face was stricken with disappointment. "Was it good?"

"It was great," said Brad. As he suspected, she appeared to have no idea who the Knicks were or when their season was. Just to be certain, he probed a little further. "The Knicks' new quarterback is great, don't you think?"

"I agree," she said with an enthusiastic smile, looping her arm through his.

"But that game they played against the Rangers was something else." He named the New York ice hockey team.

"Yeah. I didn't see it, but I heard about it."

Brad kept his expression neutral, but at least he knew what he was up against. Evidently Dr. Dickson felt comfortable lying about her interest and knowledge of sports. He'd have to listen carefully lest she try to get by with any other lies during the evening. He was fortunate he'd gotten her to reveal her source for the information about his fight with Grace. If he hadn't caught her off-guard, she probably would have lied about that as well.

"Did you see who's sitting right in front of us?" Kara leaned in to whisper. "Isn't that Alicia Winters?" Kara was almost certain she recognized the movie star. "Do you think that means we'll be on television sitting here?"

Brad stiffened and inched away. "We're right behind home plate, Kara. We're probably on television right before every pitch. That would be true even if Alicia Winters wasn't sitting here."

Kara fumed inside. This wasn't going at all the way she'd planned. Brad still seemed to have an attachment to that puny Grace, even though they'd obviously had a terrible fight. She could tell from his continuing grumpy mood, they hadn't made up with each other. And as far as she knew, Brad was unaware Grace had attempted to apologize with flowers and a card. Kara couldn't fathom why he was so attracted to Grace. She wasn't smart or pretty, and she didn't seem to have much money. Her only advantage over Kara was her preference for sports, and Brad didn't realize Kara barely tolerated sports events. But Kara had one huge advantage over his tiny ex-girlfriend—she was a really good actress. She'd been fooling her parents since a very early age, and she could make Brad believe anything she wanted. She just needed to get rid of Grace so he would see he and Kara were perfect together. And she had a really good idea how to do it.

"So where is Grace tonight? She doesn't like the Yankees?"

The muscles in his jaw flexed. "She's watching the game with her brother."

Her heart leapt. Grace would see them together tonight. As she suspected, Brad was attempting to keep his distance because he'd realized Grace might see him at the game with Kara.

*****

Grace hadn't managed to swallow a single bite of her fajita since she'd spotted Brad sitting behind home plate with the beautiful blond girl. She recognized the girl at once. "That's Leanne."

"Who's Leanne?" asked Emily.

Grace hadn't even realized she'd spoken the words aloud.

"Nobody. I mean... She's... That's who Brad is sitting with at the game. They have amazing seats. I'm happy for him."

Ben was sitting beside her on the couch. "I don't think her name is Leanne. I think it's Kara."

"No, I would never forget that girl. She's beautiful." Grace tried not to think about her short, frizzled, rusty hair as the girl sitting beside Brad flicked her heavy golden locks over her shoulder.

"So you're jealous then?" asked Ben.

Yes, she was jealous. She wanted to pull that girl's hair out by its roots.

"No, I don't have any right to be jealous. I'm the one who broke it off so I could be with Horatio."

The words tasted like cough medicine, and she fought to keep her expression calm. Her cell phone chirped a message alert. Could it be Brad? She didn't recognize the number.

U lik th dimen?

She texted back. *Who is this?*

Horatio. U hav th dimen on?

Grace felt a few more rocks land in her already heavy stomach. This was really getting out of hand. How did Horatio get her cell number? And more importantly, how was she going to discourage him without breaking his heart.

Horatio, it is a beautiful ring. But I can't wear it. She was suddenly inspired. *I already have a fiancé, and he would be jealous.* Perhaps he would feel better if he thought she'd already had a boyfriend before the school year started. Her phone beeped another message indicator.

?

He didn't understand. Of course he couldn't read well, since he'd just started first grade. She texted back. *Talk 2 U Monday.*

Ben was watching with undisguised curiosity. "Your face is white. Who are you texting? Is that Brad?"

Grace felt the blood rush into her face and lifted her hand to tug at her short hair, hoping to hide her face. "No. It's not Brad." She nodded at the baseball game. "He's too busy to be texting me."

Grace's eyes almost bulged out of her head as she watched Leanne flip her hair behind her. She had taken off her outer shirt, leaving behind a very low-cut shell with spaghetti straps. She didn't appear to be paying much attention to the game, instead turning toward Brad and leaning against him to speak in his ear. He didn't even flinch as she pressed her breasts against his arm. It suddenly occurred to Grace Leanne might not have given her card and flowers to Brad as she'd promised.

Emily must have noticed her tormented expression. "Grace, I don't think he's encouraging her."

The only way to save face was to pretend she wasn't bothered. "Oh, I don't care if he's with Leanne. After all, I've got Horatio."

"So you're not interested in Brad anymore?" asked Ben in a low voice.

"I still care about him. I want him to be happy."

"But you don't want to get back together with him?" Ben insisted. "Not ever?"

"Well, you see... I'm the one who broke it off. And he doesn't want to talk to me anymore, so I'll just stick with Horatio."

"But you said you haven't actually been out with Horatio. So you don't even know if you like him."

"What are you getting at?" asked Grace.

"I think you should go out with me," Ben whispered from the side of his mouth, with his eyes fastened on the television.

"Ohmygosh!" said Emily. "Did you see that?"

"Yes, I saw it," growled Spencer.

"What happened?" asked Grace, thinking she'd missed part of the game.

"She kissed him," said Ben, whose face looked like he'd swallowed dill pickle juice.

Leanne had kissed Brad? Grace stared at the television as if she would see an instant replay, but the camera was trained on the coach who was yelling at the umpire. She felt bile in her throat as the reality of the situation hit her. She'd gotten what she asked for a week ago, even though she'd since changed her mind. Brad had refused to consider talking to her, and he was dating another girl. And evidently, he'd given his brother the go-ahead to ask her out. She jumped up from the couch and barely made it to the bathroom before her stomach emptied its meager contents.

Emily immediately regretted mentioning the kiss. She'd spoken aloud without thinking. Grace hadn't even seen it happen—if only she'd kept her big mouth shut. She saw Grace spring off the couch and rush to the bathroom. She started to follow her when she noticed Ben was using the opportunity to peruse Grace's cell phone.

"You shouldn't do that," she scolded as she moved to look over his shoulder.

Ben made a point of covering the screen. "If you're going to criticize me, I won't tell you what she was texting about."

Spencer frowned, "Hey, that's an invasion of privacy."

Ben let out a low whistle as he scrolled through her messages. Emily said, "What? What is it?"

"I shouldn't say," said Ben, cocking an eyebrow toward Spencer. "It's an invasion of privacy."

"You've already done it, so you might as well tell us now," said Spencer.

57

Ben leaned forward and spoke in a soft voice. "The thing is, Horatio is evidently pressuring her to wear the ring, and she's telling him she's engaged to someone else. So I'm thinking she doesn't really want to date this guy. And from her reaction to that kiss, I'm pretty confident she still likes Brad, whether she admits it or not."

"So what are we going to do?" asked Emily.

"Nothing," said Spencer, with a stern set to his jaw. "It's not our place to interfere."

"Buddy," said Ben. "As I understand it, Brad saved your rear by interfering between you and Emily."

Spencer's frown relaxed. "I guess that's true. He did send me the text to warn me about that picture Becca used to sabotage our relationship. If it weren't for him, we might not be engaged."

"So we owe it to Brad to help him out," said Emily. "Let's—" She swallowed her words as the bathroom door opened and Grace emerged, looking decidedly green. She moved to put an arm around her petite friend. "Can I get something for you? Maybe a glass of water?"

Grace nodded and moved to sink onto the couch, keeping her eyes averted.

Emily strained to listen as Ben murmured to Grace. "So I'm in town until Monday. Want to catch a play with me? I've been wanting to see *Aladdin*."

Emily almost dropped the glass of water when Grace held up her left hand and wiggled her finger, flashing the large diamond at him. "I can't go out with you," she told Ben. "I'm taken."

His brows scrunched with a deep furrow between them. "I thought you said you hadn't even started dating."

Grace pulled her shoulders up and dropped them as if the effort exhausted her. "It seems I've gotten in the habit of telling lies lately."

"Maybe you're lying now," Ben suggested.

Grace stood and trudged toward the door, ignoring the water glass Emily offered. "Whatever," she said. "I'm going home."

"But the game's not over," said Spencer, clearly nonplussed his sports-fanatical sister would leave in the middle of a baseball game.

"I've lost interest," said Grace.

"Or maybe you just don't want to look at Brad with his date anymore," said Ben.

Emily saw tears rolling down Grace's face as she slipped out the door without responding to Ben's remark.

"Wait Grace!" She followed her out into the hallway and shut the door behind them. Grace was heading toward the stairs when Emily caught her and pulled her into a hug. "I know you're hurting, no matter what you say. You were there for me when Spencer and I were having a rough time. And I'm here for you now."

"It's not the same. Spencer was in love with you—Brad's not in love with me. It's so stupid." She swiped at her wet face. "I didn't even want him to be in love with me, and now I wish he was."

"Are you really engaged to Horatio?"

"What does it matter? Brad has obviously given Ben the go-ahead to ask me out. So he's finished with me for sure."

"Just because Ben is flirting doesn't mean Brad is okay with it. You know how Ben loves to antagonize his brother. I think Ben wants you two to get back together."

"He has a funny way of showing it. But really it just confirms what I already knew. When I spoke to Brad, he could barely be civil to me. I had one shot at making things right and I blew it. I left flowers and a card for Brad with Leanne, and obviously she wanted him for herself."

Emily gritted her teeth. "That girl he was with tonight? She sabotaged you? You should strangle her—I might do it myself. Why don't you just tell Brad what she did?"

Grace lifted puddled eyes her direction. "I tried to give him flowers, and he never got them. I tried to talk to him, and he didn't want to listen. Obviously Brad and I were never meant to be. You shouldn't have to work so hard if it's right."

"You don't really believe that, do you?"

"Yes. I've always believed I'll be able to tell when the right guy comes along. I'll just know—everything will feel right. That's how I knew I was supposed to break up when he first said something about being in love with me. It messed up my mind so much I could barely eat anything. In fact, I've hardly eaten for a week. I would never feel so afraid if it was meant to be—if we were supposed to be together forever."

"I think you're totally off. I was scared to death to fall in love when I met Spencer. I fought it for a long time, and you know things weren't real smooth for us. What if I'd given up when things got rough? What if I'd decided since I went to the wrong hiking area we weren't meant to be together?"

"That's different."

Emily put her hands on her hips. "How? How is my situation different from yours?"

"Because you and Spencer were destined to be together. Nothing could keep you apart. Obviously, the opposite is true for Brad and me. All the signs point to Brad and I staying apart. He didn't get my flowers. He wouldn't talk to me. He's already found someone else, and so have I." Grace held up her hand to flash her ring again before hiding it inside her purse.

Emily debated whether to push her on the subject. "Tell me the truth, Grace. Who is Horatio? Because I don't buy it—everything you've said about him is a little fishy. You broke up with Brad to date him, but you haven't actually been out with him yet. He's already given you a ring with a huge diamond, but his mother paid for it? And earlier tonight you took the ring off, so why are you wearing it again? When are we going to meet him?"

"Sunday night—you'll meet him at Sunday night dinner," said Grace as she fled down the stairs.

Where on earth was she going to find a guy to play Horatio by Sunday night? She had less than forty-eight hours to find someone. She'd seen movies where you could hire someone, an escort. But she didn't have that kind of money. She could easily pick up a guy in a bar, but not one who'd be willing to play her pretend boyfriend. Her only choice was to bring someone in on the subterfuge—Olivia. Lucky for her, Olivia was studying at home tonight.

"But I don't know if I can find a guy who's willing to do this," Olivia objected. "And I don't really want you and Brad to break up anyway. I can't believe you made up a guy just so you could have an excuse to stop dating Brad. Why didn't you just tell him you were freaked about him talking about marriage?"

"I don't know. It just happened. But I'm going to look like an idiot if I don't produce a real boyfriend now, especially since Brad has already moved on." Grace's mind was filled with an image of the tall, beautiful blond who'd been so affectionate with Brad. "And the guy needs to be really cute, too. Leanne is everything I'm not. She's smart and super tall—even taller than you. And her hair is gorgeous." Grace reached up to stroke the back of her shorn locks.

Olivia gave her a sympathetic smile. "Grace, you're smart and you're still cute, even with messed up hair. And Brad liked you just fine at five foot two. He fell in love with you, didn't he?"

Grace cocked an eyebrow. "No, he just thought he was in love."

"Well you must have been pretty sure it was true, or it wouldn't have scared the pants off you. Anyway, Leanne is a conniving, lying... witch. And it's not like Brad is going to bring her to Sunday night dinner. He might not even come—he didn't come last week."

"I know, but I told Emily I was bringing Horatio to dinner. So you know she told Spencer and Ben, and Ben will tell Brad."

Olivia made a growling sound in her throat as she pushed her hair back. "I really don't want to do this. I just want to help you get back together with Brad."

Grace wrestled with her emotions. Part of her wanted the same thing Olivia wanted. She missed him so much, and it had only been a week. But she had to face reality. "It's the rule of three, Olivia. Since I broke up with him, I've had three signs we shouldn't get back together. First, I brought him flowers, and he never got them. Second, I called him, and he wasn't interested in talking to me. Third, he went out with another girl. And actually, I'm sure the mess I made of my hair is just another sign."

"Grace, sometimes I want to strangle you! You have this stupid rule of three signs, but you twist it around to confirm anything you want. "How about the fact you've totally quit eating since you broke up? Isn't that a sign? And how about the fact you were willing to buy him flowers and give him a card and call him and try to get back together? You've never done anything like that before for any guy you broke up with. Couldn't that be a sign? And furthermore, are you going to let him end up with an evil girl who would lie and scheme to get her claws into him?"

Grace contemplated her words and blinked against watery eyes. "I just want him to be happy, whatever it takes. I don't think I'm the one who can do that for him, but I guess it would be awful for him to end up with Leanne."

"So we're in agreement you're going to tell him what she did."

"He doesn't want to talk to me." The acid words rolled off her tongue.

"Fine, then I'll talk to him."

"No, you can't do that." Grace lay on her bed, staring at the watercolors adorning her walls. She murmured, "Maybe I can get someone from my art class to play Horatio..."

"Will you forget about Horatio? We're talking about Brad, and he deserves to know the truth about Leanne."

"Yes, but he won't believe it coming from you or me." Grace pursed her lips in concentration. "There's one guy named Gavin who paints next to me, but I think he may have a crush on me."

"Every guy you meet has a crush on you, Grace. You could just bring a different guy to Sunday night dinner and say you broke up with Horatio already. It's totally believable."

"What a great idea," said Grace, perking up. "Why didn't I think of that? I'll bring Gavin to dinner and tell Emily I broke up with Horatio because he was being too pushy. She'll buy that for sure."

"That sounds kind of mean to do to Gavin," Olivia said.

"I'll be really clear we're only friends."

"You mean friends with kissing benefits? Isn't that what you told Brad?"

"Yes, but I obviously didn't make myself clear with Brad. I'll be firmer with Gavin. And anyway, I don't think I'm ready to kiss another guy yet."

"And I'll talk to Brad and tell him the truth about what happened."

Grace sat up to grip Olivia's arm. "No, you can't tell him. If he figures it out himself, it will be a sign we should get back together."

"Grace, that's stupid!"

"I mean it. I forbid you to tell him. I shouldn't have ever told you the truth. Now I don't need you to find a Horatio for me."

"You'd never have thought of switching to a different guy if it weren't for me, so you still owe me," said Olivia. "And stop rolling your eyes at me."

"I'm serious. You've already taken the Vow of Secrecy, so you can't tell Brad what Leanne did."

"I invoke the Sisterly Right of Protection."

"You know the rules for that—you made it up yourself. You can only break a promise by invoking the Sisterly Right of Protection in an emergency situation where I'm not able to talk to you. So I'd have to be unconscious or kidnapped or something."

"I'm invoking it based on the fact the person I'm talking to right now is not the normal Grace Marshall. You are beyond Grace's normal level of crazy. So since I can't talk to Grace—"

"However, you made the Vow of Secrecy with *this* Grace Marshall, and I'm the one you're talking to."

Olivia let out a scream and stomped her feet. "Grace! Why are you being so stubborn about this?"

"Don't you see? It's humiliating. I gave him flowers and a card and groveled, asking for another chance. And then I called him. When I mentioned the card and flowers, I could tell he didn't believe me. He thinks I lied to him when we broke up, and he's right. So I can't defend myself. He thinks I'm a liar because I *am* a liar. He doesn't believe anything I say anymore."

"So quit lying. Tell him the truth about everything. Don't bring a guy to Sunday night dinner."

"No, that'll just prove I kept lying about Horatio."

"So you're lying more to cover a lie you told to protect another lie you told because you're too humiliated to tell the truth now because it will prove you lied before?"

"Exactly," said Grace. "Now do you understand?"

"No. That didn't even make sense when I was saying it. I invoke the Sisterly Right of Coercion. When you're doing something really stupid, I have the right to jump in and stop you."

"You just made that up," said Grace. "That's not even a real Marshall Sisters law."

"You and I made up all the laws," Olivia reasoned. "This is just a new one that's long overdue. I should have invoked it to keep you from coloring your hair."

"So what are you going to do? You have to tell me."

"No, I invoke the Sisterly Right to Privacy."

"You can't invoke the Right of Coercion and the Right to Privacy at the same time."

"I just made it up, and I declare the Right of Coercion can be invoked at any time with any other law, and no other law can make it null and void."

"What does that mean?"

Olivia moved to slide out the bedroom door. "I don't know—I was just covering my bases. See ya later, Sister." She shut the door behind her with a soft click.

"Olivia! Olivia! Come back here!" Grace heard her laughter floating behind her like tinkling bells.

Chapter Five

"SO YOU COULD SEE US ON TV?" Brad winced as he awaited the answer he already knew would be forthcoming.

"Oh yes, little brother. You and your blond date were quite visible. And I'll save you the trouble of asking... Yes, Grace saw you with her; and yes, she saw the girl throwing herself at you. And I must say you didn't seem to object very much," Ben chuckled.

"I was leaning away as far as I could. And I swear, when she kissed me... Couldn't you tell I was trying to get away from her? I practically peeled her off me. Especially the second time."

"Grace left after the first kiss."

"She left?"

"Yes."

"As in, she left before the game was over? She didn't stay to watch the end of the game?" When had Grace ever failed to watch the end of a game?

"I'm fairly certain that first kiss upset her enough she couldn't watch anymore."

Brad felt a strange sense of pleasure because she'd been jealous. Perhaps she had feelings for him after all. "Maybe it was good then. Maybe she needed to see me with someone else."

"Oh yeah. It was great. In fact, I'm pretty sure she wretched in the bathroom." Now Ben fixed him with a cold stare. "If you're going to treat her like that and be happy when you hurt her, you don't deserve her anyway."

"I never said I wanted to hurt her."

"No, but I'm your brother, and I recognize that satisfied look on your face. Just forget it. I'm not helping you anymore."

"I never asked for your help in the first place."

"Fine!" Ben folded his arms across his chest.

"Fine!" Brad grabbed the remote and switched on the television, flipping aimlessly through the channels.

"After she came out of the bathroom, she was wearing Horatio's diamond ring."

Brad froze, cutting his eyes toward his brother. Was he fabricating a story to rile him up? But his face was impassive.

"She was wearing a ring? A diamond ring?"

"I shouldn't even tell you. All you want to do is hurt her anyway. I suppose you picked that girl on purpose. It was worse because you went with someone she knew."

Brad frowned. "She doesn't know Kara."

"Grace knows her. She said her name was Leanne."

"She's got her mixed up with someone else. The girl I was with was Dr. Kara Dickson, and Grace doesn't have any way of knowing her. But what were you saying about a ring?"

Ben gave a lazy stretch. "Nothing really. She just had this humungous diamond ring Horatio was trying to get her to wear. But according to the text I just happened to see on her cell phone, she was telling him she was already engaged to another guy. So I thought to myself, she really doesn't like this Horatio and she's already trying to blow him off. But after she saw you sucking face on television—"

"I wasn't sucking face!"

"After she saw that kiss, she came out of the bathroom with that ring on her finger. So I guess you helped her make up her mind. Good job, brother. Like I said, you don't deserve her anyway. Who knows, you might not like her with short hair anyway."

"Short hair?" It had only been a week. How could so much have happened to Grace in a week?

"Yep, she chopped it off short. She's cute, like a little elf. By the way, I asked her out."

Brad threw the remote across the room, where it hit the wall and cracked open, double-A batteries rolling across the floor. "I told you to keep away from her."

Ben didn't flinch, but raised a single eyebrow as one corner of his mouth kicked up. "Temper, temper. Once you turned your baseball game into a real date by kissing that girl, I assumed I had the go-ahead."

Something snapped inside. He grabbed his brother's shirt collar and shook him, barely resisting the urge to break his jaw.

"Hey! Ow! Man... I think you made me break a molar." Brad fished in his mouth and pulled out a small chunk of enamel. "Look at that. You broke my tooth."

"It's your own fault. You know good and well I didn't kiss her—she kissed me."

"That's just semantics."

"You don't read—you don't even know what that word means."

"Audiobooks, Brother. Who needs to read when I can simply listen? But the point is, the kiss made it a date. You are dating someone else, so you have no say in who Grace dates."

"I'm not dating Kara. And you're breaking the brotherly code by asking her out."

Ben let his mouth widen into a grin. "I'm sorry, but in my book, the brotherly code is to hassle you as much as possible."

"You've obviously never read that book, because brothers are supposed to cover each other's backs, not stab them."

"So do something about it. Stop me. If you don't want me to date Grace, call her up. Apologize for whatever stupid thing you did and patch things up."

"I didn't do anything wrong." Even as he spoke the words, he knew they weren't true. He'd known in his heart it was too soon to tell Grace about his feelings for her. Mentioning marriage after two months of dating had sent her into a panic. She'd been completely irrational after his slip-up.

"I understand you believe you're infallible, but even the great Dr. Brad Gates can make a mistake." Ben bowed in mock subservience. "Please forgive my audaciousness at making such an unsettling, though astute, observation, Your Greatness."

Brad snarled his response, "I know I'm not perfect. That's not the problem."

"Then what is the problem?"

What was the problem? Why hadn't he called her or texted her after she'd run away from him, claiming to be dating someone else?

Why hadn't he listened to her when she'd asked to talk to him? Pride—his pride was hurt. He'd never had a girl break up with him before. He'd always been the one to do the leaving.

Ben's head tilted as he watched the thought process play out on Brad's face. "Have you had an epiphany, Your Greatness?"

Brad glowered at his impudent brother. "It's none of your business." He stomped into his bedroom, slamming the door and sending a picture hurdling to the floor. He heard a faint voice call behind him.

"There's one other thing you might want to know," Ben's smug voice rang out.

Brad pulled the door open with such force it slammed against the wall, denting the sheetrock. "Tell me!"

"She's planning to bring Horatio to dinner at the Marshall's tomorrow night."

Brad grunted and shut the door on his brother's chuckling. He tried to decipher the meaning of Grace's actions. She'd been freaked out when he'd spoken of love and marriage after two months of dating, yet she'd worn an engagement ring from this new guy after only a week. Why would she do that? There was only one reason he could think of—she wanted to make him jealous. After seeing him with another girl, she must have been jealous and wanted him to feel the same way. This was good, wasn't it? If she was jealous, it meant she still cared about him. The new guy was no threat—he was simply a device to get Brad's attention. He could put an end to this pretense. All he needed to do was call Grace and arrange a meeting. He could momentarily swallow his pride and talk to her. His heart pounded as he reached for his cell phone.

*****

Grace struggled through the door with her packages. She took in the sight of Hannah and Claire lying on the floor in contorted positions as a voice on the television provoked them into further torturous movements. "Yoga?" she asked as the bags slipped from her hands to thud on the floor.

"It's some new kind of Pilates." Claire managed to squeeze out the words although her chin was wedged against her chest as her entire body curved back over her head.

"Looks comfy," Grace remarked, with inner amusement. Her two youngest sisters regularly took up every new fitness craze.

"What did you buy?" asked Hannah, twisting her neck to eye the shopping bags.

"One pair of shoes that were too cute to pass up and a bunch of hats."

"Good call on the hats," said Claire. "Model them for us."

Grace pulled out a straw hat with a white bow on one side and propped it on her head. "What do you think?"

"It's adorable," said Olivia, emerging from the kitchen with a bowl of ice cream.

Grace regarded the scoops piled high with whipped cream and chocolate syrup and topped with chocolate chips. "Aren't you hitting the hard stuff a bit early?"

Olivia eased onto the couch, balancing her bowl and spooned a huge bite into her mouth. "Mmmmm." She swallowed. "I have a six p.m. to six a.m. shift tonight. I'm stocking up energy."

"Doesn't that just make your blood sugar drop afterwards?" Grace replaced the straw hat with a floppy blue-jean hat.

"Yeah, that's what we learned in nursing school, but I don't care. It's worth it. That's pretty cute, too. Where did you find these hats?"

"Some from Century Twenty-One. Some from the resale store. I figure I need a big supply of hats to cover up this scarecrow hair."

"I'm already used to it," Hannah huffed as she stood on her head with her knees on her elbows. "It's not so bad. It's kind of the color of sweet potato casserole with brown sugar topping."

"I'll keep that in mind. If I ever want to look like a food again, I'll repeat all eight of our processing steps on my hair." Grace slipped a brown derby on her head.

"I like that one," said Claire. "The straw hat is my second favorite."

"Reserve your judgment—I've got eight more," said Grace as she dug through the packages. She spoke quietly to Olivia. "By the way, I'm hoping you haven't said anything to Brad about Leanne."

"Not yet, but I'm going to tell him if you don't."

"Tell who what?" said Hannah.

"Nothing," said Grace.

"No fair keeping secrets," said Claire, sitting up to ignore the incessant voice pleading for positional compliance in soothing tones.

"I'll tell you," said Olivia.

"Olivia, you took the Vow of Secrecy."

"But that was before the Right of Coercion allowed me to invoke the Right of Protection."

"Oooo, we've got a new law," said Claire. "I love it. What is it?"

Grace folded her arms. "I'm invoking Presidential Power."

"Aw fudge!" said Hannah.

Olivia groaned. "If you invoke that too often, you're going to have a coup on your hands."

"I haven't used it since I made you girls zip your lips about Spencer's lack of kissing experience. All I'm asking is for you to wait until after Sunday night dinner. I'm hoping to get a chance to talk to Brad in person. Then you can tell them."

"Fine," said Olivia, while her sisters moaned their protests. "But I thought you were bringing your new boyfriend to dinner."

"You have a new boyfriend?" asked Claire. "You've already dropped Horatio?"

"Horatio was too pushy," said Grace. "And I'm not bringing anyone to dinner. I had promised to bring Horatio so Emily could meet him. But since we've already broken up, I decided not to bring anyone."

When Grace gave a meaningful look to Olivia, she smiled her approval. "Finally, you're making good decisions again. Why don't you call Emily right now, and tell her about the breakup?"

"Good idea," said Grace. She burrowed through her purse in search of her cell phone. "Where's my cell? I can't find it anywhere. Did I drop it when I came in?" She and her sisters searched the floor and all the shopping bags to no avail.

Grace sat on the couch with her face buried in her hands. "I can't believe I lost it. I must have left it on the subway."

"Isn't that the second one you've lost this year?" asked Hannah.

"No, the other one was in December." Grace jutted out her chin.

"It was New Year's Eve, and I think you technically lost it after midnight," said Olivia. "So Hannah's correct."

"Do you want to borrow my phone to call Emily?" asked Claire.

"It's not really that important," said Grace. "I'll just explain it when I see her tomorrow." She gathered up all of her hats and trudged up the stairs.

Olivia called after her. "Hang in there, Grace. I'll see Josh tonight at the hospital, and I'll make sure Brad is coming to dinner tomorrow night. I know you two can work things out if you just sit down and talk."

Grace didn't respond, but her heart pounded at the prospect.

*****

Brad tried Grace's number for the fifth time, and for the fifth time it rang for a while before going to voicemail. He wasn't about to leave her a voicemail—he needed to speak directly to her. They needed to talk. For the fifth time, he sent a text message asking her to call him. Maybe she was tied up or maybe she'd forgotten her cell phone at home. She was always losing it or forgetting it. But he began to worry. Maybe she was afraid to call him because he'd been angry when they'd last talked. This time he texted, "No matter how late it is when you get this message, please call me. I want to talk to you. I need to apologize."

*****

Olivia slid into a chair beside Josh, using her coat sleeve to wipe her forehead. "That was crazy, tonight. This is the first time I've sat down in ten hours."

Josh raised bloodshot eyes toward her. "It's not usually like this. I haven't been this tired since I was a first-year resident." He gave her a crooked smile. "Do you still think this is what you want to do? You could always just stop after nursing school—we can always use more good RNs."

"No, I'm going to be a doctor."

"Well, you've got a long time to decide what branch you want to pursue. You might change your mind about Emergency Medicine before you're done."

"That's true, but I really love the adrenaline rush. I'm afraid I'm already hopelessly addicted."

They sat in companionable silence for a moment. Josh had seemed so downhearted as of late, and Olivia knew the reason. He was totally besotted with Emily's sister, Charlie, who wouldn't give him the time of day. She cut him a sideways glance. "I... uhmm... I heard from Charlie."

"Really? What did she say?" His expression was so eager and earnest, her heart broke for him.

"We didn't actually talk or anything. I just saw a Facebook post about starting her classes at University of Colorado. She says it will only take her two years to finish her prerequisites for law school."

His entire body slumped with defeat. "She unfriended me on Facebook. I can't even see her posts anymore."

"If you want, you can use my Facebook account to stalk her. Just don't tell anyone."

"No. If she doesn't want me to see the stuff she posts, I won't invade her privacy."

"Well, if it makes you feel any better, Emily still thinks she likes you. She says Charlie is just really careful about admitting her feelings. And she's coming to Emily and Spencer's wedding in December, right?"

"I know. Emily told me. And I haven't given up. I'm not a lightweight like Brad." He made a sour face like he was swallowing medicine.

"Speaking of Brad... Is he coming to dinner tomorrow?" Olivia glanced at her watch. "Oops, I mean, tonight?"

"I don't know," said Josh. "He's not scheduled to work, but do you think he should go to dinner? Will it make Grace uncomfortable?"

"I think it's really important for him to come to dinner. Grace wants him there. I'm hoping they can work everything out if they get a chance to talk face-to-face."

"I'll see what I can do, but he's been a real bear lately. We've had a few shouting matches, and we've never done that before."

Olivia smiled. She was glad Brad was out of sorts. It would be a bad thing if he were functioning well without Grace in his life.

Josh said, "You know, I'll enlist Ben's help. He can get Brad to do anything by pushing his buttons. I'm sure we can get Brad to Sunday night dinner."

"Awesome," said Olivia. "I'll be so glad to get the old Grace back. Although, she doesn't much resemble the Grace from a week ago. But eventually, everything will be back to normal."

*****

Josh came in from a five-mile run, shedding his shirt on the way to the shower. "Hey Ben. Did you talk your brother into coming to dinner at the Marshall's tonight? Spencer said there would be plenty of food."

"Well about that... He's coming to the dinner. In fact, he's already left to pick up his *date*."

"His date?"

Josh could see the muscles working in Ben's jaw. "Yes. He claims he tried to call Grace all day yesterday, and she didn't return his phone calls. And since she's bringing Horatio, he wants to have a date as well. I tried to talk him out of it, but he wouldn't listen to me."

Josh's mouth went dry. "But Grace isn't bringing Horatio. Olivia told me this morning Horatio is no more. Is he bringing Kara Dickson?"

"He's bringing that woman he took to the baseball game. But did you know Grace recognized her? She insisted her name was Leanne."

"Leanne? That's the name of the girl Grace left her flowers and card with last week. Grace told me it was a nurse named Leanne. If this means what I think it does, Kara lied to Grace and purposefully hid the card and flowers from Brad. And now Brad is bringing her to dinner at Grace's house—this is a disaster."

Ben sat forward. "Maybe this could be good. Maybe Grace will confront her and Brad will find out the truth and dump that witch."

"I can't believe she has the nerve to go to dinner at Grace's house. You'd think she'd be terrified of being exposed."

Ben rubbed his short-trimmed beard as he pondered. "Maybe she doesn't realize where she's going."

"You're probably right." Josh wondered how they might be able to work this to their advantage.

"Well, this should make for an interesting dinner. You and I may be the only ones who realize the truth. We've got to help Grace out."

"Let me get a quick shower, and I'll be ready to go." He tossed his cell phone to Ben. "Do me a favor? Call Olivia, and give her the heads up so she can warn Grace. I don't want her blindsided with this."

*****

"I don't think I can do this." Grace paced at the foot of her bed where Olivia was perched, having just delivered the news. Her stomach was churning and she couldn't imagine sitting down to dinner. The thought of food made her want to rush to the bathroom. "Don't you see? He finally called me after I lost my phone. It's another sign we aren't supposed to be together."

"I'll agree it seems like the universe is conspiring against you, but the Grace I know would never give up this easily."

"I'm not giving up. I'm trying to do the right thing."

"Do you think it's right to hurt Brad like this? Is it right to let some conniving shrew end up with him? Are you going to let him believe you ignored his phone calls? He at least deserves to know the whole truth."

"But maybe it means something he picked a girl so totally opposite of me. Maybe I'm not really his type, and it took something like this for him to figure it out. And anyway, I'm not the kind of person who likes to make a scene—I can't confront her in front of all of my family and friends."

Olivia's curls were wild from the pulling of her frustrated fingers. She lifted a pillow to her face and let out a muffled scream. *"Arghhh!"* She flung it at her sister with all her might, impacting her side, but not slowing her agitated strides. "Grace, I'm going to invoke some sisterly right that allows me to pound some sense into you. Look, here's the bottom line. You brought this on yourself when you lied to Brad instead of being honest with him. So now, you need to buck up and face the consequences. You're going to this dinner, and you're going to pull that girl into a private place and tell her off."

"I don't know..."

"Grace, do you like Brad or not? Is he worth fighting for?"

Grace swallowed a hard lump of air. Did she like Brad? No. If she'd learned anything over the past week, she'd learned she didn't like Brad. She loved him. With all of her heart and soul, she loved the man. His loss had left a yawning, aching, empty hole inside her. But as much as she wanted to be with Brad, what she wanted most was for him to be happy. And she worried she might not be able to do that for him. Still, she couldn't accept Brad would ever be happy with a devious woman like Leanne, either.

She stopped pacing and turned to face the mirror on her dresser. Her voice was plaintive when she spoke again. "Will you help me pick out a hat for tonight?"

Olivia hopped up from the bed, grinning with excitement. "I'll pick out your whole outfit, from head to toe. Brad won't know what hit him."

*****

Brad was uncomfortable bringing Kara to the Marshall's dinner, but he didn't want to be alone when he saw Grace with another man—especially a man who'd somehow already convinced her to wear his ring. Although Ben seemed to be convinced she wasn't interested in Horatio, she obviously wasn't interested in renewing her relationship with Brad either. She hadn't even returned a single phone call or text.

He kept his hands shoved into his pockets as he strolled beside Kara on the way to the Marshall's home. She'd already attempted to hold hands once as she walked beside him, her long legs matching him stride for stride. He knew inviting her to this dinner was encouraging her affections, a complication he didn't need. But he couldn't think of anyone else to bring along at the last minute. He glanced at her rather revealing top and decided he should be straightforward and warn her Grace would be at dinner.

"So I appreciate you coming to dinner with me," he began.

"I was glad you invited me. Friday night you seemed so angry with me for some reason."

"Well, I was a little angry. I thought we had an understanding. I went to the game with you to help you with a guy problem, and that kiss was not part of the deal. We're only friends, Kara. I helped you with a guy problem, and I asked you to come tonight to help me with a girl problem."

Her eyes narrowed. "What girl problem?"

"So Josh told you about Grace and I breaking up? Well, tonight the dinner is at her house, and she's bringing her new boyfriend."

"So now you want me to pretend to be your girlfriend?" she asked. Brad glanced her direction. She didn't seem offended. In fact her wide eyes and broad smile appeared all too eager.

"No, you don't need to take it that far. I think having a date will be sufficient. Her entire family will be at the dinner, and Dr. Branson will be there as well. It's a weekly tradition."

"No problem. I think I can handle a little family togetherness with your old girlfriend. You know, I never thought she was right for you anyway."

Brad pressed his lips together to hold back a biting retort. He didn't want to hear any disparaging remarks about Grace. "I still think we might get back together."

"But you really don't have much in common, with you being a doctor and her being an elementary school teacher. And she's from New York, and you're from California."

"We have plenty in common. For one thing, we're both sports fanatics." Brad worked to relax the tension that had risen in his shoulders. Kara had a habit of saying things that got under his skin.

"That's fine for you, I guess. But almost every guy is a sports fanatic. Her new boyfriend probably likes sports, too. But don't you think you'd rather end up with someone in the medical field?"

"Not necessarily. I get enough medicine at work—I need a break when I get home."

"That's because you're working your butt off in the ER. But some day you'll be in administration, and you'll have plenty of doctors to do all your grunt work. To be honest you look pretty bad this week. You're obviously working too many late hours."

He had no intention of leaving the ER to be an administrator—he loved his job. But he didn't feel like arguing with Kara.

"Right now I look bad because I haven't been sleeping well. Maybe someday I might like to move up the ladder a little, but not too far up and not any time soon. I like what I do."

"You know, my father's on the board at Central Hospital back in L.A. I'm sure he'd be willing to pull some strings to get you a great position. Wasn't that your first choice for your ER residency?"

"It was." He cringed at the admission, although she'd already known the answer. "But I like it here. I have no desire to leave."

"I only came here for the New York experience. I've always planned to go back. You should think about working in L.A. You know, I'm only a year behind you in my residency."

Was Kara actually proposing a long term relationship? Was she bribing him with a position at Central? He felt his heart rate accelerating. How could he feel trapped when he was walking out in the open?

"I like it here and I plan to stay, so I guess it's a good thing we're only friends. It sounds like we could never have a future together."

"You may change your mind about staying here. Isn't your family in L.A.?"

"My parents are there, but my brother is planning to move to New York someday. In fact, he'll be at the dinner tonight."

Kara was quiet for a moment. "My dad might be willing to live in New York half of the year. He could probably get on the board at Mercy General."

"Steven Gherring is on the board at Mercy General. I doubt your father could have any more influence than he does."

Kara waved away his objection. "Gherring's only interest is the publicity—he doesn't care about the day-to-day operations of the hospital."

Brad took a slow deep breath and counted to ten. He failed to hide his considerable irritation.

"Steven Gherring is a personal friend of mine and Dr. Branson's and a really great man. His only interest is the good of the hospital and the patients. He doesn't give a flip about publicity."

"Wow, don't bite my head off! I didn't know you knew the guy. Is that how you and Josh got in the residency?"

"No! We earned our residency positions before we ever met him. The same way I hope everyone else in the program did." He spit the words out like venom.

But Kara laughed out loud. "Oh Brad, you're hopelessly naïve if you believe that. The only way you'll ever get anywhere in life is by knowing the right people. I think it's great you know Steven Gherring—we should be able to use that to our advantage if I can't talk you into moving back to L.A."

Brad stopped before entering the Marshall's apartment building, acutely aware of his perspiration despite the cool evening air. He grabbed her elbow and pulled her toward him, using his slight height advantage to look down on her.

"Kara, I don't have time to talk about this right now, but let me make one thing perfectly clear. I'm not interested in using my friendship with Steven Gherring for personal gain. And please don't say anything about that in front of this group of people. They're all friends with him, and they'll be quite offended."

She wrenched her arm away. "Okay, don't get your panties in a wad. I wasn't going to say anything, anyway."

Brad knocked on the door, wondering if he'd made a terrible mistake bringing Kara to Sunday night dinner. But he needed her with him to face Grace and her new man, especially since Grace had ignored his phone calls and texts. Surely Kara would act properly in this social situation. He'd instructed her to keep her mouth shut about Steven Gherring. And she'd been warned about Grace's presence at the dinner. He'd been clear to Kara about maintaining their relationship at the level of friends and professional colleagues. He'd covered all his bases. What could go wrong?

Chapter Six

KARA KNEW THIS WAS HER BEST OPPORTUNITY to secure Brad Gates for herself. She was a bit disappointed he'd been reluctant to discuss more ambitious career opportunities, but he would come around eventually. He wouldn't want to deal with the stress of Emergency Medicine for long. He was a perfect match for her—intelligent, tall, handsome, well-muscled. She didn't much care for the way he cropped his hair short and wore a goatee, but that would be easy enough to change later on. She definitely wanted him to have a different style before the wedding, but that might be a year or two away.

She knew from the icy stares directed her way she wasn't very popular with Brad's friends. Of course these people were all Grace's family, so they were understandably defensive. She hadn't seen Grace's brother and his fiancée yet—they were in the kitchen cooking. But she doubted she would be well-received by them either.

Brad made introductions. "This is Dr. Kara Dickson, a colleague from work. Kara, this is Olivia Marshall. She's in her second year of nursing school, and she plans to go on to medical school."

Kara shook her hand, appraising her looks. Interesting. As petite as Grace was, her sisters were all very tall and thin. Not as tall as Kara, but all over five feet eight inches. Olivia was quite attractive, with sharp brown eyes and long brown hair flowing in loose curls. She could potentially become more competition for Brad.

Kara told Olivia, "Good luck with that. I guess if you don't get in, you can just stick to nursing." Olivia narrowed her eyes, pressing her lips together, as if biting her words.

Brad frowned and his voice was stern. "Olivia won't have any trouble getting into medical school. She has a three point nine GPA, and she's already taken Organic Chemistry and Biochemistry."

He moved Kara to the next sister. "This is Hannah. She's a sophomore in college. What are you studying, Hannah?"

"This week, it's Journalism. I'm not sure what it will be next week." She laughed, her auburn curls bouncing around in a fetching manner.

"Nice to meet you," Kara said, turning her attention to the next sister in line. This one was younger, but returned her gaze with a no-nonsense stare. She had straight brown hair, cut in a fashionable angled bob. Her lips formed a straight line as she offered her hand to Kara.

"I'm Claire," she said. "I'm a senior in high school, and I'm going to be an accountant."

Kara had a sense this girl was ready to pick a fight, so she kept her response to a stiff smile. She turned her eyes to Grace, carefully schooling her expression to give no sign of recognition.

"You must be Grace. I've heard about you." She was surprised when Grace simply turned her back and walked away.

Judging by Grace's scowl, she must have realized her deception, recognizing Kara had given a false name and neglected to pass on the flowers and card to Brad. She was prepared to deny the entire incident if she reported it to Brad. She could handle the tiny spitball, no matter how angry she was. And her tall sisters appeared hostile as well, but they were of no consequence. Kara had plenty of contacts, highly influential and wealthy people she knew through her father's business partner—the same man who'd given her *his* season tickets to the baseball game. She and Brad would have no shortage of friends. And they wouldn't have to squeeze into a small dining room in a low-rent apartment every week for dinner. But Kara knew how to play the game.

"Mrs. Marshall, you have a lovely home. Thank you so much for having me. It's so hard for me to be here in New York City while my family is all the way across the country in L.A. This just makes me feel so at home."

"Oh, you're welcome," she said, blushing at the praise. "You can call me Connie. And this is my husband Joe." Kara returned a brilliant smile. Common people were so easy to flatter.

From behind her, Brad muttered in Grace's general direction. "I thought I was going to meet your new boyfriend tonight."

"We're not together," said Grace.

"You mean he's not here? Or you broke up?" Brad asked.

"We... We never really got together." Kara saw Grace's face turn pink, contrasting with the strange orange-brown color of the hair peeking out from under the stylish hat perched on her head. She'd obviously had a hair-color mishap since she'd seen her on Tuesday. Kara was exultant Grace's mistake had played into her plans to steal Brad from her. Really, it was too easy to be called stealing—Grace had practically handed him to her.

However, the next arrivals were Brad's brother, Ben, and Josh Branson, who both regarded her with barely concealed enmity. Since Dr. Branson was her supervising physician, it wouldn't do to be on his bad side. Still, he was a man—she knew she could handle him. He would soon be eating out of her hand. In fact, if things didn't work out with Brad, she could always go for Josh instead. He was equally handsome, with blond hair instead of brown, and gorgeous green eyes. Although at the moment those intense eyes were studying her as if they could read her mind.

"Hello, Dr. Dickson," said Josh through tight lips.

"Hello, Dr. Branson. I'm so honored you and Dr. Gates are including me in your dinner. I don't think I've seen you out of scrubs. You clean up nice."

"I'm surprised you have time to go to dinner. Shouldn't you be studying for board exams?" Josh asked.

"I studied all day. I need a break." She stretched to emphasize her fatigue and draw his attention toward her low-cut blouse. To her annoyance, Josh's eyes never dropped from hers. However, Ben's eyes were bugging out of his head. "And you must be Dr. Gate's brother."

Brad said, "Yes, Dr. Dickson. This is my brother, Ben. Ben, this is my colleague, Dr. Dickson."

Ben cocked one eyebrow at his brother. "Your colleague, huh? Not your date?"

Grace appeared between them, having evidently been pushed there by one of her lanky sisters. She shifted her feet and cleared her throat a few times before she craned her head to look up at Kara. When she spoke there was a distinct quiver in her voice.

"So I thought your name was Leanne? When we met the other day at the hospital, I'm sure that was the name you gave me."

Ever the consummate actress, Kara gazed at her, blinking with confusion. "I'm sorry, but I have no idea what you're talking about."

Grace put her hands on her slim hips and straightened to her full miniscule height. "I think you know exactly what I'm talking about."

Kara continued her wide-eyed, straight-faced perusal of Grace. Despite her crazy hair-color, she was quite becoming. Her short hair only emphasized her huge hazel eyes. She knew she shouldn't underestimate her opponent's appeal. She was wearing a skirt with wedge heels that gave her a greatly needed boost in height, but Kara still had a five-inch advantage on her. Shaking her head, Kara said, "I'm really sorry, but we've never met before. You must have me confused with someone else."

Mrs. Marshall said, "Grace, perhaps you shouldn't make a scene."

"You're right, Mom. Leanne or Kara or whatever your name is... Would you mind stepping onto the porch for a moment?"

"Of course not," said Kara. "We'll get this all straightened out in a jiffy." This was perfect—she could totally manipulate this girl if she got her alone. She followed Grace outside.

Brad almost threw himself in front of Grace to prevent her from leaving the room with Kara. He felt like he was letting a kitten be alone with a wolf. He was only beginning to see the real Kara Dickson, but she seemed like a dangerous character. He was still staring at the door that closed behind them when Josh punched him on the arm.

"I can't believe you brought her here," Josh hissed in his ear.

Brad rubbed the knot on his bicep. "That was totally uncalled for. I brought her because Grace was bringing Horatio. I didn't know they'd broken up. And anyway, she ignored all my calls and texts yesterday—all five of them."

"Really?" said Josh, crossing his arms. "I don't believe you. That doesn't sound like something Grace would do."

"You don't know her like I do. Hell, I don't even know her anymore. She's changed so much in the past week—"

"She has not," Olivia hissed, pushing her way between them. "She hasn't changed at all. You guys had a good thing going and you just knocked her off the saddle. You can't tell her you love her and talk about getting married after only dating for two months. Not with Grace, anyway." She gave a pointed look to Josh, "And not with Charlie, either."

She shook her finger in Brad's face. "I can't believe you brought that woman to our dinner. If Spencer figures out who she is, you may not get to be best man at his wedding."

Brad bristled. "Grace could have at least had the decency to return my phone calls or texts. I wouldn't have brought Kara if I'd known Horatio wouldn't be here."

"When did you call Grace? Yesterday?"

"Yes—five times. Five calls and five texts. I even told her I wanted to apologize in the last text. Obviously she doesn't want to talk to me ever again."

"Well *obviously*." Olivia's voice dripped with sarcasm. "*Obviously* the girl that already brought you flowers and a card and called you and asked to get together and talk when you flat out turned her down... *Obviously* that girl would refuse to return your phone calls and texts. *Obviously* there couldn't be some other reason she didn't answer you. *Obviously,* she couldn't have left her phone on the subway yesterday."

Olivia quivered with anger.

She jumped when Josh touched her arm. "Come on. Let's go see if Spencer and Emily need help in the kitchen."

With one last disdainful look at Brad, Olivia flounced into the kitchen behind Josh.

Brad turned pleading eyes toward his smirking brother. "But you know I didn't ever get the card and flowers Grace supposedly sent."

"Yes, you imbecile, you didn't get them because Kara Dickson intercepted them and told Grace her name was Leanne."

He cursed under his breath. Why hadn't he put two and two together? He could vaguely remember seeing Kara with some flowers on Tuesday. He'd been so devastated at the time he hadn't paid close attention. He should have known Grace wouldn't lie about something like that.

Ben smiled. "Yes, you are in some pretty deep stuff, all right. And by the way, you look like it, too."

Brad knew his eyes were bloodshot. He was so desperate for sleep he was tempted to take a sleeping pill. He had to get things worked out with Grace soon. "It's not my fault—I didn't know it was Kara."

"You don't have to convince me—you have to convince Grace." Ben glanced toward the front door. "That is, if she survives this encounter with the shark."

*****

Grace swirled around to face Kara, blood beating in her temples. "Don't try to pretend with me—I remember you from Tuesday morning. I know you didn't give my flowers and card to Brad."

Kara's face was impassive. "I have to say I don't remember you at all. But that's really not the issue here. The ultimate issue here is what's best for Dr. Gates."

"Well *you* certainly aren't what's best for him. He doesn't need a lying, conniving—" Grace stopped herself before the word left her lips. She hated the way this woman made her feel out of control. "A lying, conniving *person* for a girlfriend."

Kara folded her arms across her chest and glared down her nose at Grace. "Let's talk about *your* qualifications as Brad's future wife. Surely you can see you'd be a disaster for him in the end. I mean, you're cute, or at least you were before you messed up your hair. I can only see a few strands the hat doesn't cover, but I know a bad dye-job when I see it."

"I don't believe Brad is so shallow he'd reject me based on a hair mistake." Grace said the words with a conviction she didn't quite feel.

"I'm saying your looks aren't that important, although he should be concerned his future offspring might inherit your short stature. But that's not what I'm worried about. Listen, you know Brad is from L.A., right? And that's where his family lives, right?"

Grace nodded, not sure where this conversation was going, but all too aware she'd lost her angry momentum.

"So if he stays in New York at Mercy General, he has no future. He'll never get to be head of Emergency Medicine, much less higher up in the administration."

"But he likes what he does. He's happy doing it."

"Emergency Medicine is an exhausting field. Surely you've noticed how tired he looks tonight. Are you so self-absorbed you didn't see the dark circles under his eyes? He's only thirty. Imagine how it will be when he's forty years old."

"What does that have to do with me?"

"He needs connections. That's why he sought me out in the first place. My father is on the board at Central Hospital in L.A., where Brad's family lives. Brad and I have known each other for three years since I've been in this residency. You've only known him for a few months. But since he met you, he's abandoned his aspirations of returning to L.A. with me where his future promotion is almost assured."

Grace pondered her words. Would he really give up his dreams just to please her? Did he really need Kara for her influence and connections? What about his connections here?

"He knows Steven Gherring, and he's on the board at Mercy General."

"Yes, but Brad has told me Gherring would never use his power to promote his friends at the hospital. I'm not saying that's a bad thing, but Gherring won't be any help for Brad."

"I never asked him to sacrifice anything for me. I would probably move to L.A. if we ever got to that point."

Kara's smile was anything but benevolent. "But as I said before, my father is on the board at Central. Brad has a great future in L.A. if he's with me. But if I drop Brad, someone else will inherit that great future."

"But maybe he doesn't want you, even if I'm not in the picture."

One corner of Kara's mouth lifted, a cross between a smirk and a sneer. "He was interested in me before you came along. But something tells me you're holding out on him, keeping that little treasure in your pants as an enticement."

Grace felt her face heating at Kara's crass suggestive comment.

Kara continued, "I'll tell you from experience, Brad will be interested until he gets what he wants, but eventually he'll be bored and seek greener pastures. I'm okay with that. I know my future husband and I might occasionally have a little side entertainment—I can live with it. The question is... Can you?"

"I... That's not what I think marriage should be like." Grace fumed. There was no way she believed Brad had that attitude toward marriage. Kara was lying again.

"Then we already know you're not the right woman for Brad. So how long are you going to string him along? Will you keep him on the hook until he misses his opportunity for happiness? Are you going to keep him here in New York until he burns out at the age of forty? You know, even if he's not with me, he needs to move away in order to move up the ladder. He's already turned down an opportunity just this month because of you."

"What if you're lying to me? I don't believe Brad would ever cheat on a woman he was married to. And I already know you lied to me about your name. And you lied to Brad about my card and flowers."

"Fine—I'll admit I met you before and I lied about my name. But I was only thinking about what was best for Brad, like you should if you care about him at all. Or maybe you don't care about him. Maybe you just want to marry him for his money. I didn't take you for a gold-digger, but—"

"I'm not a gold-digger—I care about Brad. But I'm saying being with me wouldn't keep him from moving away."

"You can't tell me you really want to move across the country when your whole family lives here. Brad isn't stupid—he knows it would make you miserable."

"But why didn't he tell me this himself? Why wouldn't he tell me about needing to move away from New York?"

"You could always ask him yourself if you don't believe me, but he'll probably lie to protect you. Don't you see? Brad is one of the few good guys out there. He's willing to live a life of misery to keep you from being unhappy."

"I'm willing to do that for him, as well. I don't want him to be unhappy."

"But he's not willing to let you be miserable. So the only way Brad will ever be happy in the long term, is if he's not with you. And yes, I'm sure I could make him happy, but I know he may not choose me. The point is you can't make him happy, even if you're willing to give up your family, because he won't let you."

Grace's eyes began to fill up until Kara's face was wobbling in her vision. "I don't believe you," Grace said, although she could see the logic of Kara's arguments.

"You don't have to take my word for it. Just take a close look at Brad's face when you go back inside. You'll see for yourself the toll his work schedule is taking on him. It breaks my heart." A tear spilled down Kara's face, and she swiped it away. Her voice cracked. "I'm sorry—I don't usually lose control like that. But I just hate to see what's happening to him."

"It can't be that bad," said Grace, squeezing her eyes against a deluge of tears. "He would have told me if he was unhappy in New York."

Kara sniffed a few times and dabbed at her eyes with her sleeve. "Even though you've only known him two months, you know better than that. You know he's the kind of guy who always puts other people first. He probably hasn't even told Josh the truth because he wouldn't want Josh to feel bad."

"Why would Josh feel bad?"

"Dr. Branson got promoted over Dr. Gates. If it weren't for Josh, Brad could probably stay here and move up at Mercy General. But you know Brad would never let Josh know he was disappointed."

Grace felt a tight band around her chest. It was true. She knew Josh and Brad had been in competition for the top spot after their residency. But she hadn't realized Josh's selection last month meant Brad's career in New York was stalled. It made so much sense. Brad needed to leave New York, but he'd never believe she'd be willing to go with him. Unless... Unless he believed their relationship was over, leaving him free to follow his dreams. After he found a new position in Los Angeles or whatever city he chose, she could let him know she was in love with him. If she came to him, fully aware he was leaving the city, he would understand she was willing to move with him. And it would be too late for him to turn down the job and sacrifice himself for her.

Kara sniffed a few more times. "I just... I just care so much about him. Thanks for understanding." Kara laid her hand on Grace's arm, but Grace recoiled at her touch, stepping back to glare at her.

"Don't mistake my tears for weakness. I recognize you for what you are, and I don't believe your affection for Brad in any way approaches your love for yourself. And whether or not Brad and I end up together, I promise he will be fully aware of your treachery. If he chooses you, knowing who you really are, then he deserves you."

Kara's stricken face morphed into an odious snarl. "Do you actually think I care about your opinion of me? I was trying to be nice, but now the gloves are off."

Grace laughed, stalking back inside. "Watch out... People will see your claws."

Brad knew he was in trouble with Emily and Spencer the moment he walked into the kitchen. Spencer glared silently at him, but Emily had no shortage of words.

"What were you thinking? You knew Grace saw you kiss that woman at the baseball game, and then you brought her here to dinner? Are you just trying to hurt her?" Emily's blue eyes shot daggers at Brad as she spewed out her accusations.

"You were the one who told Ben about Grace bringing Horatio to dinner," Brad objected. "I only brought Kara because I thought he was coming. I didn't know they'd already broken up."

"Yes, but you brought the woman that lied to Grace and stole her card and flowers. Olivia already told us."

"Thanks for that." Brad sent a sour scowl Olivia's direction.

"How could you? I thought you said you loved her," Emily said.

"I don't know what I'm supposed to say. Olivia told me I couldn't tell Grace I loved her because we'd only been dating for two months. But it seems I'm required to follow certain unknown rules to prove I actually do love her even though I'm not allowed to say it."

Emily coughed out her exasperation. "Ha! And what's so strange about that? Yes, girls require you demonstrate your love for a while before we're willing to accept hearing the words. It's not that difficult."

"It's difficult if you don't know the rules," Brad complained. "Was it really such a sin I said out loud the words I was feeling?"

"No, it's just hard to believe your feelings were genuine when you brought that woman with you, knowing how much it would hurt her."

"Why isn't anyone worried about Grace hurting me? She was the one who broke up with me just so she could date some other guy. And believe me, it hurt."

Emily's eyebrows lifted as she folded her arms. "You certainly seemed to recover quickly from your terrible hurt—kissing another girl on national television a week later."

"I didn't kiss her—she kissed me."

"Semantics," said Ben from behind him, dodging the fist Brad shot toward his side. "Watch it! I'm already injured."

"It's getting old, Ben," said Brad.

"No it's not," chuckled Josh. "I hadn't heard it yet."

"Why isn't anyone upset about her dating this Horatio guy and accepting a diamond ring from him in less than a week?" Brad had the distinct impression everyone had chosen sides, and no one was on his.

"I kind of figured she made him up," said Emily.

"She did make him up," said Olivia.

"And this would have all been over if Kara hadn't intercepted the card and flowers," said Josh.

"Wait a minute... She made him up? Isn't anyone upset with Grace for lying about Horatio?" asked Brad.

"Technically, she didn't lie," said Olivia. "There is a boy named Horatio who's in love with her, and he did give her a ring. But he's only six years old, so I don't think he's a real threat."

"Ha!" said Ben. "You got outmaneuvered by a six-year-old. That is so awesome." His laughter grew at Brad's outraged expression until he was rolling on the floor. His hilarity was contagious and soon the other four were chuckling, too.

"I'm glad you're all enjoying yourselves at my expense. It would be nice if someone was willing to help me out." Brad tried to control his growing irritation.

"I tried to help you, but you wouldn't listen," said Josh.

Spencer finally spoke. "I'm willing to help, but I think it may be too late. Bringing that woman to dinner may have been the last straw."

"I'll help you," said Emily. "But only because I feel sorry for you because you look so terrible. Have you been sick?"

Brad rubbed his forehead. "If you must know, I've hardly slept since she broke up with me."

"Shhhhh!" said Olivia from her listening post near the kitchen door. "I think Grace and Kara are back inside."

Ben continued in a low voice, "Maybe if we can just get through dinner, you can get Grace alone long enough to apologize and talk to her."

"I'll even distract Kara for a while," said Josh, "although you'll owe me big time. I don't know what you see in that woman."

"She's beautiful, of course. That's what Brad sees in her," said Olivia.

"I don't think she's beautiful." Brad stuffed his hands in his pockets. "I think Grace is beautiful."

Olivia's mouth quirked up on one corner. "I hope you still feel that way when she takes her hat off."

*****

Grace felt Brad's eyes on her during the entire dinner. She kept hers glued awkwardly to her plate, only speaking to give monosyllabic answers to direct questions. Kara, however, was animated and charming, flattering almost every person at the table, including all three of her sisters. She even directed a few veiled compliments toward Grace, enjoying her obvious discomfort.

"Grace, I absolutely love your hat!" said Kara. "I've tried to wear them myself, but my hair is just so long and straight they never look good on me." She flicked a heavy tress over her shoulder. "But with your short, wiry hair, hats look great."

"Gee thanks," muttered Grace, acutely aware of the blood rushing to her face.

But Olivia's expression was the epitome of *if looks could kill*. "Kara, I'm so glad we're getting to know you. When I first met you I thought you were a stuck-up... uhmm... Well, let's just say I thought you were stuck-up and malicious. But now, after seeing an example of just how kind and thoughtful you are, I know I really underestimated you. Stuck-up and malicious wouldn't even begin to describe you. I mean, you are just soooooooo malevolent! Oh, I'm sorry, I meant to say benevolent."

Hannah and Claire giggled, but their mother's eyebrows furrowed. "Olivia... I think you've said quite enough."

"But Mom," said Olivia with wide eyes. "I was only complimenting Kara, the same way she complimented Grace."

"Mom. May I be excused?" asked Grace. She couldn't handle the stress for another moment. And it was killing her to sit across the table from Brad when he was sitting with Kara.

Connie put her hand on Grace's arm. "Before dessert? Are you not feeling well?"

"I'm just not hungry." Grace spoke the truth, having pushed her food around on her plate for the duration of dinner.

"Okay, sweetheart. I'll come check on you in a bit," said Connie.

When Grace stood up to leave the table, she saw the satisfied smirk on Kara's face. But Brad rose as well. "I'll walk you out. I'd like to talk to you before you disappear." Grace saw the smirk hop from Kara's face to Olivia's.

By the time Grace slipped into the den with Brad following closely, her heart was hammering and her hands were perspiring. "Grace? Could we sit for a minute?" Brad indicated the couch with his outstretched hand.

"Okay." Her voice sounded quivery, and she took a deep breath to steady herself as she perched on the end of the couch.

Brad took up a position so close she could feel his warmth radiating from his legs. He reached out and picked up her hand between both of his, holding it firmly when she tried to pull away. "Grace, we need to talk." He closed his eyes as he drew in a lungful of air and let it whistle through his lips. "I tried to call you yesterday, but you didn't answer or return my calls."

"That's because I lost my phone. I left it—"

"On the subway," he finished for her. "I know that now. But I didn't know that when I invited Kara to come to dinner. I also didn't know Horatio wasn't coming or that Kara was the one who prevented me from getting your card and flowers."

"It's okay. I'm not mad at you. I can understand why you would date her. I mean, she's smart and beautiful and tall."

"I'm not dating her."

"Well, I know you quit dating her when you started dating me, so it's natural that—"

"Did she tell you that? Did Kara say we were dating before I started dating you?" Brad's blue eyes glinted like steel as his jaw clenched.

Grace swallowed hard at his palpable fury. "I... I think she just said you were interested in her before I came along, but she implied you and she had... that you were... you know... together." She felt her cheeks burning.

Grace was shocked to hear him curse. "Look Grace, she lies—you shouldn't believe anything she said. I'm just now realizing how low she'll stoop to get her way."

"So... You never considered going back to Los Angeles with her to work at Central Hospital?"

"No way! As far as I'm concerned, Kara Dickson would be a major deterrent to working at Central Hospital. And I'm sorry I brought her here. Okay? And I'm sorry I didn't talk to you Thursday night. And I'm sorry I talked to you about being in love and getting married. I know it's too early to think about that. Okay?"

"Okay." Grace felt hope blooming as he squeezed her hand.

"Grace?"

"Huh?" She looked up through her lashes to find his face close to hers.

"Can I kiss you?"

"Uhmm... I don't know—"

Brad swallowed her protest as he pressed his lips to hers. All objections flew out of her head as a dizzying sensation overwhelmed her. With only the lightest tender touch of his mouth against her lips, she felt a tingle spread from her neck down her spine. His fingers rose to gently caress her cheek. He pulled back a fraction and whispered, so close she could feel his breath on her face.

"Grace, I like you a lot."

The warm feeling building inside Grace was replaced by a sudden chill. Had he changed his mind about loving her? Her crazy reaction to his profession of love must have caused him to take a step back. Now she recognized her own feelings of love for Brad, he no longer felt the same. Before panic could overtake her, Grace clamped down on her emotions. She had to be sane and rational—she couldn't afford to overreact again. If he loved her before, he would come to love her again once he knew he could trust her.

Brad rested his forehead against hers, with one hand holding her face toward him. He moved slightly to brush his lips against hers again. "Do you like me too?" he asked, his voice sounding uncertain in the wake of her silence.

"Yes, I do."

"Uhmm, I'm glad." He smiled as he kissed her again, torturing her by bestowing only the softest amounts of pressure on her mouth, feathery caresses against her desperately seeking lips.

Grace pulled away from his embrace to force a sense of reason into her head. She attempted to slow her breathing as she studied Brad with wary eyes. To her great distress she realized he looked exhausted, as if he were recovering from some lingering illness. There were shadows under his bloodshot eyes, and his face appeared thin and drawn. So at least one of the things Kara had told her was factual. Grace had to find out if anything else she'd said was true. Was his job schedule wearing him out? Was he really giving up his hopes and dreams by remaining in New York City? Was he sacrificing his happiness for hers? She had to find out the truth. She would do whatever it took to ensure Brad got the life he deserved, even if she risked not being a part of his future.

Brad felt like a bundle of dynamite waiting for a spark. His nerve endings were on high alert, sending out lightning bolts each time his lips contacted hers. He was determined to stay in check, holding himself back from the urges that almost overwhelmed him. He had to take it slow with Grace. Now that he had her back, he had to be careful not to scare her off again. He wouldn't be foolish enough to speak of love again for a long time, and he certainly wouldn't mention marriage. He was so relieved there hadn't actually been another guy.

Well, technically there was another guy, but he was only a six-year-old. He tried to relax his tense muscles as he eased against the back of the couch, keeping a close eye on Grace lest she attempt to flee his presence.

He saw her chewing on her bottom lip the way she always did when she was worried about something. To him it was an adorable habit. He spied the funny-colored hair peeking out the hat he'd knocked askew. He grinned and cocked his head to the side.

"Let me see it. Take your hat off."

She grabbed it and tugged it down tight over her hair. "No way."

He laughed and tickled her side until she tried to fight him off, leaving her hat unguarded. He snatched the hat from her head and held it out of reach.

"You rat!" She covered her head with her hands.

"Stop," he said, pulling at her hands. "It's not that bad."

"It's awful," she moaned, giving up and collapsing against the couch in defeat.

"It's just hair," he said, grinning. "It would take a lot more than that to make you look bad. And anyway, it'll grow back."

"I look like an orange wicked witch."

He laughed and shook his head, "No, Kara is the wicked witch. I'm so sorry I didn't realize what she was like. Can you forgive me?"

"Sure, but..."

"But what?"

"Well, Kara mentioned something about you going back to Los Angeles to get a job."

"Don't believe anything she said. I'm not going to Los Angeles. Don't worry. I'm staying right here in New York City."

"Okay, but don't you need to move somewhere in order to move up?" Grace sat up straight, holding herself stiff and unyielding with a scrutinizing gaze as she awaited his answer.

Brad considered how he should respond. He knew she wouldn't want to stay in a long term relationship if he left the city, and he loved New York. He had no desire to leave, especially since his brother was making noise about moving there. In fact, he knew he had a good chance of eventually making chief of the Emergency Medicine Department at Mercy General. Most people assumed Josh would eventually snag the job, but he knew Josh had become enamored with surgery and had plans to work a few years in emergency medicine before doing a cardiac surgery residency. This was privileged information, and he couldn't share the secret with Grace. But all he really needed to do was assure Grace he wouldn't move away from New York City.

"I might be able to move up at Mercy General."

"But what if the only way you could advance was to move somewhere."

"Look, I don't want to scare you again by talking about us in the long term. But if we stay together, I promise not to move from New York City."

"But that's the thing, I'm telling you I'd be willing to move if we stayed together." Grace's eyes were wide and she had a stubborn tilt to her chin.

"But Grace, you wouldn't be happy if you left the city—all of your family is here."

"I'm telling you, I'd be fine. I would even move to Los Angeles if I needed to." Why did she look so frantic? Why was she so concerned he would break up with her and leave the city?

"No Grace, you wouldn't be happy, at least not in the long term. But I understand that, and I would never ask you to leave. I'm not planning to break up with you for any reason. I'll keep working at Mercy General. If I get an offer from some other city, I won't accept it. In fact, I had a good offer last month and turned it down."

"But what if it was your dream job? What if it was exactly what you wanted? What if it was the best job in the country, with really good pay and really good hours? Then you would need to move somewhere, and I'm telling you I'm perfectly willing to move. I could Skype with my family every day. I would be happy. You don't have to sacrifice your happiness for mine."

Now her eyes were shimmering with tears and her breathing was rapid. Why was she so upset about this issue? He had to reassure her somehow. He reached out his hand to cup her jaw gently, smoothing her tightened lips with his thumb until he felt them relax. He gradually slid his hand around to the back of her head and pulled her forward as he leaned in to place a chaste kiss on her soft, pliant lips.

He willed her to feel all the assurance and security he could give her in the promise of his kiss. He held his passion in check. Perhaps the hair mishap had made her feel more insecure. She mustn't think his sentiments were built on base, physical desire and attraction. She needed to know his feelings wouldn't change if she gained weight or changed her hair. He put all of his love and devotion into the caress of lips against hers.

He could sense when the tension left her body and she began to lean into him, responding with a sincere, urgent passion. His heart exulted. He'd done it—he'd broken the anxious barrier she'd erected. Her lips parted, and he heard the faintest of whimpers. He deepened the kiss, unable to resist her earnest invitation. Her hands rose to lock around his neck, holding tight as if to keep him from moving away. When he felt her tongue teasing tentatively against his, he couldn't help the groan that erupted from his chest. He could feel his hunger building into a threatening tidal wave, and he broke the kiss before he lost control. But instead of pulling away, he wrapped his arms around her and pulled her trembling body into a sweet embrace.

Holding her as his heart pounded against her and her breathing began a gradual slowing from frantic pants, he chuckled. "Wow Grace, I have to fight with every ounce of strength to keep control with you."

"Me too," she whispered, with her head still relaxed against his chest.

"So we're good right?" Brad spoke the words into her hair. "You just need to know, as long as we're together, I won't even consider taking a job away from New York. I won't apply and I won't look at any other offers. No matter what. Even if it's my dream job. Okay? So just quit worrying."

As he spoke the words he felt her stiffen in his arms, and he heard a small sob escape her lips. How did he mess up this time?"

Chapter Seven

"She refuses to talk to me," Olivia told Brad when she returned downstairs. She saw the hope drain from his expression, and she felt a wave of sympathy. "What happened?"

Kara had left, albeit unwillingly. Josh and Ben, who volunteered for the duty when Brad had interrupted dessert in a panic, begging for help, had escorted her home.

"I have no idea what happened." Brad rubbed his hand on the top of his head, pulling in frustration at the cropped hair. "One minute everything was fine, and the next minute she told me we couldn't see each other anymore."

"Did you scare her off? Were you talking about marriage again?"

"No, I swear! I didn't even say the word love. She seemed really worried I might want to leave New York City. I thought I had her convinced I wouldn't move."

"Why would she think you wanted to move?" Olivia drummed her fingers on her arm. Would Grace go crazy over the idea of leaving New York? It was certainly possible—she'd never spent any significant time away from her family.

His shoulders shrugged. "I don't know. Maybe it was something Kara said. She kept offering to move with me."

"Move with you? So you were talking about marriage?"

"Well, not really. We were talking about the future if we stayed together. We never mentioned marriage at all."

"But that must be it." Olivia tapped her front tooth with her fingernail. What else would make her sister panic but the thought of commitment? Maybe it wasn't the commitment, but the idea she would voluntarily give up the control she held so dear. "She seems to freak out thinking about marriage—only *her* marriage. She's fine with Spencer and Emily getting married in a few months."

"But I wasn't pushing her at all, and we never mentioned marriage."

"What else could it be?"

"I don't know. Maybe she still didn't believe I would stay in New York City. Kara told her I wanted to move to Los Angeles, and nothing could be farther from the truth. I shouldn't have let her talk to Grace—I realize now she's a big time con artist."

"I encouraged her to talk to Kara alone. I wanted Grace to tell her off." Olivia regretted giving that sisterly advice to Grace, but it was too late to change what had happened.

"What am I going to do?"

"For now, you need to go home and get some sleep. You really do look bad."

"I know I look horrible, but I've hardly slept since Grace broke up with me the first time. I'm not likely to be successful in sleeping now that she's done it again."

Olivia gave him a side hug and patted his arm. "Don't worry too much. I happen to know Grace likes you a lot. She's not talking to me right now, but she'll eventually give in. I'll get to the bottom of this one way or another. By tomorrow night we'll all probably be laughing about it."

"I hope you're right," said Brad, blinking his glistening eyes. Oh no—Olivia couldn't stand to see a guy cry. She punched him in the arm.

"Ow! What was that for?"

Ha—it worked. Brad was completely sidetracked by his smarting arm, and the weepy expression was gone. In its place were confusion and irritation—much better.

"That's because I believe in my heart you'll eventually be my brother, and I always punch my brother in the arm. Better get used to it."

"I already have a brother who does that kind of thing. I was kind of hoping sisters would be more gentle and sweet."

"You've got Hannah and Claire for that. I'll probably be Ben's female counterpart."

"Great," said Brad in a voice sounding anything but pleased. "Just what I wanted—Ben in a female body. *Not!*"

*****

It was so much harder this time, eight long weeks since Grace had admitted to herself she loved Brad. But this time, she knew she was doing the right thing. When she'd finally recognized the toll Brad's schedule was taking on him, she'd known she had to do something. She'd never seen him look so tired and drained before. He'd always managed to cover up the effect of his work strain, hiding it from her so she wouldn't worry. Or perhaps, since she was commonly oblivious to her surroundings, she'd simply failed to notice the problem. He was so selfless, willing to sacrifice his own health so she could stay near her family. And no matter how hard she'd argued she would be fine in another place, he wouldn't give in. He was determined to martyr himself for her benefit, even though it wasn't necessary. She knew she was taking an awful chance by breaking up with Brad. But he had to believe they had no future together before he would accept a position that promised him a better opportunity. Timing was everything. She had to suspend all contact, but somehow keep a close watch on his life. In her fervent prayers each night, she begged God to let them be together in the end.

She had no one to talk to—no one understood her motives. Her sisters were mad at her. Her parents were clueless. She couldn't talk to Josh. He'd only feel guilty his advancement over Brad had resulted in this insolvable situation. Emily had attempted on multiple occasions to sway her toward renewing her relationship with Brad. Spencer had said point blank, "Gracie, I love you, but I think you're making a big mistake."

The hardest obstacle she faced each week was Sunday night dinner. Although Brad had customarily attended about half of the dinners due to schedule conflicts, he'd been miraculously available for every single dinner since the fateful dinner with Kara. And eight weeks had accomplished no change in Brad's beleaguered appearance. If anything, the circles under his eyes were even darker than before. Every week without fail he endeavored to get her alone for a conversation. Well aware of her lack of willpower in Brad's presence, Grace carefully thwarted his efforts.

She simultaneously dreaded and cherished the weekly visits, starved as she was for news about him. But this week's dinner promised to be more entertaining than usual since Ben was back in town.

*****

"Don't tell me you still haven't patched things up with Grace," Ben said. "It's been like six months since she dumped you again."

"Two months," Brad corrected, glaring at his brother. It seemed to him he adopted a permanent scowl when Ben was in town.

"So what's the deal? What did you do to scare her off? Are you that bad of a kisser? I could probably give you some lessons, but you'll just have to watch and learn. I'm not demonstrating on you."

Josh busted out a laugh, choking on his water. "Ben, I think you should just move in here. It's so much more entertaining when you're around."

"I beg to differ," Brad snapped.

"Come on, lighten up little brother," said Ben. "I'm just kidding you."

Brad responded with a grunt as he bent over to retie his shoe, hoping to disguise the rush of blood to his face.

"Are you dating someone else?" Ben asked, scrunching his nose in distaste.

"No. I'm not interested in anyone else."

"Did she break up because of her hair? Did you give her a hard time?" asked Ben.

He noticed Ben rubbing the short hair on his head, as was his own habit when he was caught in a quandary. Despite Ben's tendency to intentionally irritate him, they had a lot in common.

"No *little brother*. You're the Gates brother who gives people a hard time, not me."

"Oh yes, please play the *I'm-older-smarter-nicer-stronger-doctor-better-at-everything-er-than-you-are* card."

"Which is only trumped by the *poor-pitiful-younger-brother-whose-older-brother-picks-on-me* card." Brad gestured with flailing hands.

"Watch it! You almost put my eye out," said Josh, ducking to avoid the onslaught of Brad's thrashing knuckles. "Seriously Brad, you don't seem to be making any headway with Grace. Maybe we can help."

"Yeah, and you look like crap," said Ben. "If this lasts much longer, your deteriorated condition is going to be a source of embarrassment. You need to uphold the 'Brawny and Beautiful Brothers' reputation."

"I don't think my looks are hurting your reputation."

Josh said, "I have to say, Brad, you really do look fatigued all the time. Is it the ER schedule?"

Brad collapsed onto the couch, allowing his head to flop back. "No, the ER is fine. I'm just not sleeping well."

"Have you tried taking Ambien?" asked Josh.

"I don't want to be dependent on a prescription drug. Medication's going to be the last resort."

"Well you look half-dead, so you might want to try that last resort before it's too late," said Ben.

"Thanks a lot, brother."

"So back to the original subject—Grace. Will she be at the dinner tonight?" asked Ben.

"She's been there every week so far," said Brad.

"Grace has been there every week? And you haven't worked out your differences yet?"

"She won't talk to him," Josh said. "And she won't talk to me or anyone else, for that matter."

A Cheshire cat grin split Ben's face. "Ah-ha! Challenge accepted. Grace will talk to me, and I will solve the riddle of Brad Gates' fall-from-Grace. Pun intended."

Brad started to object, but realized he'd exhausted all of his other resources. Like it or not, Ben was his best hope. He glanced at his brother, still sporting the wide smile and waggling his eyebrows. He didn't like it.

*****

Ben tried to secure a chair next to Grace at the Marshall dinner table, but she snagged a seat between her parents on the far end of the table from Brad. However, his place directly opposite her allowed him a perfect position to observe her during the meal. While she seldom spoke and trained her eyes on her plate for the majority of the dinnertime, when her glance arose from her food it always darted toward Brad and back downward. In fact, she didn't even notice Ben's scrutiny for the first fifteen minutes. She was definitely preoccupied with his brother's presence even while she pretended otherwise.

Olivia asked, "Ben, when is your shoulder surgery?"

"I have it scheduled in two weeks. Poor Brad and Josh are going to play nurse to me for the first week after surgery."

"You'll probably be begging for a real nurse after having two doctors do that duty. They're not the most nurturing guys in the world," Olivia teased.

"I've never pretended to be a good nurse. He'll mostly be fending for himself," said Josh.

"I'm giving up my bed for a week so he won't have to sleep on the couch," said Brad. "That'll have to be enough."

Ben said, "I intend to ring a little bell to fetch you when I need something."

"I'll tell you where you'll find that bell the first time you ring it," said Brad, glowering at his brother through squinted eyes.

Ben chortled at his remark, stealing a glance at Grace. She was utilizing the teasing exchange as an opportunity to study Brad, and her frown indicated she was unhappy with her observations. Ben caught her eyes, and they widened as she realized she'd been discovered. He saw two bright red patches appear on her cheeks as she returned her gaze to her food, which had been artfully rearranged on her plate rather than eaten.

"Grace, you're awfully quiet tonight," Ben ventured.

She mumbled something unintelligible, and Hannah said, "She never talks at Sunday night dinner anymore."

"Grace hardly talks at all anymore," said Claire, with her lower lip pooching out. "It's like I've lost my sister."

"That's not true," Grace murmured, as the flush spread to encompass her entire head and neck.

"It is true," said Olivia.

"Mom. May I be excused?" asked Grace, turning pleading eyes toward Connie Marshall.

Connie's sigh was audible. "Can't you make it through dinner?"

"Please?" she whispered.

"Okay, but I think you might need to see a doctor," said Connie.

"Mom, can we not discuss this in front of company?" asked Grace as she rose and fled from the room.

"Excuse me," Ben said, realizing he had to catch her before she disappeared. He jumped up and scrambled through the door, barely managing to catch her by the elbow at the foot of the stairs.

"Grace, wait!"

"I... I can't talk to you," she said, blinking at tears.

Ben kept a firm hold on her arm.

"No, you *can* talk to me. It seems to me you can't talk to anyone else." He watched her troubled expressions fleeting across her face as she considered his suggestion. He almost had her.

"You can talk to me, Grace. I'll keep it to myself, I promise. I won't tell Brad or anyone else. And you can ask me about Brad—I know you want to."

She pulled her lips in and bit them. "You really won't tell anyone—not Brad or Josh?"

"Cross my heart." Ben drew an imaginary "x" on his chest. He nodded his head toward the door. "Let's take a walk."

Grace stood frozen, her eyes darting toward the dining room and back. She sucked in a huge breath and held it, clenching her eyes shut. When she opened her eyes and let the air out, she straightened her back and lifted her chin, firming her lips.

"Let's go before I change my mind."

She strode out the front door with amazing speed considering her pint size, and Ben struggled to keep up.

"Okay, start talking."

She shot him a squinty scowl. "If I ever find out you told anyone anything I tell you, I'm going to cause you great pain."

Her threat seemed both serious and plausible. "I've already promised. Anyway, I'll love telling Brad I can't reveal the content of our conversation. It'll drive him crazy." He grinned at the thought. "So why did you break up with him this time?"

"For his own good."

Ben strolled beside her in silence, waiting for her to continue. "That's it? *For his own good*?"

Her brows drew together. "Yes. Have you seen him? He looks terrible. His job is killing him, but he won't tell anyone."

103

"But he said he hasn't been sleeping."

Grace shook her head. "It's like this. Remember a few months ago when Brad and Josh were up for the same position at Mercy General and Josh beat him out?"

"Vaguely. I think I remember giving him a hard time about it. It's not often someone manages to get the better of him."

"Well, that's the reason Brad has such a strained schedule. And he doesn't have any prospects of moving up because Josh is above him and they're the same age. When the time comes to appoint a new head of Emergency Medicine, it'll go to Josh."

"So maybe Brad needs to go somewhere else."

"Exactly—that's what I told him. But he told me he wouldn't even consider it, no matter how great the opportunity. In fact he told me he wouldn't move even if it was his dream job."

"Why not?"

"Because of us. Because of me. He thinks I wouldn't be happy if I moved away from my family. But I tried telling him I'd be fine as long as I could Skype with them. He refused to listen."

"So are you telling me you broke up with him so he'll give up on you and take a better job in some other city?"

"Yes, I'm hoping to get back together with him once he's accepted another job."

Ben rubbed the back of his neck. "I see some flaws in your plan."

"I know... I know it's possible he'll be so hurt or angry he won't take me back at all."

Ben grimaced. "I'm afraid that's pretty likely. Why don't you just tell him straight out you'll date him if he promises to search for a position at another hospital where he has better opportunities?"

The look she gave him must have been the one she used on her first graders when she was losing patience with them. "He'll just say the words he thinks I want to hear. Think about it! You know him. If he really believes I'll be unhappy living somewhere else, he'll never actually move me. He'll just sacrifice himself—you know I'm right."

"Why hasn't Josh figured it out?"

"Josh hasn't realized the implications for Brad's future, and Brad doesn't want to make him feel guilty. So Brad's never said anything to Josh about it."

"You know, Grace, not every doctor gets to be department head. Brad seems to love his work. Maybe he'd be perfectly happy living in New York and working where he is. He's never said anything to me about wanting to move."

"Haven't you seen how bad he looks? He needs better hours. He can't keep this up forever."

"Like I said, he told us he hasn't been sleeping well."

Grace shook her head. "That's because he doesn't want Josh to know. If it was just a sleep issue, he could prescribe himself a sleeping pill."

"Josh suggested he take a prescription drug to help with sleep, but he said that would be a last resort."

"He's just covering up to protect Josh."

Ben rubbed his temples. "Okay—I can follow your logic. And I have to say, that alone is kind of a scary thing. In fact, I don't usually mention girls in the same sentence with logic."

Grace's elbow almost knocked him off the sidewalk. "Hey!" Ben chuckled. "I'm glad you're short or that would've hurt my shoulder. As it is, my knee may never recover."

"I'm not that short, and I'm about to knock your head off to prove it."

"That might be good. I've been told my current head is too big."

Grace's pout dissolved into a reluctant grin.

Ben continued, "So I understand your logic, but I'm not convinced. And I think the whole thing will backfire if you keep it up. Let's say you finally make him give up completely and take a job somewhere else. How are you going to convince him to trust you enough to even date you again?"

"I don't know." Grace's teeth worried her lip. "I was kind of hoping you could help me figure that part out."

"So let me get this straight, you actually still like my brother? You only dumped him for his own good?"

"That's right. And I was thinking maybe after enough time passed, he'd look for a new job. And then when he found one, I'd just explain I only dumped him... I mean, I only broke up with him so he would do what was best for himself without considering me. Don't you think he'll understand?"

"I don't know, Grace. I barely understand it myself, and I'm not emotionally involved. What if instead you let me talk to him? I think I could convince him he needs to find a job with better prospects for the future. And I can convince him you'll be fine living in another city. There's no guarantee your siblings are all going to stay in the city anyway."

"Okay, you can do that, but you can't tell him anything I told you."

"Look Grace, why can't you two just date and then worry about the job thing later. You're not talking about marriage yet are you? At least not since Brad accidentally said the word. He swore he wouldn't bring it up again."

Grace was quiet for a minute as they walked. Ben looked down to find her swiping a tear off her cheek.

"Wait! Don't start crying—I'm not good with emotions. I try not to feel any more than I absolutely have to. What did I say to make you cry?"

She sniffed. "I... I think he's going to kill himself."

"Brad would never do that!"

"No, I don't mean literally kill himself. I just think he's stubborn enough to work until he doesn't have anything left. I thought he would've already given up and at least started looking for another job by now. He looks so tired and..." Salty tears trailed down her cheeks.

"Okay, okay. Don't cry. I'll talk to him and make him look for another job. I can probably trick him into it. If I tell him I'm moving to New York City, he'll probably start looking for a new position right away."

"Can't you just convince him I'm totally over him and there's no hope for us?"

"I just don't think that's the best approach. It hasn't worked so far, has it?"

"No, but..."

"Look, I'll think of something. I'll persuade him to believe he needs to find a job somewhere else. I think the best thing would be to tell him you want to move away for some reason."

"He won't believe you."

"I'll think of something. Trust me—I've been manipulating him since I learned how to talk. I'll call you and tell you when I get it worked out in my head."

Chapter Eight

"I'm sorry, Mom. What did you say?" Emily snapped her attention back to the woman who was watching her with a quizzical expression. Emily was having lunch with her mother, Anne Best Gherring, and her stepdad, Steven Gherring, at the small diner next door to Gherring Inc. where they worked.

"I was asking if you wanted to come over this weekend and address wedding invitations. We were thinking you and Spencer could come over Friday night."

Steven picked up his wife's hand from her lap and gave it an affectionate squeeze. "Your mom is finally feeling well enough to really enjoy all of this wedding planning."

Emily smiled as she watched her mom rubbing her swollen tummy with her other hand. "I'm so glad you finally quit feeling sick all the time. And it least now you actually look pregnant."

She recalled her shock when she first learned her mother was expecting, and then her further shock when they announced they were having twins. For the first half of her untimely pregnancy, her mother had suffered greatly from hyperemesis gravidarum, to the point of multiple hospitalizations. Spencer's mother, Connie Marshall, had served as her private nurse until the symptoms subsided. Thus the Marshalls and Gherrings had developed even tighter ties than those of the average in-laws-to-be.

"What has you so distracted today?" The lines on her forehead marked her concern.

Emily forced the corners of her mouth up and raised her eyebrows. "It's nothing, really. Don't worry."

"You don't have to protect me from everything. It's not like I'm going to lose the babies because I'm stressing a bit."

Emily hesitated. It would feel good to get it off her chest. She hadn't been able to stop thinking about it since last night's dinner.

"It's just that I'm worried about Grace and Brad."

"Are they still on the outs with each other? Are you worried because they're both in the wedding?"

"Sort of. See, I never told you about the doctor that works with Brad and Josh. Her name is Kara Dickson, and she's a real piece of work. She actually intercepted Grace's flowers and card a couple months ago at the hospital. Grace was trying to make up with Brad the first week after she broke up with him. And Dr. Dickson is the reason they didn't get back together. She lied to Grace and gave her a fake name and everything. And she threw herself all over Brad at the Yankees game, and we all saw it on TV."

Anne gasped. "And Grace saw it?"

"She did. It was awful."

Steven's brows drew together over his sharp blue eyes. "So now Brad is dating this woman?"

"No, he's not. At least I'm pretty sure he's not. But she just seems so... so unethical to me. And she really seemed to have her sights set on Brad. I'm worried she's going to do something else to keep them from getting back together."

Anne cocked her head. "Why are you suddenly bothered about this? Did something happen?"

"It's just a feeling. Sunday night, Brad's brother was there, and he talked to Grace for a long time. I feel like they're so close to getting back together. And I'm just afraid Dr. Dickson is going to jump in and spoil everything. But really, I don't have anything to go on, and maybe Brad wouldn't be fooled again."

"Dr. Dickson... Are you talking about Kara Dickson who works in the ER with Brad and Josh?" asked Steven, his jaw muscles flexing in a slow rhythm.

"Yes, her first name is Kara. I think maybe she's still a resident. Like she's a year behind them? I'm not sure how all that works."

Steven squinted as his breath whistled through his lips. "I know who she is. I'm surprised Josh hasn't gotten rid of her if she's that unethical."

Emily chuckled. "I guess you can't kick someone out of the residency program for intercepting another girl's flowers. It's not like she did anything illegal, but she seems so underhanded to me. The good news is Josh seems to be totally on to her."

"I don't suppose Charlie would be impressed to hear that about Josh?" asked Anne. "Maybe if you mentioned it to her, she'd be more willing to give him a chance."

Emily let her cheeks balloon out with air before she blew it out. "Mom, you know how Charlie is. She's so stubborn—she's convinced Josh is only interested in her because she's the first girl to turn him down."

"Is she right? Is she the first girl to turn him down?"

"Probably." Emily suppressed a laugh. "But I think he really cares about her. I feel sorry for him because she'll probably never give him a chance."

"So back to Kara Dickson," Gherring interrupted. "What is Josh doing about her? He's the attending—he ought to have some power."

Emily shrugged. "I don't think there's much he can do since she hasn't broken any laws or rules."

Steven's eyes glinted hard as steel. "She's already demonstrated a distinct lack of scruples. I'm certain a little digging below the surface would unearth other unethical actions. Even if she finishes the residency, she's not the type of doctor we want working at Mercy General."

"I shouldn't have said anything in front of you—I forgot you're on the board at the hospital." Emily paused with her fork suspended in the air. "But if she does anything else to interfere between Brad and Grace, I'm going to... to pull her hair out!" She stabbed a meatball with savage force.

Steven lifted his brows as he chuckled, "Girls fight so dirty."

*****

Monday afternoon Ben found himself in a standoff with Brad and Josh. He had put it off as long as possible, and he still hadn't come up with a fail-proof plan to convince Brad he should leave New York and explain why Grace would be happy to go with him. He'd simply have to go with his instincts and wing it if his brother didn't respond as predicted.

"I'm waiting. Tell me what she said." Brad paced in front of the couch where Ben was lounging. Josh, insisting he deserved to know as well, was sitting on the other end of the couch.

"I can't tell you exactly what she said, but..." Ben racked his brain. What could he say? He'd had the whole day to come up with a story, and so far he'd drawn a blank.

"But what? Does she like me? Does she hate me? Is there another guy? Is there any hope at all?"

"She's... Uhmm, she's afraid..." He felt perspiration beading on his forehead. He had to think fast. What could he say?

Brad stopped, swirling to face Ben with a look of alarm. "Afraid of what? Or is it a who? Is she afraid of me?"

A plot from his favorite television series popped into Ben's head. "It's not you. She's not afraid of you, but it's someone... I'm sorry. I shouldn't say. She made me promise." He stalled as the idea crystallized in his mind. This could work, if he could just remember what had happened on the show.

"Who is she afraid of? Is someone threatening her or blackmailing her? Is it Kara?"

"You have to promise—both of you—promise you won't tell her I said anything."

"I'm not telling her," said Josh, sitting up on the edge of the couch.

"I won't tell her," said Brad, lurching over his brother with his hands clenched into fists. "I just need to know. What is she afraid of?"

Ben took a deep breath. "It's a stalker."

"A stalker?" Brad's eyes were wide. "Like someone's following her? Or someone is calling her? How is he stalking her?"

"I don't know all the details. But that's why she wants to leave New York."

Josh said, "She wants to leave New York?"

"I thought she *didn't* want to leave New York," said Brad.

Ben leaned back and crossed his arms. "Tell me, brother. Did she or did she not try to talk you into leaving New York City?"

Brad said, "She never said she wanted to leave the city. She just tried to convince me she would still be happy if she left. She asked if I would take a job in another place if I had a better prospect of advancing." He began to pace again. "Why wouldn't she tell me if someone was stalking her? I don't get it."

"Has she reported it to the police?" asked Josh. He furrowed his brows as he fingered his cell phone.

"What are you doing?" Ben asked, snatching the cell phone from Josh's hand. "You can't call her."

"I'm going to call her or else I'm calling the police." Josh grabbed at the phone while Ben tried unsuccessfully to hold it out of reach.

"No you can't," said Ben as Josh recovered the phone. "You promised. She can't know I told you."

"I'm with Josh. We have to report it to the police or get her to report it. Her life may be in danger." Brad was losing control, and Josh was already punching in Grace's number. He had to think fast or they would call Grace and confront her about the stalker.

"You can't! Don't do it! Wait... I didn't tell you everything!"

Josh froze, holding the cell phone with Grace's name on the screen. "What? What else?"

Brad made a loud, strangled noise in the back of his throat as he pushed the heels of his hands into his eyes. "Just tell us what she said, Ben."

"She hasn't actually seen him. She doesn't have any actual evidence. She got a strange phone call, but she thought it was a wrong number. Then she... she thought a car was following her when she running. But she didn't get the make or the license plate. She only saw it was a black sedan. And then there was the little boy who gave her a message on the street corner."

Ben paused, swallowing half a bottle of water while buying time to formulate a message in his mind.

"The kid said, 'That guy gave me five dollars to tell you he knows where you live and he thinks you're cute.' But there was no one standing where the kid pointed and then he ran off. Since then, she just gets a feeling someone is staring at her or following her, but she's never actually seen the guy. He could be anybody."

Josh stared at the phone in his hands.

"So you see, Josh, there's no point calling and getting her more upset. There's really nothing to tell the police."

"I don't understand why she wouldn't just tell me she was afraid," said Brad.

"Because she didn't want to make you leave the city if you were happy here. She knew you would sacrifice your own happiness for her safety if she told you the truth. Once she realized you were determined to stay here, she broke it off."

"She really is psycho," said Josh. "That makes no sense whatsoever. She should just tell everyone what happened so we can help protect her."

"So what is she doing to protect herself if she's not telling anyone about it and she's not reporting it to the authorities?" asked Brad, rubbing his hair with his hand as he took up his pacing again.

"I can't tell you. I don't think I can trust you not to say something to her." Ben debated whether to continue with the next part of the television show because the plot got rather strange for a real life scenario.

"You've already told us part of it. You might as well tell us everything. I'm not going to tell her you told me," said Brad.

Josh slid his phone into his pocket. "I won't say anything to her, either. Go ahead. Give!"

"Well... You know she changed her hair—that was part of it. She's considering plastic surgery to change her appearance."

"No!" shouted Brad, and Ben flinched at the force of his anger. Hmmm, maybe he should have chosen a different TV show. Brad gestured wildly while kicking at the floor. "She is not screwing up her face! I won't let her!"

"This is crazy," said Josh, covering his face with his hands. "Even for Grace, this is crazy. I can't believe she would do something this stupid."

"I don't think she's actually going to do it," Ben hurried to say. "I think I talked her out of it. But don't you see? You can fix everything, and she'll never know I told you."

"How?" said Brad, with a sideways look.

"Just tell her you're looking for a job somewhere else."

"And that won't make her suspicious? That I'm suddenly looking for a job outside of New York City when I swore I would never move? Why couldn't she have just told me why she wanted to leave the city to begin with?"

"Like I said, she wants you to be happy, so she didn't want you to change your plans for her. Can't you follow her logic?"

"We can't follow her logic because she's not logical," said Josh.

"Women don't think in a linear fashion," Ben explained.

"Who told you that?" asked Brad.

"I read it in a book."

"Ha! You? Reading a book? Now I know you're lying to me."

*****

"Mom, can I talk to you about something?" asked Grace, relieved to find her Mom at home alone. After the jarring news she'd gotten at her doctor's visit that afternoon, she really needed her mother's comfort. And the fact her mom was a registered nurse was an added bonus. She would've normally talked to her sisters first, but they had all been a little stiff with her ever since she refused to talk about the reasons for her breakup with Brad. It smarted more than a little to think they were taking his side in a matter they didn't even understand. Perhaps they preferred Brad to their own sister.

"Sure honey. Come sit down." Connie patted the couch beside her while closing the book she'd been reading. "So you're finally going to tell me what happened with Brad? I didn't want to push you. You're so darned independent—you've been that way since the day you were born."

"No, it's not about Brad." Grace felt her eyes begin to water, and she fought for control. "It's... I have to have a procedure done." Tears began to roll down her face. "Why am I such a baby about this? It's not really a big deal." She wiped her face on her sleeve.

Connie hugged her. "Oh Gracie. It's okay. You don't have to be brave for me. What are you talking about? What procedure are you having done?"

"I went to the doctor because I found a lump in my breast. It was kind of sore—that's how I found it." Grace sniffed.

"Actually, it's good it was sore. It's more likely to be a benign cyst filled with fluid. I'm sorry, but you know I've had quite a few of these. Are they going to do a mammogram?"

"That's the thing. This was a few weeks ago, and I had the mammogram done already. I went back to the doctor today, and that's when she told me..." She couldn't stop the tears from falling.

Connie held Grace's shoulders and peered at her with wide eyes. "What did the doctor tell you? Does it look like cancer?"

"There was another one, farther in, one she couldn't feel. It's probably not cancer, but they're going to do a needle biopsy on both of them."

Connie patted her arms. "That's no big deal, sweetie. They'll get you numb, so it won't hurt. And then they'll probably use an ultrasound to guide the needle to the right place."

Grace felt a wave of nausea. "Stop, Mom. Don't talk about it." She flattened her hand on her stomach.

"Are you that worried about it?"

"It's so embarrassing, Mom. I started crying when she told me about it. I'm so afraid of needles, and I hate blood and all of that stuff."

"I'm sure you're not the first nervous patient the doctor has dealt with."

"I think I'm the first one she's decided to use IV sedation on."

"Oh." Connie wrinkled her nose in an attempt to hide her smile. "But sweetie, you have to get a needle in your arm to get an IV. I don't see how that will be any better."

"I'm going an extra hour early, and they're giving me a sedative in the waiting room. The doctor promised me I'd be so relaxed they would scoop me up out of the waiting room, and I wouldn't even remember getting the IV."

"I guess it's a good thing you didn't go to nursing school like Olivia and me," Connie chuckled. "It sounds like you have it all under control. You probably won't remember anything at all. And I'll come hold your hand. When are you getting it done?"

"That's the thing. It's tomorrow afternoon, and I know you're working. I'll be fine once I take the sedative, but I'll need someone to get me home."

"I'm finished with my shift at two. I can probably get off earlier if I need to. Where will you be?"

"I'll be in the outpatient surgery at Mercy General."

"It'll be fine, Grace. Don't worry." Connie hesitated, and her brows knitted. "But Gracie, aren't you going to tell your sisters? They'll be so upset if you don't."

"I don't want to tell them."

Connie let out a heavy sigh. "What happened? Why did you break up with Brad? And why are you on the outs with your sisters? You girls have always been so close. You've never stayed upset with each other for this long."

"Mom, you have to trust me. I broke up with him to protect him."

"To protect him? But—"

"Please Mom, not now. I'll explain later. I just can't handle any more stress right now."

"But honey, I think Brad would want to know you're having this procedure done. He's obviously still in love with you."

"He's not in love with me," Grace protested, feeling her cheeks heat up. "We haven't even known each other that long."

"Grace, I'm not as oblivious as you think I am. I know you think I'm unaware, but I'm not deaf and blind. I know when a boy is in love with my daughter." She wrapped her arms around Grace and kissed her hair. "And I know when my daughter is in love with a boy."

Grace couldn't hold back her tears any longer. And she couldn't keep denying her feelings, either. "Why does it have to be so complicated?"

"It's not that complicated. You love each other, and then you work things out so you can be together."

"But he needs to leave New York City so he can have an opportunity to advance. He's working himself into the ground at Mercy General."

Connie shrugged. "He's young, Grace. He chose this life—this branch of medicine. And if he wants to work somewhere else, you can always move, can't you?"

"He won't even discuss it. He's sacrificing himself so I can stay in New York when I'm perfectly willing to move."

"Gracie, you're doing this in the wrong order."

"Huh? What do you mean?"

"It's way too early to work out all the details. You need to spend time together and get to know each other. And once you're committed to each other... Well, I'm not saying everything is easy, but all these problems will work themselves out. You'll decide together, as a couple, the best place for you to live. But you don't have the right to make that decision for him any more than he has the right to make it for you. You have to decide together."

Her mother made it sounds so simple—too simple. It couldn't be that easy. "What if he still refuses to move? I wouldn't be able to bear watching him wear himself out, knowing it was my fault. It's already breaking my heart."

Connie groaned out loud. "I love you, sweetie. But you do have a few faults. And one of them is you think you should make all the decisions. You've been bossing your siblings around since you learned to talk. I've got news for you—in marriage there's not going to be a boss. You'll find out it's actually fun to share that responsibility. And on occasion, Brad might actually be right about something."

"But..."

She held up a finger. "Just think about it. I think you ought to tell Brad about your biopsy. But if you're not ready, I won't press you on it. It's your decision. But when this is all over, you've got to talk to him. Both of you are miserable, and there's no reason for it. Okay?"

Grace inhaled a shuddery breath. Why hadn't she talked to her mom weeks ago? Her mother had a way of making her feel like everything would work out for the best.

"Okay." She hugged her tight and grinned. "Thanks Mom. You're pretty smart for an old lady."

"I'm going to remember that remark next month when your birthday comes along."

*****

Emily knew something was wrong from listening to Spencer's side of the conversation. He'd taken the call while walking her up to her apartment, but now he stood outside her door, listening and asking scary questions like, "How long will it take you to recover?" and "Does Brad know?" It was something about Grace, and his alarmed expression made her heart race. What could it be? Had she been in an accident?

When he hung up the phone he turned to her, rubbing his temples. "That was Grace. She's having a biopsy tomorrow afternoon. I can't believe she waited this long to tell me."

"A biopsy? For cancer?"

"Yes. It's called a needle biopsy. She said it's most likely a couple of cysts, but there's a chance it's cancer. I mean, that's why they do a biopsy, right?"

"Tomorrow afternoon? Is she scared?"

"She's terrified. She didn't talk about it, but I know her. She's afraid of blood and needles and surgery. It's like a phobia with her. She tries to cover it up since she's grown, but it's still there."

"Ohmygosh! Maybe I can go sit with her. What time is she having it done? And where?"

"She said it's tomorrow afternoon. I've got an accounting test, so I can't go." He closed his eyes tight, pushing his hand through his hair. It hurt to watch the worry on his face. He was so close to his little sister."

"I'm sure I can get off work. Where is she doing it?"

"She said she's going at two o'clock to the outpatient surgery at Mercy General, and she thinks the procedure will be at three. Oh, and Mom is supposed to go over as soon as she gets off work."

"But no one will be there when she's waiting to go in? That'll be the worst time. I'm going for sure—she doesn't need to be alone."

Spencer's face relaxed a little as he wrapped her in his arms. "Thanks so much. I'll feel better knowing you're with her."

Emily felt a warm glow as she reveled in the security of his embrace. "She's going to be my sister in a few months. What did she say about Brad? Has she told him?"

"No, but she said she's going to talk to him tomorrow night after she wakes up."

"After she wakes up? Is she going under general anesthesia for this?"

"No, but she's taking a sedative and they're giving her an IV."

"I'll be sure to be there by two o'clock."

"Thanks Emily." He lifted her chin, and his kiss took her breath away.

When he released her, she stayed in his arms until her heart rate returned to normal. With her head against his chest, she could hear his own heart pounding.

"Wow. I really like these 'gratitude kisses'. I'll try to earn them as often as possible."

*****

Olivia was exhausted when she went up to her room. Her clinical rotation in NICU was intense, and she'd stayed at the library to study until eight p.m. Knowing her alarm would go off at five a.m., she'd planned to shower and fall into bed. But when she opened the door and found Grace looking up at her with red-rimmed eyes, she knew it was finally time to clear the air. Despite her fatigue, her heart rejoiced. She'd missed her sister—they'd never stayed angry at each other for this long. Not that they'd actually been angry, but they weren't communicating about anything of importance. Olivia missed that closeness so much. She'd almost felt like she'd lost a limb—everything seemed off-kilter without Grace.

Olivia opened her arms and in a blink, Grace was hugging her, both of them weeping.

"I'm sorry," sobbed Grace. "I just couldn't explain it to you, and I didn't want you to disapprove."

"But I'm your sister. I'm on your side, no matter what."

"I know, I know. I'm sorry. Do you forgive me?"

"Yes, but I expect you to tell me everything."

Grace lowered her voice. "Can I wait on that? I've got something kind of important to tell you."

The door cracked open and a head covered in auburn curls appeared. "Wait—we can't hear very well." Hannah tumbled into the room with Claire on her heels.

Grace mumbled something about paper-thin walls, and Claire said, "It's about time you came back to us—I've been missing my Grace." She squeezed between them to steal a hug, glaring when Olivia opened her mouth to object to the intrusion. "No pulling rank, Olivia. We've missed her, too. And I've got a boy problem, and I need her."

"So what were you saying? Something important? Is it Brad? Are you engaged?" Hannah asked.

"Shamazzle! No! We're not even dating right now, and we agreed not to talk about marriage or anything," said Grace.

"Then what is it?" asked Olivia. "Do I need to get rid of the junior sisters so we can talk?"

"No, it's okay," said Grace before Claire and Hannah could protest. "I'm... I'm having a biopsy done tomorrow afternoon."

"What kind of biopsy?" asked Olivia, as the other two gasped.

"It's not a big deal, really," said Grace, but the quiver in her voice belied her nonchalance. "It's a needle biopsy. I've got two lumps in Flopsy."

"Now which one is Flopsy and which one is Mopsy?" asked Claire. "I always forget."

"Flopsy on the left. Mopsy on the right," said Grace.

"Is it cancer?" asked Hannah.

Grace flinched at the word. "They're probably just cysts, but I'm kind of nervous."

"No kidding," said Olivia. "Your face is almost white just from talking about it. When is the biopsy? And where? Do you want us to be there?"

"I'll gladly skip school," offered Claire.

"It's tomorrow afternoon, and Mom's coming after she finishes her shift. I need you more tonight so I don't think about it too much."

"Is it going to hurt?" asked Hannah. "How big is the needle they stick in there?"

Olivia saw Grace's blanched face grow even whiter as her hand rose to her mouth. "Come on, Grace. Let's sit down." She shook her head at Hannah, mouthing the words, "Don't say needle."

"I'm sure it will be fine—probably hardly any blood." Claire didn't seem to notice how Grace flinched at the word 'blood', continuing on merrily. "So tell us about Brad. Are you back together yet? And why did you break up this time?"

Hannah brightened. "Hey! I thought of something good that's coming out of this biopsy thing. Didn't you always say Flopsy was bigger than Mopsy? Maybe this will even them out."

Claire giggled and let out a snort. Soon all four were laughing and rolling around on the beds.

Grace wiped away tears of laughter. "Oh man! I needed this."

"We're glad to have our president back," said Olivia. "It was like you'd fled the country."

"Yeah, Olivia's not as much fun as you." Claire ducked when Olivia took a swing at her.

"I fled the country because I thought I might get assassinated," Grace teased. "No one was talking to me."

"You weren't talking to us," said Olivia. "You used to tell us everything. Why did you quit talking to us?"

Grace worried her lower lip. "It made perfect sense at the time, but after talking to Mom... I don't know. Now, I have to admit it's possible I overreacted."

"What! *Our* Grace? Overreacting to something?" Olivia threw her head back in dramatic fashion and held the back of her hand to her forehead. "It can't be true! I think I may faint!" When Grace swung a pillow her way, she dashed out of reach.

Claire copied Olivia's pose, "No... No... Say it isn't so!" Grace lunged for Claire and caught her, tickling her until she begged for mercy.

"So are you finally getting back together with Brad? Because like I've said before, I'll take him if you don't want him." Hannah bobbed her eyebrows up and down.

"He's too old for you," said Claire.

"I like older men," said Hannah. "In fact, I'll take Josh if Charlie doesn't want him."

"Either one, huh? Something makes me doubt your level of commitment," Grace jested.

Hannah crossed her arms. "I'm not going to let you lecture me about commitment. You've turned out to be a commitophobe."

"That's not even a real word," Grace objected.

"It's in Wikipedia, and your picture is on the page." Olivia sidestepped the pillow Grace threw at her.

"Stop it! I'm not afraid to commit, I just want to be careful about it."

"I think you're not willing to give up being president of the Marshall Sisters for a lesser post. You're addicted to power," said Claire.

Grace raised an eyebrow. "I have no intention of relinquishing my post as president if I ever commit to some guy. I will always be the head honcho around here, and don't you forget it."

"So you're going to commit to Brad now? You've been skirting around our questions this whole time. What are you going to do about him?" asked Hannah.

"She's in love with him." Olivia turned a wry grin toward Grace. "Aren't you, Grace?"

Olivia saw Grace's face turn beet-red. "Enough about me... Let's talk about Claire's new boyfriend."

Olivia held up her hand before Claire could respond. "Wait. I'm invoking the Truth or Dare law. Either you tell us the truth now, or you have to accept any dare of our making."

Grace threw herself face down on the bed and let out a muffled, agonized moan. "Why God? Why did you give me sisters? Spencer is so nice—he'd never do something like this."

"You know you love us," said Olivia. "But you still have to make a choice right now. Which one will it be? Truth or dare?"

Grace flipped over. "Dare. I'll take the dare. What is it? I want to get it over with."

"Oh no you don't." Olivia motioned her younger sisters into a huddle. "We get to take our time deciding what it will be. We're not going to waste our dare on something lame. You're going to wish you'd chosen truth."

Grace's eyebrows drew together. "Maybe I'll just change my choice. Fine. I'll tell you the truth."

"No way," chuckled Hannah. "We figured out the truth as soon as you refused to answer. You're in love with Brad or you wouldn't have minded telling us. Now we know the truth, and we still get to give you a dare." She turned toward Olivia and Claire, jumping up and down, her reddish curls bouncing. "I've got a great idea."

Olivia felt the grin growing on her face as Hannah explained her plan in a low whisper. She glanced across the room at Grace, who appeared more than a bit anxious about the turn of events. Oh well, at least they'd gotten her mind off the biopsy. This was going to be fun.

*****

"Olivia? Olivia? Are you awake?" Grace whispered into the darkness.

Olivia groaned, "I am now. What's wrong? You can't sleep?"

"No. I'm still nervous."

"Are you worried about the IV? Or is it the biopsy that scares you?"

"I'm worried about the dare. I can't believe you're making me talk to Brad right after the procedure."

Olivia chuckled. "Oh, that—it'll be so easy. You'll be under the influence of the drugs. You probably won't remember anything you said."

"It's so unfair! I think there must be some exception. Didn't we pass an amendment on that Truth or Dare law when Hannah sprained her ankle that time?"

"Yes, but it only applies to the endangerment of life and limb. Embarrassment doesn't count."

"What about mortification? I'm pretty certain I'm going to die when I find out what I actually said. And having all of you witness it will make it even worse."

"You could always go with the other alternative. You could talk to him before you have the procedure done. But then you have to confess everything, and we get to be there."

"No, I'll take my chances. I'm hoping I'll be so sleepy I won't say anything to him. Or even better, he'll be in the middle of some emergency procedure and he won't be able to come. Or maybe he's working tonight and he'll be asleep tomorrow afternoon."

"Maybe, but I'm betting he'll be there. Once he finds out you're having some sort of procedure done, he'll find a way. And you're not allowed to tell him ahead of time, because I know he would come before the biopsy starts and spoil our fun." She let out a long slow, "Hmmmmmm." She continued in a teasing tone, "I think I'm going to video it and put it up on YouTube. I bet we'll get a million hits."

"No way! That was not part of the dare."

"Oh, well of course I won't make a video."

Grace was disconcerted by the ease of Olivia's acquiescence. "Do you promise?"

"I promise."

"You promise what? What exactly are you promising?"

"I promise I won't make a video and post it on YouTube."

"Okay." Grace was quiet for a moment. "What about Hannah and Claire?"

"Of course I can't promise for our sisters. They've gotten really out of control, in my opinion. You've really fallen down on your job lately."

"Olivia," Grace growled.

"What? It's true. I can't control them." Olivia began to giggle, and she continued to laugh over Grace's protests.

"Olivia, please! Don't let anyone make a video! If you love me—"

Olivia howled with laughter until she had to gasp for breath. "This is the most fun ever—I'm so glad you're my sister!"

"That makes one of us," Grace muttered.

Chapter Nine

Brad cornered Josh before he left the apartment. "What do you think I should do? Should I apply for a position in another city?"

After learning about Grace's stalker, he'd spent a sleepless night. He needed to protect her, and he couldn't do that from a distance. Now, more than ever, he was desperate to restore their relationship.

"Don't you need to talk to her first? I mean, before you change your whole life around for her, shouldn't you make sure she even still wants you?"

"I don't know what to say to her. I can't even explain why I want to stay in New York, because you haven't told anyone you're planning to change tracks in a few years. Unless you've changed your mind?"

"No, a couple more years of this, and then I'm looking into surgical residencies. By the time Dr. Cooper retires, I'll probably be gone. Anyway, just because I beat you out for attending doesn't mean I'd get the head of Emergency Medicine."

"Yes, but to be honest, I don't want to compete against my best friend."

Josh hesitated. "To be honest, I'm hoping Charlie and I will get together before I go into surgery. There's no telling where I might end up. If I'm not in New York when she moves here, my chances with her go from slim to none."

"You still think you have a chance with her? I thought she pretty much blew you off."

"Of course I still have a chance—as long as I'm willing to wait for her. And believe me, I'm willing. Plus, I'll see her at Spencer and Emily's wedding."

Brad didn't want to discourage his friend, but he knew Charlie hadn't been responding to his calls and texts. "How do you know she'll come to New York when she graduates?"

"Emily's keeping me informed. She's planning to come here for law school if she gets accepted." He frowned and crossed his arms. "But we're not discussing Charlie and me—we're talking about you and Grace. I don't think moving away from New York is a solution to her stalker problem, anyway."

"I agree, but once Grace gets an idea in her head, it's hard to convince her otherwise. I thought I might tell her I've decided to go back to L.A. And once we're together again, I'd be able to protect her. After we get rid of this stalker, I could tell her I changed my mind. By then she won't care—she'll probably be glad to stay in New York."

"That might work. In fact, you could tell her that was the only reason you went out with Kara."

"I didn't go out with Kara." Brad bristled. "We went to the baseball game as friends—that's all."

"Except for that kiss..."

"She may have kissed me, but I didn't kiss her back. That woman is psycho!"

"I thought you said Grace was psycho."

"Well Kara is more psycho... A lot more!"

Josh laughed. "That's what you get for cheating on Grace."

Brad's blood was beginning to boil. "I didn't cheat on Grace. She broke up with me. Remember?"

"Calm down. I'm just kidding you. But are you sure you want to keep dating her if she has plastic surgery?" Josh chuckled.

"That's not even funny. I'm sure that was never a serious consideration. She's scared to death of needles and surgery. And Ben said he'd talked her out of it already."

"I hope you're right. But she has been acting kind of crazy lately."

"Well, all of that stops today. I'm going to talk to her and straighten everything out."

"Good luck, buddy. Hasn't she blocked your phone number? I don't see how you're going to make that happen."

"My shift doesn't start until noon. I'm going to see her at her school. I'll stand outside her classroom until she gives in."

"Will they even let you inside the school? With all the safety hype, I'm not sure you can get to her."

"I met her principal the first week of school. Surely she'll let me in to see her. I'll wear my hospital ID."

"Why don't you just go to her house tonight? Now you know what's actually going on, you'll know the right things to say. But you promised Ben you wouldn't tell her you know about the stalker."

"I won't tell her, but I have to see her this morning. I can't explain it, but I feel like something terrible is going to happen. I can't take a chance, waiting until tonight."

Josh grinned. "Be careful. If you run into Horatio, you might have a fight on your hands."

*****

The bell rang and Grace fought to calm her students who were exceptionally rambunctious on this rainy day. Her substitute was scheduled to arrive by eleven o'clock, and she hoped the high-spirited children would settle down before her arrival.

"Ms. Marshall! Ms. Marshall!" Horatio called out. "Cord has a bloody nose!"

Grace grabbed a wad of tissues and rushed to hand them to the boy. Accustomed to the problem, Cord already had his head back and his nose pinched, but there seemed to be an extraordinary amount of blood.

"Come on, Cord," said Grace, taking his hand to walk him to the nurse. "I'll be back in two minutes. We're playing the still and silent game until I get back. Briana is the monitor. No one moves unless the fire alarm goes off."

Her stomach heaving each time she glanced at the bloody ball of Kleenex, Grace hurried him along to the nurse's station. Upon her arrival, she felt her cell phone vibrating a reminder alarm. Expecting to see the message prompting her to remember her one o'clock appointment, Grace viewed the screen. *Mercy General, biopsy, 11a.m.*

Eleven a.m.? It couldn't be. Wasn't it one p.m.? She scrolled into her appointment book as her heart thudded in her chest. There it was, plain as day. Her appointment was at eleven and the surgery was at one o'clock. She'd gotten the one o'clock time stuck in her head, and remembered it as the time she was supposed to arrive at the hospital.

With a frantic pounding of blood in her ears she patted the boy's arm. "Cord, Ms. Livingston will take care of you. I've got to run to the office for a minute. Okay?" Dashing down the hallway to the office, she found the office staff was in conference with the principal, leaving the receptionist alone left to man the front.

"Danna! You have to help me! I got my appointment times mixed up. My sub is coming at eleven, but I have to be there by eleven."

Danna's mouth formed a big O as her eyebrows flew up. "What do I do? I don't know what I'm supposed to do. I'm new—"

"I know—you're new. But you need to find the sub who's scheduled to come to my room and get them to come early."

"Oh... Oh..." She began to shuffle through papers on her desk, her hands trembling.

"It's probably in the computer," said Grace. "Do you want me to look?"

Relief flowed over Danna's face, and she gave Grace a grateful smile. "Would you please? It's just that I'm—"

"Yes, I know—you're new." Grace thought Danna ought to have learned something during her month-long term as the receptionist, but she kept the opinion to herself. She could hardly criticize the flighty girl, when she had a tendency to make such crazy blunders, herself. She located the substitute schedule and the phone number for Danna. But at her panicked expression, Grace decided to make the call herself.

"Hello? Is this Brian Taylor?"

"Yes."

"This is Harbinger Elementary. I know you're scheduled to substitute at eleven o'clock, but I'm hoping you can come early." At his hesitation she added, "It's kind of an emergency."

"Uhmm... I could probably be there by ten."

Grace sucked in a deep breath and held it. Ten o'clock would have to do. "Okay, thanks so much."

Danna was still regarding her with wide eyes. "Where are you going?"

"To the hospital." Grace held her hand to her throat, feeling the rapid pulse in her neck. "And I wish I already had that sedative they're giving me. I need it now."

The door opened behind Danna, and the principal peered outside. She frowned when she saw Grace and stepped to the desk, shutting the door behind her.

"What's wrong, Grace? You're white as a sheet."

"Oh Ms. Garcia, I'm such an air-head! I thought my appointment was for one o'clock, but it's really at eleven. I just called to get my sub to come early. He said he could get here by ten."

"Grace, your hands are shaking. Don't fret about this—I'll cover your classroom as soon as I handle a few things up here. You don't have to wait until ten o'clock to leave."

"Thank you so much! I'm so nervous about getting there on time. If I'm late I won't have time to get checked in and get the sedative. I want to make sure it has time to work before they give me an IV. I'm so afraid of the needle."

She chuckled. "Poor Grace. I don't know how you're going to handle having children."

"I may have to adopt," said Grace, only half-teasing.

"You're having surgery?" asked Danna. "What are they doing to you? You don't look sick."

Ms. Garcia stopped her. "Danna, all health issues are private. You aren't supposed to ask these questions unless you need to know. And if anyone shares health information with you, you're not allowed to give that information to anyone else. Do you understand?"

Danna started blinking rapidly, and Grace thought she might start crying. She decided to diffuse the tense situation with humor. "It's okay, Danna. You might as well know. I'm having plastic surgery." She winked at her principal. "The next time you see me, you won't even recognize me."

Ms. Garcia played along with her. "Yes, I'm hoping you've decided to go with a bigger nose to balance out those cheek implants you're getting."

"The breast reduction is going to be the best part," Grace chuckled. "It'll be so much easier to find clothes to fit."

Ms. Garcia placed a hand on her arm. "Seriously Grace, I'll be praying for you. I'm sure everything will be fine. And who's your sub?"

"I've never met him. His name is Brian Taylor."

"Brian's great—he's quite intimidating. He used to be in the marines, and he's great with discipline. He's about six foot four and he's built like a cinder-block."

"I'm sorry I'm going to miss him." She remembered her abandoned classroom and gasped. "Yikes! I've got to get back to my classroom. Thanks so much, Ms. Garcia."

On her walk back to class, Grace began to feel guilty Brad wouldn't hear about her biopsy until after it was over. After all, he hadn't really done anything wrong. She couldn't even be angry with him about the Kara (a.k.a. Leanne) situation since she'd already broken up with him when they went to the baseball game together. She retrieved her phone and entered a text with trembling fingers. *Call me when you get a chance. I have something important to tell you.* She thought for a moment. They hadn't really talked in a month—he was probably angry with her. *And I'm sorry!* There—now he would know she was taking the blame. She pressed send before she could chicken out and made sure her phone was in her pocket where she could feel it vibrate.

Adrenaline working overtime, she took a few deep breaths to slow her heart and squeezed her hands into fists. She couldn't wait to take that sedative.

*****

Kara checked the schedule again. Brad Gates wasn't due to arrive until noon, but Josh Branson was already here. This was her best opportunity to get the scoop on Brad and his girlfriend. She'd been laying low for a month since Brad had been giving her the cold-shoulder, but she was almost certain he and Grace had remained estranged. She was dating another doctor, but he wasn't as brilliant or good-looking as Brad. Plus, she was almost certain he was more interested in her connections than he was in her. She didn't mind using her father's wealth and influence to her own ends, but it was unflattering to think the man wasn't spellbound by her looks and personality.

She found Josh alone in the lounge. He regarded her with wary eyes as she approached him. He'd certainly turned out to be more astute than she'd realized. She'd have to be careful—throw him off-track.

"Dr. Branson, I wonder if you might give me some advice. It's about..." She put on her most tentative face. "It's about a guy."

"Why me, Dr. Dickson?" His expression was inscrutable. "Why not ask one of your girlfriends for advice?"

"To be honest, I don't have any girlfriends. Girls always distrust me—they think I'm going to steal their boyfriends or husbands." Her laugh was humorless. "But look at me. I'm thirty-two and still single. If I were going to steal a guy, don't you think I would have done it by now?"

Apparently disarmed, Josh chuckled. "Okay, I'll do my best to help. But I've been told I'm not that great at understanding women—at least, not all of them."

"I don't need help understanding women... I need help understanding men." She flashed her smile-of-gratitude, which he accepted and returned. Men were so easy to manipulate.

"Well then, fire away."

"There's this guy I like, but it seems like I always do everything wrong with him. I know he's attracted to me, but he holds himself at a distance."

Josh frowned. "Are you sure he's not married or otherwise attached?"

"I'm sure he's not married, and I don't think he's attached. I've backed off, but I just can't stop thinking about him. I really wish I understood... I thought you could help me learn what I did wrong with Brad, and that might help me with this guy."

He sat back, crossing his arms over his chest, and let out a heavy breath. "Kara, you never had a chance with Brad. He's in love with Grace. But barring that, you were too aggressive for him. Some guys like that, but not Brad. And then there was the matter of you lying and keeping the flowers Grace brought him. I doubt he'd ever forgive you for doing something like that."

"It was just an impulse, and I regret it now. I know I shouldn't have done that, but I thought it might be my only chance. He's dating Grace again, right? I hope I didn't do any permanent damage." She tucked her chin down and gazed at Josh through her lashes. Did he buy her story? She needed Josh on her side if she was going to bag Brad. "I really wish I could make it up to him. If he and Grace wanted to move back to California, I'd still be willing to put in a good word for him with my father."

His brows arched high on his forehead. "Really? You'd help him get a job even if he wasn't with you?"

"Of course I would—he's highly qualified. Do you think he might be interested in moving? He and Grace?"

Josh scratched his chin. "It's crazy, but I think he might actually consider it."

"So they'd be interested in moving to California? And they're dating again?" She held her breath. Was it too late?

"Well, yes and no. They're not quite back together yet, but that could change by the end of the day. And I think Brad may have changed his mind about the position in California."

She almost sagged in relief. She still had a chance at Brad. Josh narrowed his eyes. "Didn't you say this was about some other guy?"

"It is. I want to know how to get his attention."

Josh cocked his head. "What if the two of you aren't meant to be together?"

"I can't accept that answer."

"I have to admit, I know how you feel."

"Just tell me... If it were you, what would it take to get your attention?"

"Nothing you did would work on me."

Kara reeled at the insult, but kept the anger out of her expression.

"Someone else already has my attention," Josh explained. So he was in love with another woman—that's why she hadn't been able to manipulate him. She wasn't losing her touch after all.

"But this is a great guy—I don't want to lose him. You have to help me."

"I don't know. Hmmm… Somehow showing him some kind of selfless love. You know…" He rubbed the back of his neck. "Like staying up late to make cookies for him. Or taking care of him when he's sick. Or if he saw you doing that for someone else, he'd know you were that kind of person. To be honest, Kara, a lot of people think money and power are your only motivations. You need to show him that's not the real you."

Her mind churned as she turned over possible actions. She might only have a day to make herself look selfless for Brad.

At her silence Josh added, "I hope I haven't offended you by saying what people perceive about you. That doesn't mean I share their opinions."

Kara waved him off. "No, that's okay. I'm used to it, having grown up in my family. It's never bothered me before now." In fact, she was surprised he felt the observation might be an insult. She'd always been taught money and power were the ultimate goals in life, and she'd met very few people in her life who weren't similarly motivated. And she'd certainly never dated such a man.

Now she realized why she'd been so attracted to both of these men. They were genuinely unselfish—a rare commodity. She wanted to kick the door, realizing she was probably too late. But if she couldn't snag Brad or Josh, she'd at least be more prepared before the next good one came along. She was convinced this type of man would spoil her like no other. And she enjoyed being spoiled. Although not well versed at attracting altruistic men, she wouldn't be satisfied with less, now she realized they existed. She always got what she wanted, and she enjoyed a good challenge.

*****

Brad was on route to Grace's school when he received her text. Thrilled she'd finally communicated with him, he immediately called her back. But the busy signal in his ear indicated she still had him blocked in her cell phone. He almost screamed in frustration. What could she mean by her message? Why was she sorry? Was it something she'd done or something she was going to do? He hurried down into the subway station only to find he'd just missed the train and would have six minutes to wait for the next one.

By the time he arrived at Harbinger Elementary, having run from the station to the school, he was drenched in sweat. He'd have to shower before he went to work.

"Excuse me." He caught the attention of a young woman behind the front desk, gasping for air as he spoke. "I need to see Grace Marshall."

She looked him over. "Are you Brian Taylor?"

"No, I'm Brad Gates. Doctor Brad Gates—Grace's boyfriend. Who's Brian Taylor?"

"I didn't think you were him. He's supposed to be coming in this morning, and evidently he's pretty scary-looking. He's like huge and strong, six-feet-six inches or something like that."

"Is he the guy that's been bothering her?"

"Uhmm... I don't know."

"Never mind. Can you let me in?"

"Oh, I'm sorry. Grace just left."

"She left? Did she know this Brian guy was coming here?"

"Of course she knew he was coming. That's why she left. Well, Ms. Garcia told her she could leave early. She's covering her class for her."

"Where did she go?"

"She's gone to her surgery appointment."

The heartbeat, which had just begun to slow, picked up its pace again. "Surgery appointment?"

The girl's face paled. "You didn't know? Oh, please don't tell anyone I told you. I could be fired. Ms. Garcia just told me not to share anyone's health information, but you got me so rattled with all your questions."

"You can tell me—I'm a doctor."

She studied him with furrowed brows. "You don't look like a doctor."

"Look, here's my ID card."

She examined the card, comparing him to the picture. "I guess that could be you."

"Of course it's me! It's my picture. Now tell me where Grace has gone." With great difficulty, Brad kept his voice even.

"I'm not stupid, you know. People can fake ID cards. How do I really know you're a doctor?"

"Please." He paused, reading her nametag. "Please, Danna. I need to know where Grace is. It's a matter of life and death."

"How do I even know you're her boyfriend? If you were her boyfriend, you'd think she would have told you she was having plastic surgery."

"Plastic surgery? She actually said that? That's where she's going today?"

Danna's eyes welled with tears. "You don't have to yell at me. It's not my fault."

Brad took a deep breath and unclenched his fists. He spoke in a soft, low voice. "Danna, I'm sorry I yelled, but I'm worried about Grace. Can you please tell me where she went?"

She sniffed. "I don't even know. She just said her appointment was at eleven."

He groaned, checking the time. It was nine-thirty. He still had time to stop her if he could find her. "I can't believe she's really doing this."

"It's probably your fault, you know." Danna's lifted her chin as she spoke the harsh accusation. "If she was secure in your love, she wouldn't feel the need to change."

"That's so not true! I love her just like she is. She's beautiful, and I don't want her to change. But you'd better call the police before this stalker shows up."

"What stalker?" she asked, with wide eyes.

"Brian Whatever-his-name-is. He's stalking her."

"He is?"

"Never mind! I've got to go stop Grace before she makes a huge mistake." He ran outside to flag a taxi.

"Where to?" asked the driver.

"I don't know yet," Brad said, pulling out his cell phone as another text came in from Grace.

Please call me soon. I need to tell you something before you find out from someone else.

He dialed her number, cursing when the expected busy signal sounded in his ear. "Just drive toward Mercy General Hospital for now."

He called Olivia, reaching her voice mail. "Please call me about Grace and, if you talk to her, tell her to call me. She still has my number blocked."

He covered his face with his hands, mumbling his frustration, before trying Spencer's number. Again he left a message. The pattern continued through all four of Grace's siblings. He called Josh, planning to leave a message, and was surprised when he answered the call.

"What's up?"

"Josh, have you heard from Grace?"

"No, but I thought you went to see her at her school this morning."

"I did but... You won't believe it when I tell you."

"Tell me what? What happened? She wouldn't talk to you? Or they wouldn't even let you in the school to see her?"

"No. She left the school to go to a surgery appointment—a plastic surgery appointment."

"There's no way, Brad. Did you get this story from Ben? Because I think he may have been kidding us about that whole thing. Grace would never—"

"The girl at the front desk at her school told me. And she specifically mentioned plastic surgery."

"Okay, now hold on, Brad. This couldn't be happening without her family knowing about it. Maybe she's just going for a consult. I don't believe she'd ever have the nerve to do something like that, even if she was actually crazy enough to consider it."

Brad felt his tight chest ease a bit. "You're right. She couldn't possibly be having the surgery today. She's probably just going for a consult. I've still got time to talk her out of it. She texted me and asked me to call her, but she still has me blocked. Can you call her and ask her to call me or unblock me or both?"

"What did her text say?"

"Just that she wanted me to call her and she was sorry and she didn't want me to hear something from someone else. I assume she's planning to tell me about this crazy plastic surgery idea. I know I'll be able to talk her out of it. And at this point, I don't care what kind of promise I made to Ben. She's going to tell me about this stalker. I think the guy has figured out where she works now."

"How do you..." Josh's voice cut off, and Brad heard muffled voices in the background. "Brad, I gotta go. Bad accident. Multi-car. You should come in early."

The phone disconnected.

"Hey Mister," said the cab driver. "You decide where you want to go yet?"

If he'd had anything but half-inch stubble on his head, he would have pulled all of his hair out. He grunted, "Just take me to Mercy General."

Out of desperation, he called his brother, but again was forced to leave a message. He growled into the phone, "Ben! You told me you had talked Grace out of this stupid plastic surgery. She has an appointment somewhere this morning at eleven, and if I find out it's anything more than a consult, I might take a scalpel to your neck. Not only that, but it appears her stalker has discovered where she works. So all bets are off—I'm not keeping anything a secret anymore!" He hung up, feeling a little better. He always felt a better after yelling at his brother—it was quite satisfying. Not as satisfying as doing it in person, but still satisfying.

He tried Grace's number three more times with a futile hope she might have removed his block in her phone. He prayed Josh's assertion was correct since he wouldn't have another chance to talk to her before her eleven o'clock appointment. Time to switch off his emotions and go to work.

Chapter Ten

Spencer frowned as he listened to Brad's message. He must have called during his accounting class. According to Brad, Grace had called him and left a message, but still had his number blocked in her cell phone. He felt a sense of relief Grace had finally come to her senses. Spencer would've been upset if Emily had had a biopsy without telling him about it. He was certainly glad she'd decided to tell Brad before the procedure. He glanced at the time—eleven o'clock. He had another class, but he could text Grace to unblock Brad's number and call him again. She still had a few hours to reach him before her biopsy appointment. His stomach felt tight as he thought about Grace. He really loved his little sister, and he couldn't help but worry about her. Even though she'd assured him it was unlikely to be cancer, he felt like a rock was wedged inside his stomach. He was glad he had another class to distract him from his anxious musings.

*****

The man's voice droned on and on while Grace drummed her fingers on her knee. When he stopped speaking, Grace knew he must have asked another question.

"I'm sorry. What did you ask me?"

The hospital admissions clerk repeated the question as she fidgeted with her phone. He seemed unaware of her tension. Or perhaps he simply didn't care.

"Excuse me, Mark?" She read his name from is ID badge. "It's almost eleven o'clock now, and I'm supposed to take my premedication right at eleven so it will have time to work." Her heart felt like it was trying to leap out of her chest.

"Yes, well this will only take ten minutes or so."

"You don't understand. I need that medicine now, or I may not be able to stay for my procedure." She tried unsuccessfully to slow her breathing.

"Do you have another appointment after this?"

"No, but I need to have that medicine." Grace felt the room closing in on her. "I think I may be about to pass out."

Now she had his attention. "Oh! Okay! I'm going to get someone. Do you think you're having a heart attack? Does your chest hurt?"

Grace leaned down to stick her head between her knees. Her voice was muffled when she answered. "Please just get the nurse with my premedication. I talked to him a minute ago. He has it ready to go."

She was answered with silence. And the room grew dark.

Grace cracked her eyes open, blinking at the light glaring from the ceiling. After a moment she managed to focus on the suspended ceiling tiles. Where was she? She was lying down somewhere. She remembered... She was having a biopsy. She was at Mercy General.

"Ughh! Is it over?"

She heard a male voice chuckling. "No, Ms. Marshall. It's not over. You haven't even taken your premedication yet. We couldn't give it to you while you were unconscious."

"Is it too late to take it? I've got to have plenty of time for it to work before they give me the IV."

"It's only eleven-o-five. I'm sure you'll be out of it long before twelve o'clock with what your doctor has prescribed for you. Let me help you sit up and swallow this pill. Luckily you got through enough of the registration for us to give you your meds. But now you're going to need to finish answering questions before this takes effect."

He helped her to her feet, and she wobbled a bit before regaining her balance. "I don't feel any calmer yet. How long before I'm relaxed?"

"You should start feeling it in about twenty minutes. Believe me. You'll probably be sound asleep by twelve."

"What if I can't wake up to get ready?"

"You'll be able to wake up and respond to us, but you probably won't remember any of it. Once you finish your admission, you can get ready and wait in here if you'd like."

"No, this room is scary. I'd rather fall asleep in the waiting room. Is that okay?"

"Sure. But don't wander off or we'll never find you."

With the knowledge the sedative was in her system, Grace already felt less tension. She managed to finish her admission interview with Mark, who regarded her with trepidation.

Fearing she'd missed Brad's call, Grace checked her cell phone and discovered Spencer's message. She gave herself a mental kick for forgetting to unblock Brad's number and another for forgetting to tell her family about her error concerning the surgery time. She was about to send a group message when a thought occurred to her. If her sisters didn't realize the time had been changed, they would arrive too late to embarrass her while she was under the influence of the IV drugs. She couldn't help the smile that slid onto her face—she'd outfoxed her sisters.

She confessed to her mother in a text. *Mom. Got surgery time wrong. Starts at twelve. Don't tell the family. Will wait here until you get off work. Took premed already. Please pray.*

With that done, she unblocked Brad's number and sent another message. *Unblocked your number. Please call soon.*

She settled in to wait, attempting to concentrate on the mystery on her kindle. She reread the same paragraph multiple times before abandoning her book to watch the news on the waiting room television while her mind drifted into oblivion. When her head jerked, she woke with a start to discover thirty minutes had passed. A band tightened around her chest with the realization she might not be able to speak to Brad before the procedure. Her mind was getting foggy, but she knew she needed to communicate with him somehow.

She opened the message screen and forced her numb mind to move her fingers. *brad. i am having a needle biopsy. mercy general at 12. i am sorry i didn't tell you before. in case i never wake up, i love you.*

She strained her eyes in a hopeless attempt to focus on the small words. Should she really leave that last sentence in there? It was kind of lame to say it for the first time in a text message. But what if she didn't survive the procedure and he never knew the truth? She took a deep breath and sent the message to Brad.

*****

Kara was totally frustrated. The emergency room had been so hectic due to the accident victims she hadn't had a single moment to speak to Brad alone. She had to talk to him soon before he had a chance to make up with Grace. She needed to tell him her big news. The inspired idea had come to her after her earlier conversation with Josh Branson. She'd dug the application forms from a discard pile in her locker, and she couldn't wait to reveal them to Brad. It was a surefire way to prove she was selfless and altruistic. In light of her revelation, he was bound to find her much more appealing than Grace. She couldn't think of any other reason he would be attracted to the diminutive girl who toiled as a first grade teacher other than the self-sacrificing nature of her job. Once he discovered Kara's philanthropic plans, he'd be open to dating her. And after she'd bedded him, she could use her ample skills to control him. Later, when her application mysteriously *fell-through*, he wouldn't realize she'd never actually sent the forms into the agency. By that time, he wouldn't want her to go overseas anyway.

"Brad! I mean, Dr. Gates! Do you have a second?" She pulled the papers out of her coat pocket and cut him off before he entered the lounge."

"Actually Dr. Dickson, this isn't a good time." He slipped past her and through the door.

"It will only take a second. I only need your recommendation on this form. I'm applying for Physicians Across Borders."

He halted while reaching for his cell phone and turned to face her. "Really? That doesn't seem like your cup of tea."

She shrugged and lowered her eyes. "I know. No one knows the real me. I really want this. But I've got to get some great recommendations or I won't have a chance."

"A chance at what?" Josh's voice rang out behind her.

"Kara's applying for Physicians Across Borders. Did you know that?"

"No, I didn't," said Josh, squinting as he regarded her. She felt her face getting hot. She'd hoped to keep Dr. Branson out of it. He might be suspicious.

"What is this?" Brad was staring at his cell phone with his mouth hanging open.

Josh said, "Did you hear from Grace?"

"Yes... But what do you make of this text?"

Kara cleared her throat. "About my application..."

Josh snatched the papers from her grasp. "Don't worry, Dr. Dickson. I'll make sure this application gets completed before the deadline. And I'll secure your recommendations as well." His smile was genuine. In fact he was almost chuckling. Perhaps he believed her after all.

"Well, can I just—"

"Dr. Dickson, could you please give me a private moment to consult with Dr. Gates? Thank you. I'll get back to you about your application."

Kara found herself staring at the outside of the locked lounge door.

Brad showed the text to Josh. *Brad . i an having a meddle noisy merry general at 12   i am spray i didn't yell you before. On case i beverage wake ipod , i live you.*

Josh scrunched his eyebrows as he studied the text. "I'm not sure. Does it say Mercy General at twelve? But the one above this says she unblocked you. Call her!"

"Right," said Brad, punching in her number. His heart tapped a wild rhythm while he listened to it ringing. He'd almost given up when a garbled voice answered.

"Br-r-raad! You called me! I'm sorrr-r-r-ry. I know-w-w I should've tolded you."

Brad covered the phone to speak to Josh. "She's drugged—she can't even talk." He spoke into his cell, "Grace, where are you?"

"I'm-m-m r-ri-i-ight he-e-er-re. I'm-m getting my pro-ce-dure dun-n-n."

"Where is here? Are you at Mercy General?"

"Yes-s-s-s." Brad heard her dissolve into giggles. "I s-s-sound like a s-s-snake."

"Are you having surgery? Today? Right now?" The words strangled from his dry throat.

"At tw-w-welve." She giggled again. "My s-s-sisters-s-s think it's-s-s at two."

Josh said, "Where is she? What floor? We can stop her."

"Grace. Listen to me. Where are you? What floor? What surgery unit?"

"Uhmmm… I don-n-n't kn-n-n-ow."

"Look around. What do you see? Do you see any numbers? What color are the walls?"

"I s-s-see a r-r-re-volv… a r-r-re-vol-ving door-r-r."

"She sees a revolving door!"

"Outpatient surgery?" Josh furrowed his brows. "Who does plastic surgery in Outpatient?"

"But she sees a revolving door. Where else could it be?"

Grace said, "I n-n-need to hang-g-g up. M-m-my boy-fr-r-riend m-m-may cal-l-l."

"No Grace!" Brad started running. "Don't hang up! Stay on the phone. Don't you hang up on me. I'm your boyfriend."

"You ar-r-r-e? Is-s-s-s this-s-s Br-r-rad? I'm-m-m s-s-sor-ry…" Her voice trailed off.

"Grace? Grace? Are you there?" Brad huffed out the words as he dashed through the hospital hallway, dodging people like an obstacle course, with Josh on his heels. "Josh, what time is it?"

"It's almost twelve. Three minutes 'til," came the breathless reply.

Minutes felt like hours as he ran, his lungs burning with effort. Brad scanned the waiting room as he rounded the corner, stumbling to a halt. "Do you see her?" he gasped.

"No. She's not here," said Josh, panting as he paced.

"Maybe we're too late."

"Or we're in the wrong place."

Brad bent over, trying to catch his breath. From the corner of his eye he spied a small foot extending from a shapely leg dangling over the arm of a couch. He reached the sofa in two bounds. "Grace! Hey Grace, wake up!"

She groaned and turned on her side.

"She's been mostly asleep for the last thirty minutes or so," said an elderly woman, watching with interest as Brad attempted to revive her. "But she has a bracelet on, so I think she's going to have surgery. Are you her doctor?"

"I... No... I mean, yes. Yes, I'm her doctor. And we're going to postpone her surgery."

"What are you planning to do?" asked Josh. "They'll probably come for her any minute now."

Brad pulled Grace into a sitting position and slapped the palm of her hand. "Grace. Wake up, baby."

She blinked her eyes open into an unfocused stare. "Is it over? Can I go home now? I need to leave before my sisters find out." She blinked a few more times and scrunched her nose. "Are you my doctor?"

Brad pulled her to her feet. "Come on. I'm taking you home." She moved with him in a drunken stumble, leaning heavily on his arm.

Josh blocked the way. "What are you doing, Brad? You can't take her out of the hospital."

"I can't let her go through with it, either. What do you suggest?"

"We can confront the doctor. Force him to postpone until she has certified counseling. Make him jump through the hoops."

"But she's already signed the papers. What if he won't listen? I can't take a chance." He pushed past Josh, guiding Grace in the direction of the revolving door.

"Brad, don't be ridiculous. You can't take an admitted patient out of the hospital."

"I'm a doctor."

"It doesn't matter, and you know it. Now let's do this the right way. We'll talk to her physician—"

A voice called out behind him. "Grace Marshall! Grace Mar— Hey, where are you taking her?" Brad glanced over his shoulder at the male nurse who glared back at him. He had to act fast. He scooped her up in his arms and trotted toward the exit.

"Wait! You can't take her out of here! She's admitted to the hospital already." The nurse was bounding behind him.

Grace mumbled and burrowed into his chest as he scurried on, ignoring the alarmed cries that followed him. Through the door. Down the sidewalk. Where was his car parked? The doctor's lot was around the building. He almost ran over a slim girl running toward him as he rounded the corner, skidding to a halt just in time.

"Brad? Is that you? Is that Grace? What happened to her?" Emily's eyes were wide, and her hand was covering her mouth.

"I don't have time to explain," said Brad, glancing behind him at the nurse who'd continued the pursuit outside the building.

"Did she already have the procedure? Did something go wrong?"

"No, I stopped it. I'm not going to let her do it. I've gotta go." He started running again, hefting Grace's dead weight up to get a better grip.

Emily ran behind him. "Stop, Brad! She needs this. You're a doctor—you should know."

"I'm not letting her ruin her face! There has to be another way. We'll get the police involved. We can even move away if we have to."

"What are you talking about?"

The nurse, unfettered by any burden, was gaining on him. "Stop right there! That's my patient!"

Pain shot through his ankle as his right foot caught on the curb, propelling him forward. Time slowed in his mind. He had to protect Grace—he couldn't fall on her. Attempting and failing to regain his footing, twisting and turning, his body landed with a heavy thud on his back, cushioning Grace from the fall. He heard, rather than felt, his head hit the pavement.

Chapter Eleven

Josh's face was inches away when Brad opened his eyes. "Good. You're finally awake. Now I can yell at you. No, no, no—don't close your eyes. You have to stay awake. Can you follow my finger with your eyes?"

Brad blinked at the blurry images before his face. "Where's Grace?"

"Amazing... You remember that?"

"Remember what? Did something happen? I know I was looking for her." He tried to ignore the throbbing pain in the back of his head. He was in the emergency room, but for some reason he was lying on one of the beds instead of working. "What happened?"

"What day is it?"

"It's... uhmm... I don't know. You answer my question first. What happened? Where's Grace?"

"Grace is fine," Josh spat the words. "No thanks to you. You are certifiable. Do you know that?" He began a furious tapping on the computer keyboard adjacent to Brad's bed.

"What are you talking about?"

"That's right—you're just as psycho as Grace. No, even more psycho. You only *thought* Grace was doing something crazy. You actually did something crazy. You two deserve each other. Now what day is it?"

"It's... uhmm... My head really hurts." He pushed up on his elbows and strained into a sitting position. Reaching to the back of his throbbing head, he discovered a large piece of gauze taped in place. "Did someone hit me?"

"No, but I thought about it. Someone should knock some sense into you. Who's the president of the United States?"

"Uhmm... Wait... I know this."

"What month is it?"

"Slow down, okay? I need a second."

"Let's try an easy one. What's your name?"

"It's uhmm... It's... Wait, where's Grace?"

"I told you, she's fine. Look at me." Josh aimed a bright light at his eye.

"Ow!" Brad squeezed his eyes shut.

"Keep your eyes open. I have to check your pupils." Josh reached over to force his eye open and shine the light toward it.

"Ow!"

"Stop being a baby. Let me check the other one... And... There. Got it."

"Ouch. My eyes are fine. But where's Grace?"

"Do you remember why you were looking for her?"

"Because I... She, uhmm... Wait... What did you ask me?"

"Great. It's Ten-Second Tom."

"Oh, the guy from *Fifty First Dates*?"

"How can you remember that, but you don't remember who the president is?"

Brad rubbed his temples. "I think I need to sleep for a while." He started to lie down again.

Josh pushed him back up. "Nope. No you don't. Sit up. Stay awake, and I'll tell you about Grace."

"Grace? Why? Is something wrong with Grace?"

A gargled oath emerged from Josh's throat. "Maybe I'll wait and explain it after you come back from your CT scan."

"Why am I getting a CT scan?"

"Can you tell me when a CT scan is necessary for patients who have or are suspected of having a concussion?"

"Sure. Suspicion of intracranial structural injury. Diploplia. Seizure activity. Loss of consciousness for more than a minute. Severe headache..."

"That's enough. You were unconscious for more than a minute."

"I was unconscious?"

"Yes, you were."

Brad was quiet while watching Josh entering more data into the computer. "Can I ask you one question?"

"Sure." Josh never looked up from the computer.

"Who are you?"

Ben was accosted when he made his way into the outpatient surgery waiting room.

"Ben! Do you know how Brad's doing? Have you heard from him?" asked Emily. He was surprised to see all of four of Grace's siblings along with her mother and father.

"Brad? Did something happen to him? I just got a message from him that... that Grace was... that she had a... uhmm... medical appointment." He coughed into his hands, attempting to hide the rush of blood to his face. He hadn't understood Brad's message, but he knew his brother was upset about Ben's fabricated story. He'd arrived to do damage control, hoping to avoid having his cockamamie story leaked to Grace and her family. Grace would kill him if she found out.

"You heard from Brad?" asked Spencer. "Was it before or after the accident?"

"What accident?"

Emily explained. "The one where Brad was running away from the hospital while carrying Grace and fell and busted his head open. Josh took him to the emergency room, and we're still waiting to hear how he is. I thought he would come tell us or call us or something."

"Why aren't you over at the emergency room?"

"We're still waiting for Grace to come out of her biopsy," said Olivia.

"Grace is having a biopsy? I didn't know that."

"Then why are you here, anyway?" asked Olivia, with a shrewd stare through lowered brows. "Do you know something about why your brother tried to kidnap our sister from outpatient surgery?"

"Yeah," Emily tilted her head as she spoke. "He didn't seem to know she was having a biopsy. He said something about 'not letting her mess up her face.' Do you know what he was referring to?"

Ben felt sweat trickling down his back. "Uhmm, no. I promise, I didn't know she was having surgery at all. She didn't tell me about the biopsy or anything. I thought she was teaching school today."

Emily's shoulder's drooped. "I just don't understand what could have happened."

Hannah said, "Oh look! They changed the status on her number." The family rushed to stare at the screen.

"In recovery," said Spencer. "I thought this was a simple procedure. Why does she have to be in recovery?"

"Because she insisted on an IV. She has to recover from the anesthesia," his mother explained.

"This spoils all our plans," said Claire. "We can't get Brad to come talk to her because he's in the emergency room."

Ben was still trying to decipher the meaning behind Claire's comments, when he felt a tap on his shoulder. He turned to face Olivia, who drew him to the side.

"I want you to know I'm on to you."

He slapped his most convincing innocent expression on his face. "What are you talking about?"

"Don't think I didn't notice you didn't answer Emily's question. You talked around it instead."

"I have no idea—"

"Nope, that won't work—I recognize word manipulation. I've honed that skill by necessity as a younger sibling with a bossy older sibling. I suspect you've done the same. Pushing buttons, making suggestions, influencing emotions, skirting the truth." She lifted an eyebrow and leaned back with her hip cocked and arms crossed. "Am I right?"

His mouth twitched into a grin before he could stop it. "Sometimes I go a bit farther with Brad than skirting the truth. It's possible this is one of those times." He bent forward to lock his eyes with hers. "But you can't let Grace find out. Brad, I can handle, but I'm a bit afraid of Grace."

"Spill it." She didn't flinch at his intense stare.

"I may have... sort of... suggested Grace was considering plastic surgery."

"What?"

"Shhhh! Keep your voice down—they're all staring."

Olivia threw a look over her shoulder and smiled at her siblings. She spoke without moving her lips. "Why would you suggest such a thing?"

"I only said she'd considered it, but I had talked her out of it. It was to protect her from her stalker."

Olivia's whisper was strident. "Grace had a stalker?"

"No. Actually, Jasmine Colter's client had a stalker on *Colt 57*. Have you seen that show? And her client had plastic surgery to hide from her stalker. I used the plot to convince Brad to tell Grace he was willing to move away from New York City. I was only trying to help them get back together where they belong."

Her mouth was hanging open. "And Brad believed you?"

He rolled his lips in across his teeth in an effort to stop his smile. "Brad and Josh both believed me."

"*Oh... my... great... grandma*. You are in so much *trouble*."

"But everything's okay, right? I mean, Grace doesn't have to know. And it's not my fault Brad thought she was having plastic surgery instead of a biopsy. I told him I'd talked her out of it. I've just got to talk to Brad and Josh before she wakes up. I haven't quite figured out my story yet. Have you got any advice? You know, as a younger sibling with years of experience? Can you help me come up with an explanation for Josh and Brad? Or maybe I should fly back to California before Josh comes out of the ER."

"Uhmm..." Olivia's wide eyes were fixed over his shoulder.

The hair stood up on the back of Ben's neck. "Josh is standing behind me, isn't he?"

"Yep! Nice knowing you." Olivia melted away like butter.

He felt an iron hand clasp his bicep. "Ben, I hope you're working hard on that explanation."

"Josh!" Emily cried out, rushing to join them. "What happened? How's Brad?"

Josh leaned over to speak in his ear. "This conversation isn't finished." He emphasized his words with a vice-like compression on Ben's arm before turning to Emily and the rest of Grace's family.

"He's got a concussion, but he'll live. The CT scan was clear of intracranial bleeding. I'm not sure he's ever going to remember the details very well."

His scowl deepened. "So why are all of you here? And what's Grace doing here? She had some kind of biopsy?"

Connie answered, "She had a breast biopsy—a needle biopsy on a couple of cysts. And yes, I know most people don't have sedation for that procedure, but Grace is a little spastic about these things."

"She told all of us the wrong time for the procedure—two hours later than the real time." Hannah pressed her lips together.

"She texted me with the right time," Connie defended.

"But not me," said Hannah. "Or any of the rest of us. If you hadn't told us, we wouldn't even be here yet."

Josh shook his head. "I know this is a supportive family, but still... All of you here for a needle biopsy? Is there something you're not telling me? Do they think it's cancer?"

Emily said, "I was supposed to be here early to sit with her so she wouldn't be nervous, but I didn't find out about the time change until eleven thirty."

"I was coming for the show," Claire chuckled. "Ow!" Olivia elbowed her ribs.

"What show?" Ben asked.

Connie seared Claire with a 'we'll-talk-about-this-later' look. "I assume Claire is referring to the fact Grace will probably be a little loopy when she comes out of surgery."

"I can't believe her own sisters would take advantage of her compromised state," Spencer declared.

Emily raised an eyebrow. "Says the brother who has a flip-video in his rear pocket."

"Ha! I knew it." Olivia stabbed her index finger at Spencer's chest. "You're itching for a chance to get her back for making that video of you after you got your wisdom teeth out."

He chuckled. "I do owe her big time. After all, she posted it on Facebook."

Ben rubbed his tongue over a sharp tooth. "Speaking of teeth, I've got a chipped molar that needs fixing. Brad shook me senseless and made me break it. You know a good dentist?"

"I've got a friend who just graduated from dental school," said Olivia.

"Is he any good?" asked Ben.

"He's a she—Shanna Williams."

"Is she cute? Is she single?" asked Ben.

"Yes and yes." Olivia laughed. "Suddenly you don't care if she's good or not?"

"Hmmm... I don't know. How cute is she? In this case the cute factor could really make up for the skill factor."

"Well, you're in luck. She's cute and she's a great dentist. I'll hook you up."

"That's what I'm hoping." He winked at her.

"Eh-hem!" Josh cleared his throat and grasped Ben's arm.

"Right now, I think Ben wants to go see his brother in the ER. Isn't that why you came here, Ben? Brad's really confused right now. I'm hoping you can straighten some things out."

Ben mouthed a silent "Help me!" toward Olivia as Josh dragged him away. He spoke aloud. "Maybe I should wait until Grace is out of recovery."

"Oh no, Ben." Olivia stifled a giggle. "We'll take care of Grace. You can go with Josh to check on Brad."

Ben pantomimed having his throat slashed before he disappeared around the corner. He heard Olivia's laughter tinkling and one of the sisters asking, "What was that about?"

"I'm glad you think this is so funny." Josh's humorless eyes were full of contempt.

"Look. I have no idea how this got so out-of-hand. All I meant to do was convince Brad to tell Grace he was planning to leave New York City. She wouldn't let me tell him the truth—she swore me to secrecy."

"And what was the truth?"

He hesitated. "No, I still have my honor. I promised her I wouldn't tell anyone, and I won't betray her confidence."

"Honor? How can you have honor after lying about Grace having plastic surgery?"

"But that's not what I said. I said she'd considered it and I'd talked her out of it."

"What about the stalker? You said she didn't have any idea of his identity, but Brad said the stalker had located Grace's school."

"I don't know where that came from. There is no stalker."

"So the entire thing was a lie?"

"I wouldn't exactly call it a lie."

"What exactly would you call it?"

"A slight departure from the absolute truth with completely honorable intentions."

"A slight departure?" Josh's jaw and neck muscles were flexing. "What part of your story was truth?"

"Uhmm... the part where I told you Grace wanted to leave New York City."

He muttered a few unintelligible words. "Why did she want to leave New York City?"

"Yes. That's the million-dollar question only Grace has the right to answer." Ben pulled Josh to a stop before they entered the next hallway. "Look. I know you may not believe this, but I love my brother. I was only trying to prevent a huge tragedy. I've never seen him like this about a girl before, and I think Grace is really good for him. So I took a few liberties with the truth. As long as they end up together, that's all that matters. Right?"

Josh grunted. "That remains to be seen—they're not back together yet." He shook off Ben's arm and marched onward. "They were together again... in a way. But I doubt either of them will remember."

*****

Brad's head was pounding, but the pain didn't bother him as much as his muddled brain. He was really upset about Grace. But why? Something was wrong. If only he could remember. He had to find Grace, and he was wasting time sitting in this room. He'd already heard his CT scan was clear. So why were they making him stay? If he could hide his confusion, he could stop wasting time and find Grace.

He was pulling on his shirt when a female doctor opened the curtain. "Hi, Dr. Gates. How are you feeling?"

He frowned at her. She seemed vaguely familiar, but he couldn't quite place her. He read her ID tag. "Hello, Dr. Dickson. I'm fine, thanks. CT scan showed no intracranial bleeding. In fact, I'm ready to go."

"That's great. Hey, I just got off my shift. Can I walk out with you?"

He shrugged his shoulders as he buttoned his shirt. "Sure. Let's go."

"Do you have your release papers signed?"

"I don't know if he remembered to sign them," Brad lied. "It doesn't matter."

"Are you kidding? Dr. Branson is a stickler for the rules." She chuckled. "Usually, you're pretty uptight about the rules, too. I guess that concussion made you a little more relaxed. I'll do the release for you." She brought up his information on the computer while he paced.

"I think I'll go on outside."

"What's your rush? Hang on just a minute—I'm almost done. Anyway, I wanted to talk to you about my application to Physicians Across Borders. Do you think it's a good idea?"

The topic didn't ring a bell, but he could cover his lapse. "I think it's a great idea. You'll be wonderful, Dr. Dickson."

"Aren't you surprised at all? I mean, would you have pictured me doing something like that?"

"Absolutely. You've always been self-sacrificing and giving with all the patients." Were his words true? For all he knew this woman was a selfish shrew. Oh well—it couldn't hurt to say something nice. Her beaming smile indicated he'd spoken the right words.

"There. It's done." She signed off the computer. "Now we can leave without ticking Josh off. I'm so glad you're excited about the Physicians Across Borders application. Maybe we could go to dinner and talk about it. I want to get your advice about asking for recommendations."

He was already out the door and hurrying toward the exit. "Uhmm... I think I should go home and rest."

"But you have a bad concussion. You're not supposed to be alone tonight."

"Oh, right. Well, I'm not going straight home." They'd almost made it to the exit when he spotted Josh making a beeline for his vacated room. He ducked his head and slipped outside.

She followed him through the door. "Wait up! What's your hurry?"

"I need to get somewhere." He was almost running down the sidewalk, but she kept pace with him.

"Where are you headed?"

He slowed as the pain in his head swelled to a crescendo.

"I'm going..." Where was he going? He needed to find Grace but he couldn't quite remember where she lived. "I'm not really sure."

"Let me help you. I'll go with you—just tell me where you want to go."

"I need to find Grace. Something's wrong, but I can't remember. Do you know her?"

She paused, tilting her head as she regarded him. "I know her, and I know where she lives. Let's catch a cab."

Brad was squinting against the bright afternoon sunshine that sent another ache into his thumping head. Grateful for her help, he let her hail a cab and guide him inside. She gave the cab driver an address.

"Grace teaches first grade, right?" she said.

"Right." He hadn't remembered that fact, but he didn't want Dr. Dickson to know.

"Well, she won't be out of school yet. I live fairly close to her house. Why don't we go by my place for an hour or so until she gets out of school?"

"I don't know. Maybe I'll just wait outside her place. Where did you say she lives?"

She cleared her throat and chewed on her lip. "Uhmm... Brad, did you remember you and Grace are broken up? I think it's been a month or two."

A sharp pain shot through his head causing a wave of nausea. He and Grace weren't together. Could that be the thing that had him so worried? He must have forgotten. He tried to remember the last time he'd seen her. He could picture it in his mind—holding her close, kissing her soft lips. Had it really been months since that had happened? Anything was possible—he couldn't even remember where his own apartment was located.

"I still think I need to see her. It's important."

"Okay. We'll just wait at my apartment until she gets out of teaching, and then I'll walk over with you."

He couldn't think of a valid reason to object to her idea. But the nauseated feeling hadn't subsided. Was it the concussion? Or was it knowing he was no longer with Grace?

*****

"Wow, Josh. You lost him?" Ben grinned at Josh who hadn't stopped yelling since they'd arrived to find Brad's empty room.

"Shut up, Ben." Josh marched out to the nurse's station. "Where did Dr. Gates go?"

Ben couldn't help but sympathize with the slight girl with pale skin that grew even whiter at Josh's fierce tone.

"I don't know, Dr. Branson. I didn't see him leave."

"You didn't see him leave? He had to walk right past here to go anywhere."

Her lower lip began to tremble. "But I was gone part of the time, checking on another patient. I didn't know I was supposed to watch him."

"Why don't you call his cell phone?" Ben suggested, attempting to divert Josh's attention from the timorous nurse.

Josh stuck a phone in front of Ben's face and shook it with such ferocity Ben dodged backwards. "Because he left his cell phone! That's why! He took everything else he owned, but he forgot his cell phone." He began to pace. "I can't believe he's breaking all these rules today—I hadn't signed his release papers."

"Excuse me, Dr. Branson?" the timid girl interrupted, flinching when he turned his gaze toward her. She indicated her computer screen. "It looks like Dr. Dickson signed him out."

The veins on the side of Josh's red face were bulging. "Kara Dickson signed his release form?" His next words were unintelligible, but delivered with venom. He pulled out his cell phone and punched a few buttons, listening while it rang. When forced to leave a message, he ground out the words.

"Dr. Dickson, this is Dr. Branson. You'd better have a really good explanation for why you signed a release for Dr. Gates without my permission. And if you have any idea where he went, I expect you to let me know immediately." Josh stomped down the hallway, sticking his head in the unoccupied rooms, muttering about how Brad was "probably lost somewhere."

"Did Dr. Dickson hear about how the accident happened? Does she know Grace is in outpatient surgery right now?"

"I don't think so," said Josh. "I tried to keep that detail out of the accident report, and smooth things over with Grace's nurse. He wasn't quite as angry after Brad fell and knocked himself out."

"Would Brad have gone home with her or maybe home to your apartment?"

Josh pressed his fingers to his temples. "He could have gone with Kara, I guess, but she didn't answer when I called. I don't think he could find our apartment. He could be anywhere. But I guarantee he's looking for Grace—she's the only thing he's talked about since he woke up."

"So maybe he's at the outpatient surgery waiting room."

"One—we just came from there and we didn't pass him. And two—he had no idea she was having a biopsy today."

"But he knew she was having some kind of surgery. Didn't I hear he tried to kidnap her from her biopsy?"

"Yes, but he didn't remember any of that after the accident. I tried to explain it to him. But ten seconds later, he'd give me this blank expression and forget everything I'd just told him."

"But maybe he remembered more than you thought. We should check there first in case he circled around on the outside of the hospital somehow. And then we'll split up and check all the places you can think of. Maybe some of the Marshalls will help us look. And really, what's the worst that can happen?"

Josh tilted his head down, glaring at Ben from beneath pinched brows. "Really?"

A chill rippled down his spine. "Uhmm... Forget I asked that."

Chapter Twelve

"Why don't you come sit down? You know you shouldn't move around so much after a concussion," Kara reasoned.

Brad ignored her, continuing to pace the floor. "What time is it?"

Her sigh was labored. "It's five minutes later than the last time you asked. It's way too early to go to Grace's house. Come sit down and I'll get us a drink."

After she disappeared into the kitchen, he perched on the edge of the couch, leaning his elbows on his knees and burying his face in his hands. He couldn't think. He was feeling more agitated with each passing moment. He battled nausea as another dizzy wave swept through his head.

He felt hands on his shoulders, kneading his muscles. "This should help. Are you feeling tense?"

He melted under her ministrations. "Yes. That feels great. But my head... I'm so dizzy."

"Why don't you come lay down for a bit? I'll wake you up when it's time to go see Grace."

The room swirled around his head as she helped him to his feet. Leaning heavily on her shoulder he stumbled to the bed and collapsed. "What did you say your name was?"

"I'm Kara. You don't remember me?" Her voice was petulant, but Brad kept his eyes closed against the light shining in his eyes.

"Could you turn the light off? It really hurts my eyes."

"Fine. Here, let me help you. Do you want to take your shoes off?"

"My head is spinning." He squeezed his eyes shut, and blessed darkness filled his mind.

Kara flipped through the channels on the television. Nothing was going according to plan. She had Brad in her bed, but a fat lot of good that did. He'd been asleep for an hour. Her cell phone rang... Again. Josh was calling... Again. And she ignored it... Again. She needed to return his call, but she had to make some headway with Brad, first.

The idea came to her like a flash. She had an amazing opportunity—a gift. And she wasn't about to waste it.

She tiptoed into the bedroom where he lay sound asleep on his back. Even in sleep, his face held an expression of pain. She made quick work of the buttons on his shirt, opening it and admiring the view presented. He looked even better than she'd imagined. She considered attempting to remove his pants, but she couldn't take a chance on waking him. Unbuttoning her own shirt and stripping off her pants and shoes, she eased into the bed beside him.

"Hey, Brad! Wake up!" She shook him until he opened his eyes. "Come on, it's time to wake up."

He pushed up on his elbows, blinking his eyes at her. "Who are you? Where am I?"

"Brad! Are you kidding me? I'm Kara—Kara Dickson." She turned it on—batting her eyes against sudden tears and allowing her lower lip to tremble.

"Why am I here? Did I sleep with you?"

"Yes, of course you did. I mean, we did. I can't believe you don't remember." She sniffed.

"I don't... I'm sorry... Who are you again?"

"Brad. We just made love. How can you not remember my name?" A tear slid down her cheek.

He slid out of the bed onto his knees. "Where... Where is the bathroom?" Oh no—he was going to be sick.

"In here. It's right here."

He crawled behind her and made it to the toilet before he threw up.

Great—so much for her big plan. "It looks like we're going back to the emergency room." She was startled by a loud banging on the front door. "Just stay here." As if he could do anything else. She threw a towel at him and made for the door, fastening her shirt on the way.

"Hello, Dr. Dickson." Josh pushed his way inside when she opened the door. "Is something wrong with your phone?"

"I... I didn't hear it. I've been rather preoccupied."

"So you didn't get my message?"

"Uhmm... No, I'm sorry. But actually it's good you're here. I think Brad's gotten worse."

"So he's with you? We've been looking for him." For the first time he noticed her state of undress.

"We were... This is strictly confidential, of course. We were in bed, and well... Afterwards, he started feeling nauseous."

"You were in bed? With Dr. Gates?"

"I don't know what came over us. It was a moment of weakness, I guess."

Josh's eyes were hard as flint. "Where is he?"

"In here." She led him into the bathroom.

Josh took in the scene and mumbled something before bending to speak to him where he lay on the floor. "Brad! Let's go. Can you get up?"

His eyes fluttered open. "My head. Stabbing."

Josh said, "Dr. Dickson. Help me get him up."

She pulled her pants back on, and together they got him to his feet.

"I've got him from here," said Josh. "You go get a cab."

She dashed to the street, still in bare feet, to secure a ride, hoping Brad wouldn't vomit on her carpet before Josh got him outside.

"Do you want me to come with you?" Kara asked as Josh deposited Brad's wobbly, moaning form into the cab, his shirt still flapping open.

She couldn't help wincing at his ferocious tone. "No, Dr. Dickson. I don't want you to come to the hospital with Dr. Gates."

"Look, I'm sorry about sleeping with Brad. But these things happen, you know. He may want me with him when he comes back out of this."

"I doubt that very much." Josh's jaw was clenched as tight as his fists. She hadn't foreseen his virulent reaction to her revelation. But no matter—she should be able to manipulate both of them with her claim. After all, no one could refute it.

*****

Both Hannah and Claire regarded Grace with rather triumphant expressions when she opened her eyes, blinking against the bright lights.

"Is it over?" Her voice sounded as raspy as it felt.

"Here Gracie." Connie placed a straw to her mouth. The cool water soothed its way down her parched throat. "Yes, it's over. But you need to wake up a little more before we can take you home."

"Are you surprised to see Hannah and me?" asked Claire, with one corner of her mouth twitching in a smile. "You thought you could get away with it, didn't you? You sent Mom a text about the biopsy time, but not the rest of us."

"It was an accident."

"You accidentally forgot to send a text to a single one of your siblings? And you accidentally told Mom not to tell the family? Ha! *Right*. But your little ploy failed anyway—I've got the video right here." Hannah held up her phone.

"But I just now woke up."

"Yes, it was the stuff you said before you were really awake that made it all worthwhile." Hannah chuckled.

"Mom, why didn't you stop them?"

"Me? I can't control your sisters. I thought you were the sister president—at least that's what you've told me in the past. It sounds like you have a small insurrection going on, but that's not my problem. I'm Switzerland."

"What about Brad? Was he here? Did you make me say something embarrassing to him?"

Claire said, "Hmmm... Brad? Let's see. Are you talking about the guy you broke up with and refused to talk to for a couple of months? That Brad? The one you were supposed to talk to immediately after your biopsy because you agreed to take the dare? Is that the Brad you're talking about?"

"Please don't torture me any longer. Did you or did you not totally embarrass me by letting Brad talk to me while I was *under-the-influence*?"

Hannah's cell phone buzzed. "It's Olivia! Hey Olivia, did you find him? What? Yes, she's pretty much awake now. Sure… Here she is."

Hannah's eyes were wide as she handed Grace her phone. Olivia's excited voice rang out in her ear. "Grace, did you really tell the receptionist at your school you were having plastic surgery?"

"What? No, of course not. I mean, I joked about it, but I wasn't serious. She couldn't possibly be that dense."

"Well, she evidently took you seriously. And then, when Brad came to the school—"

"Brad came to my school? When? This afternoon?"

"No, he came looking for you this morning. And that's when he found out you were having plastic surgery. And that's also when he told her to call the police about your stalker."

"My stalker? Brad said I had a stalker? I didn't even know I had one."

"Well, this stalker turned out to be an innocent substitute teacher who didn't appreciate getting handcuffed at the elementary school. I think you may have to find a different sub next time you need one."

"It sounds like I may have to find a different job."

"We've got quite a few things to ask Brad about when we finally find him. I don't suppose you've heard from the others."

"What others? What are you talking about?"

"Didn't they tell you Brad was missing?"

Her stomach began to churn. "No. No one said he was missing."

"Yeah, he disappeared from the ER."

"Before his shift was over?"

"No, he wasn't working. He was recovering from busting his head on the concrete when he was rescuing you from your biopsy, which he thought was plastic surgery. So everybody else is out looking for him. Emily and Spencer, Pop and I, Ben, Josh… Wait! That's Josh calling. I've gotta go."

"What are you talking about?" Grace's voice raised an octave. But Olivia was gone.

*****

"Yes, I found him. We're headed back to the ER," Josh told Olivia. "Can you let the others know?"

"How is he? I assume he's not too good if you're going back to the hospital."

"He's..." Josh glanced toward Brad, but his eyes were glassy. "Honestly, I'm worried. But I need to go."

Stashing his cell, he tapped the taxi driver on the shoulder. "I know the traffic's bad, but if there's any way we can get there faster..."

The cabbie answered with an outraged explanation of the impossibilities of his request, complete with a few expletives.

"Sorry. I just thought it might be bad for business if he died in your back seat."

"Why are you in my cab and not an ambulance?" Josh ignored him as he tended to Brad, but he noticed the driver was honking and changing lanes more often as he weaved his way down the busy streets.

"Brad. Hey, how are you feeling?"

He answered with a foul word Josh had never heard him utter.

"Still nauseated?"

He turned his head and focused his eyes on Josh, blinking rapidly. "I can't find Grace."

"I know where she is. I'm taking you to her right now."

"I'm going to see Grace?"

"Right now, buddy."

He squeezed his eyes tight as both hands raised to hold his head. "My head hurts."

"I know it does. Brad, I need to know. Did you sleep with Kara Dickson?"

His brows furrowed. "No. Who is that?"

"Dr. Dickson. You were at her apartment just now—in her bed."

He shook his head, squinting his direction. "I don't know her. I know you, but I don't remember your name."

"Josh. I'm Josh. We're roommates. So you didn't sleep with her?"

"Who? Grace?"

"No, Kara Dickson."

"Excuse me." Brad rolled his window down, hanging his head out before retching.

"Yeah, that's how I feel about her, too."

*****

"Why am I getting a spinal tap?" Josh tried not to show his exasperation at Brad's continual barrage of questions. Brad was lying on his side, while Josh worked behind him with a resident assistant.

"You tell me. That seems to be the only part of your brain that's still working right. Of course, that was true even before you hit your head on the sidewalk."

"I hit my head?"

Josh bit back a smart response. "You fell and hit your head. You were unconscious for about seven minutes."

"Did we do a CT scan?"

"Done. No ICB detected. Continued worsening headache, dizziness, and nausea with emesis."

"So I need a tap to see if there's bleeding missed by the CT."

"And we're doing that now."

"You shouldn't have released me."

This time an expletive slipped out before he could stop it. "I didn't release you—you left and I wasted an hour looking for you!"

He noticed Brad's shoulders shaking and repented of his harsh words. Now he was crying, an emotional response from his worsening condition.

"I'm sorry, Brad. It's okay, man."

But Brad broke out laughing. "Ow! It hurts to laugh." He breathed rapidly through his mouth. "I'm sorry, I couldn't resist teasing you. I know you wouldn't have released me." Teasing? Was he coming back to his senses?

"That was a joke? Don't move. Big pinch."

"Sorry, Josh. Ow!"

"You know who I am?"

"Do I know who you are? What are you talking about? Are you trying to remind me of the fact you got promoted over me? Because you're not really my boss, you know. You're not *my* attending."

"No... How do we know each other?"

"Are you asking about being roommates or about doing our residency together?"

"What's your brother's name?"

"I can't say it in polite company."

Josh chuckled as he sealed the last vial of fluid. "Okay, done." Josh handed the vials to the resident. "Get these to the lab right away."

He turned back to Brad. "I'm glad you're a bit more lucid, but you're not out of the woods yet. What do you remember?"

He grimaced. "I think my head hurts too much to remember anything."

"Do you remember riding in the taxi with me?"

"Fuzzy."

"Do you remember going to Kara Dickson's apartment?"

"No way. I would never do that."

"Well, you did. That's where I found you."

"Ughh! Why did I do that?"

"How about throwing up?"

"Sounds like a good idea."

"No, do you remember throwing up?"

"Not so much."

"Leaving the ER with Kara?"

"Nope"

"Sleeping with her?"

"What! I didn't sleep with her." Brad started to sit up, but Josh held him down.

"Don't move—you just had a spinal tap. You're head's going to hurt even worse if you don't lie still. You know that."

"But I didn't sleep with her."

Josh lifted his eyebrows. "She claims you did."

"And you believe her?" His voice was miserable.

"I didn't say I believe her, but there's no way to prove it didn't happen."

"This is ridiculous. Why does God hate me?"

"Let's drop it for now. What else do you remember?"

His face creased in concentration. "I remember looking for Grace... And you were helping me. But... but I was looking for her here at Mercy General. Why would she be here?"

"What else? Do you remember falling and hitting your head?"

"No. Just bits and pieces of being in the emergency room. What about Grace? Did we find her?"

Josh saw Brad straining to watch him without moving his head, so he pulled up a chair and sat eye-level with him. "I hope your memory is functioning again, because this is a long story. I'm hoping I'll only have to tell it once."

*****

"And so you see, I kept my promise. I didn't tell Brad what you told me, and I got him to agree to look for work somewhere else." Ben found no encouragement in the look of shock on Grace's face. Thank goodness she was still a bit groggy from the medication. Maybe she wouldn't remember anything he told her. He glanced over his shoulder where Olivia leaned against the wall with her arms crossed. At least no one else was in the room to witness his confessions.

"You told him I was going to have plastic surgery?"

"No, no, no. I only told him you considered it. And only as a way to escape the stalker. I told him I'd already talked you out of it."

"Oh great—that's so much better." Olivia laughed at her sarcasm, but it didn't seem funny to Ben.

"I still don't understand," said Grace. "What happened to Brad? How did he get hurt?"

Olivia spoke up, "Brad went to the school to talk to you and heard you'd gone to have surgery—plastic surgery."

"I can't believe that girl seriously thought I was having plastic surgery. Has she never heard sarcasm before? I was so obviously kidding, and my principal went right along with it."

"Brad believed it because he'd already heard it from Mr. Storyteller, here. He wanted to stop you, but he didn't know where you were. And you texted him to call you, but you had his number blocked. And then when he got your last message, he figured out you were at Mercy General. He found you in the waiting room and was in the process of kidnapping you when he fell on the sidewalk and knocked himself out." Olivia pulled up a chair and sat beside her sister's bed.

"Not quite the knight in shining armor," said Ben. "But at least it proves he cares."

"Emily said it was obvious he was using his body to cushion you from the fall," Olivia remarked. "And Claire wanted me to remind you she'd be glad to take Brad off your hands if you aren't interested."

"No one is taking him off my hands. I think it's kind of romantic he tried to save me, even if he did fall while he was doing it."

"Well, you're not back together yet," said Olivia. "And Ben still needs to go confess the truth to his brother."

"If you look at this whole thing objectively, everything has worked out rather well," said Ben. "I mean, my methods were a bit unconventional, but I managed to get the results you wanted without breaking my confidence. Right? Doesn't that count for something?" He tried to read Grace's expression. He knew he was in trouble with Brad. No big deal—he was always in trouble with his brother. But he couldn't stand having Grace mad at him. When she smiled at him, he felt the tension flow out of his shoulders.

"Yes, it counts for something." She arched her brows. "But you're not off the hook. When you said you would 'think of something' you didn't say you were going to make up something that involved me. Your 'something' was only supposed to be about Brad."

"But Grace," said Olivia. "You got yourself in this mess when you weren't honest with Brad in the beginning. You should have just talked to him."

"Ha! Easy for you to say, Miss Perfect. I don't see you with a boyfriend. You're not any better at relationships than I am."

"I think you'll find I'm quite skilled at what I do. I keep all of them at arm's length. I don't have time for them. I've got nursing school, and then I've got—"

"The M-CAT and medical school," Grace interrupted. "I know. I've heard it plenty of times. Are you going to wait until you're in your thirties before you date a guy seriously?"

"What's wrong with that? In my thirties, I'll have my career going and I'll be more mature."

"All the good ones will be gone by then," Grace quipped.

Ben observed the exchange in silence, but he couldn't help grinning.

Olivia gave his arm a playful punch. "What are you smiling about?"

"I was thinking I might enjoy having a sister."

*****

"Don't worry, Grace. You look fine," said Ben.

She pulled her hands down from her hair and held them at her sides, her hands balled into fists. She wasn't ready to see Brad yet. Why had she agreed to go with Ben?

"Could you slow down a little? My legs are a lot shorter than yours."

"Oh, sorry. I promise he'll be so glad to finally get to talk to you, he won't care about anything else. In fact, I'm hoping he won't even ask me to explain my story." Ben shortened his stride as he patted her on the back.

"I don't know. What if he's mad? I didn't talk to him for a long time. I know I had a good reason for it—or at least it seemed like a good reason at the time—but he doesn't know that."

"I'm telling you, he won't care. Stop worrying."

"Maybe I should wait until he's released from the hospital."

"No, I already told Josh I was bringing you. Brad will be disappointed if you don't come."

She rubbed her sweaty palms on her pants and followed Ben through an open door. Josh was sitting in a chair talking quietly on his cell phone. Then her eyes fell on Brad, and her heart clenched. There he was lying in a hospital bed, so still he almost looked dead. And he'd hurt himself trying to protect her. Within seconds, her eyes were swimming.

"Hey Grace. Come here, baby. I can't lift my head."

"Why not? Is your neck broken?" She moved to stand beside him.

"No, I had a spinal tap, so I need to lay flat on my back to prevent a bad headache. Well, in this case, to prevent my headache from getting worse." He reached out to take her hand, pulling her fingers to his lips and pressing a tender kiss. "I'm glad you're here."

"I'm sorry you're hurt." She squeezed his fingers.

"I'm just glad you didn't mess up your face."

"Eh-hem," Ben cleared his throat. "Looks like you don't need me. I guess I'll leave you two alone."

"No you don't," said Brad. "Why would you tell me she had a stalker when it wasn't true? You knew how upset that would make me. Why would you make up something like that?"

Ben chuckled. "I thought by now you wouldn't be so gullible. No, wait—I'm kidding. It was Grace's fault... She wouldn't let me tell you the truth. I had to do something. And the way I see it, you should be grateful. My story was ultimately what brought you back together."

"Are we back together?" asked Brad, his eyes searching hers. "I still don't know why you broke up with me again. I told you I wouldn't push you or say the L-word anymore."

"It seemed like the only alternative at the time, but well... After I talked to Mom I realized I was trying to control things."

"What things? What were you trying to control?"

She glanced at Josh who was still concentrating on his phone conference with intense tones. Good—he wasn't listening. She lowered her voice.

"I didn't want you to stay in New York for me. I knew you were wearing yourself out working here, and you couldn't move to a better position as long as you stayed here."

Brad frowned. "I'm not wearing myself out here. I love my work, and the hours aren't that bad. I need the experience before I can hope to head up an emergency medicine department anyway."

"But I think you're working too hard. You hadn't been sleeping well, and you looked really tired." She didn't want to bring up the fact Josh would be in line to get the department head position.

He began to chuckle. "You're right—I haven't slept well in months."

"You see, I was right." Grace stuck out her chin. "I'm a woman and we're sensitive to these kinds of things."

"Yeah, but you were wrong about the reason. It's not work—it's you. I haven't slept well since you first broke up with me. You screwed up my mind."

"What? Are you saying I'm the reason you look so bad?"

"I didn't know I looked *that* bad."

"You do!" Ben smirked; "You look like..." He stopped, glancing at Grace, before he continued. "Uhmm, you look like something that comes out of the south end of a chicken."

Brad rolled his eyes toward his brother. "Thanks so much, Ben. As always, your input is so helpful."

"I'm sorry I tried to control everything myself. I'm kind of used to being in charge. Yesterday, Mom told me everything would work out if we made the decisions together."

"I wish you would've talked to your mom a long time ago." His smile was devastating. How could she have kept herself away from him for so long?

Grace leaned over to press her lips gently against his forehead.

"Really?" he teased. "After risking my body to save you from the evil plastic surgeon, all I get is a forehead kiss?" He pulled on her arm, reeling her in. "Come here."

She pulled against him, her face burning with the knowledge Ben was watching them, but she didn't resist too hard. She really missed kissing him. He was grinning and she was giggling as she let him win the battle. His hand slipped behind her neck, dragging her face toward his waiting lips.

"Brad?" A feminine voice interrupted their game. "What's going on?"

Grace jerked out of his grasp, straightening to stare at Kara Dickson.

"Kara? What are you doing here?" Brad asked.

She ignored his question. "Are you back with her? I can't believe it! When we made love this afternoon, you told me you weren't dating anymore."

Grace felt the blood draining from her face, as revulsion boiled in the pit of her stomach. She looked at Brad, waiting for him to deny the accusation.

"Kara, I don't believe that happened," said Brad. "In fact, I don't even remember being at your apartment."

"You don't remember? You don't remember being with me?" Tears began to streak down her face. "You don't remember any of those things you said to me?"

Josh stashed his phone and stepped forward to take Kara's elbow. "Dr. Dickson, this isn't the time—"

"Not the time?" She shook her arm from his grasp. "When is the time? After I find out I'm pregnant? We didn't use protection, so it could happen. What were you planning to do? Did you think I would get an abortion? Because I won't do it!"

Grace didn't realize she was moving until she heard Brad's voice calling behind her, "Grace! Wait, Grace! Don't go!"

Brad was struggling against Josh, who was holding him down. "Don't move! You can't move! I'll go after her! Just promise me you'll lay here!"

"Please," he gasped for breath. "Please stop her. Bring her back." He felt a sharp pain in his chest as if someone had ripped his heart from his body.

"Okay. Just don't move!" Josh flashed a deadly look at Kara before running out the door.

Brad squeezed his eyes shut, embarrassed to realize there were tears on his cheeks. He felt a cool hand caressing his arm and opened his eyes to find Kara at his bedside. He jerked his arm away. "Don't touch me!"

"How can you say that? How can you simply turn your emotions off like that? You said we had something special—something real."

He had no answer for her. Part of him didn't believe her story, but he couldn't remember most of what he'd done that day. If he'd truly slept with her, he would despise himself. He wouldn't even use the concussion as an excuse. A chill of death settled in his bones. Life was cruel to tease him with hope and jerk it away.

"Hi. I'm Ben. Remember me?" Ben had a silly grin on his face as he offered his hand to Kara.

"Yes, Ben. I remember meeting you at the Marshall's dinner." She smiled and Brad was reminded of Kaa in Jungle Book. He half expected her to break out into a round of *Trust Me*.

"So Brad's finally found a girl who'll take him—flaws and all. It's been so long since he dated Leah."

Brad speared his brother with his eyes and growled a warning, but Ben ignored him.

"I didn't notice any flaws," she proclaimed. "In fact, he's got a great body."

"Runs in the family," Ben said, puffing out his chest. "But his tattoo on his hip didn't bother you?"

Brad would have beaten his brother if he could have moved from the bed. He yelled, "Ben, wh—"

"No Brad." Ben laughed out loud. "I've got you this time. You can't make me be quiet, Bro. I'll just take her outside and grill her. Anyway, you should thank your lucky stars. I can't believe you found a girl who doesn't care."

"I like tattoos," said Kara. "It didn't bother me at all."

"You don't mind he's got another girl's name on his hip? It's not like he can change 'Leah' into 'Kara'. It's a permanent thing."

"Uh... No... I suppose it bothered me at first. But then I realized it simply means he's extremely devoted. Maybe someday he'll have my name tattooed over his heart."

"Let me get this straight," said Ben. "You saw that tattoo and you had sex with him anyway? Didn't you at least make him explain it?"

"In the heat of the moment, I didn't want to stop and talk." Kara winked at Ben. "I mentioned it afterward, and he explained Leah was from a long time ago." She shrugged. "I'm not the kind of girl who'd hold something like that against a guy. How many years did you say it had been?" She held Brad's gaze with an expectant stare, waiting for his answer.

"I didn't say," said Brad.

"Yes, you did. You explained about dating Leah and breaking up with her, but I don't remember how many years you said it had been."

Brad smiled. "I don't think so, because Leah was my dog. I did love her a lot, but I didn't date her."

Her smile faltered. "I guess you were confused from the concussion. Or maybe you were embarrassed you had a dog's name on your hip."

Brad turned to Ben. "Okay. You've totally redeemed yourself. I hereby forgive you for all the lies you told me."

"All of them? *Awesome.*"

"No wait—just the lies about Grace."

"Too late. You said all of them, and I'm holding you to it."

Kara's face was turning redder by the minute. "I'm telling you, you really did say Leah was your girlfriend. You just don't remember it."

Ben began chuckling. "Kara, the gig is up. There's no tattoo."

Her jaw dropped, "No tattoo? I mean... I knew that. I was just..." Her eyes narrowed on Ben's. "You! You're a—"

"I wouldn't complete that thought if I were you," said Brad. "I think you'd better cut your losses and leave now. And believe me, you've got some losses built up."

Her gaze was cold. "You don't know what you're throwing away. We could have been good together."

"I thought you might want to know, I recorded our conversation." Ben winked, wagging his cell phone in his hand. "I'm just sayin'..."

*****

Josh caught up with Grace before she made it to the end of the hall. "Grace, wait. Let me talk to you. You need to know some things about Dr. Dickson."

She gave no resistance when he led her to a consultation room. She sat quietly, studying her fingernails.

Wishing he could reveal everything he knew about Kara Dickson, he finally decided to keep it simple.

"She's dishonest—you can't trust anything she says. It's quite possible she made the whole story up. We have no way of knowing Brad slept with her."

She regarded him with wide eyes, but didn't respond. He tried to imagine what she was thinking. But she was a woman—she could be thinking almost anything.

"Grace, did you hear me? I said it might not even be true."

She sat up straight and lifted her chin. He detected only a slight tremble in her chin when she spoke. "By the rules of logic, you're saying what she said might actually be true. Right?"

He groaned. "Technically, yes. But since when do women think logically? It's just Brad was totally out of it today after he hit his head. He doesn't remember anything. Nothing he said or did made any sense whatsoever."

She pressed her lips together, giving a small nod and lowering her head to hide the tears that began to puddle.

"But Grace, the only thing he thought about from the moment he woke up until now, was you."

She looked up through her lashes with wide eyes. "Really?"

"I've never lied to you, and I'm not about to start now. I can tell you truthfully I got really tired of having him ask me where you were, over and over and over again. Especially when he couldn't even remember who I was."

One corner of her mouth kicked up. "He didn't remember you?"

"He didn't remember me or anyone else. He couldn't remember his own name. He certainly didn't remember Kara Dickson. But he kept asking about you. Where were you? Were you okay? Only you, Grace. Only you."

He watched her trace the seam on the arm of the chair with one finger, while she chewed on her cheek. "I love him, you know. I won't stop loving him. Even if I find out he slept with her. I know he wasn't in his right mind."

It wasn't until Josh released a breath he realized he'd been holding it. "That's great, Grace. Come back with me and tell him that yourself."

"But Josh." Her brows knotted on her forehead. "If she's pregnant with his baby... that would change everything. Not because I wouldn't love him or I couldn't forgive him, but because of the child."

"He wouldn't marry her, Grace. He would support the child and be a father, but he wouldn't marry her. Could you love a man who had a child with another woman? If it was a man who loved you with all his heart? One who broke all of his own rules to save you from some imaginary threat and then busted his head to protect you from falling?"

Her eyes closed, and a tear rolled down her cheek leaving a salty, wet track. She whispered, "Only if it was Brad. But it would be hard... really, really hard."

He took her hands and lifted her to her feet. "You can do it, Grace. I believe in you."

His breath whooshed out as she lunged into his arms and hugged him. "Thanks Josh. You're pretty good at this."

He chuckled, patting the top of her head. "Wow, I forget how short you are."

Grace straightened and pulled her shoulders back. "I may be short, but I'm action-packed. I'm gonna go fight for my man. Kara Dickson won't know what hit her!"

She followed him back down the hall toward Brad's room. The closer she got, the faster her heart was beating. She wasn't afraid of facing Kara. She was terrified of expressing her feelings to Brad. After all, only a short time ago she broke up with him because he told her he loved her. And now she'd decided she felt the same way. Could she really say the words? Should she? Did he still feel the same way? She wanted to talk to him in private, and she didn't want to talk to him in front of Kara Dickson. Maybe she would sock that woman in the stomach when she saw her. Though she knew she'd never do it, the thought gave her extreme pleasure.

A man in a white coat came hurrying from Brad's room. "Dr. Branson. I got the lab results on that lumbar puncture."

Josh scanned the report with a pained expression. "Grace, we need to postpone your confrontation. Brad needs another test right away."

"Is something wrong? Did he get a bad report?"

"It's not what I hoped for. But I don't have time to explain it. I'm sorry, Grace."

"Dr. Branson? Isn't it possible the blood is from trauma from the puncture?"

"That's why we took four vials. With consistent levels even in the last vial, we lessen the chance of a false positive."

He nodded. "Okay, so what's our next step? Find the blood source?"

"That's right. And can you tell me the test of choice?"

"CT angiography?"

"Right. Can you set that up right away? I'll talk to Dr. Gates."

"But Dr. Branson? Doesn't this indicate a much higher morbidity rate, no matter what the source of the blood?"

"Not as long as his Glasgow score is over twelve. And it's currently fifteen."

"But I was just in there, and he's getting confused again."

Only the sudden pallor of Josh's face gave away his concern. "Then let's hurry up with that angiogram." He disappeared into Brad's room while the other doctor scurried through a set of double doors.

Grace found herself alone in the cold, hard hallway, with tears threatening once again. She pulled out her cell phone and punched a number, her tight control slipping at the familiar sound of her sister's voice. "Grace? Grace, are you there?"

"Olivia... I need you."

*****

Ben's heart was in his throat. Josh sent him away while he sedated Brad, who was moaning in agony. He walked out of the room like a blind man, not even noticing Grace until she tugged on his arm.

"What's going on?"

"I don't know." His voice rasped, and he realized his mouth was dry. "Everything was just fine and then all of a sudden he started groaning and holding his head. And then he started saying over and over, 'No feeding tube. No feeding tube.'"

"Is Dr. Dickson still in there?"

"No, she's gone. And Grace... He didn't sleep with her."

"We can't really know that, Ben, but I already decided it didn't matter to me. Well, it matters, but I won't break up with him over it."

"No, I mean he really didn't sleep with her. I tricked her into a confession of sorts. That's why she's gone already."

She might have looked relieved if she hadn't been so upset. Her eyes were watery, and he could tell she was hanging by a thread. He put an arm around her shoulder, and she melted into him.

"I love him," she said.

"I know. I do too." Had he ever actually told his brother? When this was over, he'd make sure Brad knew.

A man entered the room and emerged with Josh, pushing Brad's bed toward the double doors. Ben was rooted in place, but Grace moved to intercept them. "Can I see him?"

Josh nodded. "Just for a second."

She held his hand between hers and squeezed it. "Brad?"

He opened his eyes and, after a moment, focused on her. "Grace... I didn't..." His speech was slurred and weak.

"I know you didn't sleep with her. It's okay. I didn't even care."

"So sorry... No tube... I..."

She leaned over to place a kiss on his lips, her tears falling to wet his face.

"Goodbye... Grace... So sorry..."

"Grace," Josh interrupted. "We need to hurry."

She pulled away and dropped his hand, wiping her face with her sleeve. Josh spoke in soft tones to the man, and he continued on with Brad while Josh remained behind. He rubbed his forehead before he spoke.

"I have to be honest, I'm really worried."

"I don't understand what happened," said Ben. "He was fine one second, and then in terrible pain the next."

"It doesn't make sense, really. The first CT looked fine—we couldn't see any intracranial hemorrhage. But after he had continuing symptoms and vomiting, we did a lumbar puncture to look for blood we might have missed. It's not a hundred percent accurate before the twelve-hour mark, but we couldn't afford to wait. He seemed to be improving significantly and cognitive functions were good. But the test result showed blood, which could still possibly be from spinal tap trauma even though the levels were consistent over four vials. But also, his headache came back with a vengeance."

Ben said, "He was talking crazy. He kept saying, 'No feeding tube.' Why would he say that?"

Josh's forehead creased with tension. "That's not crazy. If it's a subarachnoid hemorrhage, the outcome can deteriorate rapidly. He was saying he didn't want to be kept alive if that happened. He told me that as well."

Grace choked. "What are you saying? Are you saying he could die?"

The double doors opened and a woman called out, "Dr. Branson? They're ready for you."

"I've got to go," Josh said, giving Grace a quick hug. "I'm not doing the procedure, but I want to be there. I'll come out to the waiting room and talk to you as soon as we know something."

Ben grabbed his arm before he left. "Should I call our parents?"

Josh shook his head. "I'll be out in less than an hour."

Ben tried to swallow, but his cottony mouth made the act impossible.

Chapter Thirteen

GRACE SAT ON THE WAITING ROOM COUCH, surrounded by all three of her sisters while Ben paced before them. She was so nervous she almost wished she could take another of those pills she'd taken before her procedure.

"Ben, you should sit down. It's going to take a while," said Olivia. "And your shoes are squeaking."

He picked up a foot and examined the bottom of his tennis shoe, as if expecting to find some artificial noisemaker on its sole. He flopped into a chair and dropped his head in his hands.

"I can't believe I made such a big fuss over a little biopsy. Right now, I'd be willing to have a hundred needles stuck in my body if I knew Brad would be okay."

"Perspective," said Olivia. "It's all about perspective."

Grace felt her chin tremble. "What if I never get to tell him I love him? What if he never wakes up?"

"The important thing is you've finally admitted you're in love with him," said Hannah.

Claire frowned at Grace. "What a hypocrite. Aren't you the one who broke up with him for saying those words?"

"That's different—I wasn't dying at the time."

"Stop being negative," said Olivia. "He's not going to die. And we're all going to pray for him right now."

The group fell into silence. Grace tried to pray, but it felt so desperate—more like begging.

Finally she spoke into the quiet. "I feel responsible. If I'd talked to him before the surgery, this wouldn't have happened."

Ben stood and began to pace again. "If you feel responsible, think how I feel. It was my story that made him think he needed to carry you out of the hospital."

"Ben... Sit," Olivia ordered. "Squeaky shoes, remember? It was a crazy set of circumstances, and it won't do any good to mete out blame."

Spencer trotted into the waiting room, obviously out of breath, with Emily close behind. "We got here as soon as we could. What's going on?"

"Ohmygosh! We wouldn't have even left if we'd known he was getting worse. I thought it was just a concussion." Emily's face was red from running.

"He was improving—in fact he seemed to be a lot better. But then his headache spiked and they found blood in his spinal tap." Ben was tapping his feet and patting his hands on his legs in a random pattern.

"So what does that mean?" asked Spencer. "Like his skull cracked open or something?"

Olivia fielded the question. "Josh said they were worried it might be subarachnoid hemorrhage. Right, Grace? I had to look it up. But if I understand correctly, the danger is blood can build up pressure and damage the brain."

"But he's going to be okay, right?" Emily asked Grace.

Only the reassurance of her sisters' hands squeezing hers kept Grace from crying at the question.

Ben answered for her, "He's going to be fine. He's way too stubborn to die."

No one refuted his claim. Grace prayed the humorless jest would prove true.

And then they waited. And waited. No one seemed to feel like talking.

"Hasn't it been an hour?" asked Grace.

Every minute felt like an eternity. As the words left her mouth, the door opened and Josh came out. He was surrounded before he made it three feet. Grace tried to read his expression. He didn't seem too upset, but then again, he didn't look happy either. Her stomach was in knots.

He pulled off a scrub cap and rubbed his head. "So we didn't find anything."

Ben frowned, "That's good news, isn't it?"

"Well, it's good we didn't find an aneurism or a big bleed, but we still don't know the source of the blood in the tap."

"But he's going to be okay, right?" said Spencer.

"We can't know until we do another spinal tap at the twelve hour mark. That's the only way we can be absolutely positive whether the blood came from trauma from the lumbar puncture or another source. I don't want to be too optimistic because we can't explain his symptoms apart from a slow bleed somewhere. If we get another positive tap, we'll probably do an MRI."

"Can I talk to him?" Grace asked.

"I don't know. We have to keep him from getting too excited." Josh winked at her.

She felt her face flushing. "Josh, don't tease me. I need to talk to him—he still doesn't know."

"He knows he didn't sleep with Kara," said Ben. "That conversation happened before his head started hurting."

Grace saw Emily's eyes bugging out at Ben's words. "It's a long story, Emily. We'll tell you later."

As Josh turned to go back into the surgical area, she put a hand on his arm. "Wait, Josh. He doesn't know I love him yet. Everyone else knows, but I haven't told him."

His eyes crinkled at the corners and he chuckled. "Yes, you did. Well, it took some interpretation, but I'm pretty sure he figured it out, anyway."

"What are you talking about?"

"Check your messages." He grinned before he disappeared again.

She frowned as she pulled out her cell phone and opened the messages. Olivia and Emily peered over her shoulder.

"Open the messages to Brad," Olivia ordered.

She complied and was astonished to see the nonsensical message she had sent to Brad, evidently while under the influence of her premedication.

"Ohmygosh!" cried Emily. "At the end of that message you told him you loved him."

"No she didn't," chuckled Olivia. "She said she *lived* him."

Grace wished the floor would swallow her whole.

*****

"Hi." Brad spoke in a soft voice as he blinked his eyes open.

He'd appeared to be sleeping when she'd entered the room and slipped to his bedside on silent feet. She'd watched him breathing for a while and thought to leave and let him sleep. But his eyes opened and he reached out to take her hand, his grasp firmer than she expected for having been sedated.

"Hi back." She felt heat radiating from her cheeks. Why was she suddenly feeling awkward? "How do you feel?"

"Great, since you're here." His forehead wrinkled and he closed his eyes for a moment, drawing a deep breath. "Grace, I'm sorry about Kara."

"It's okay. Ben already told me you didn't sleep with her. And I'd already decided I didn't care. You can ask Josh."

"You didn't care?" He grinned. "So does that mean you're into open relationships?"

"No, it doesn't. And you're not funny."

"But you're smiling."

"No, this is a grimace of distaste."

The smile dropped off his face. "Seriously Grace, I'm sorry about her. I'm sorry I ever agreed to go to that stupid Yankees game with her."

"Hey... Don't insult the Yankees."

He chuckled. "You're right. Let me restate that. I'm sorry I was stupid enough to agree to go to a Yankees game with that stupid woman."

"Much better." She bobbed her head. "And I'm sorry I ever broke up with you."

"And I'm sorry I told you I loved you." His eyes twinkled. "Because it's too soon to say that. Right?"

"That's right." She bit her lips as her cheeks reddened.

"So I won't say it again. But Grace..." He caressed her hand with his thumb, causing tingles to race up her arm. He spoke in a voice so soft she had to lean in to hear him. "I *live* you, too."

*****

Brad had sent Ben, Grace, and the rest of the Marshall clan home, promising someone would call as soon as there was new information. Grace was still acting pretty awkward. He couldn't tell if she was unsure about her feelings or simply concerned about his injury. That part of his memory was still a blank, but he'd been told the details of his actions leading up to the fall. It sounded like the script in a bad movie, and he couldn't believe he'd been so reckless.

He was waiting for the pinch in his back, but that wasn't what worried him. He knew too much. Josh was trying to keep up a cheery banter, but Brad could tell he was uptight, too.

"You don't have to pretend," Brad said. "I know it could be bad news." He tried not to flinch as he felt the needle pierce his skin.

Josh was quiet as he drew the fluid out and handed it to the doctor at his side. When she had departed to the lab with the crucial tubes, he took off his gloves and sank into a chair next to him with a groan. It was one a.m. and the toll of the incredibly long and stressful day showed on his face.

"The fact you know it could be bad news is good news. At least we aren't seeing any further deterioration in your cognitive abilities."

"Any further deterioration?"

Josh chuckled. "Sorry. I should have said continuing evidence of deterioration. You were certainly not the brightest crayon in the box yesterday. But your stupidity started before you hit your head."

Brad wanted to object, but he knew Josh was right. "I don't know what came over me. I'm usually so sensible—Ben is the impulsive brother."

"I think you two are more alike than you admit."

"You're probably right. Maybe that's why he gets under my skin."

"Your problem is you have an Achilles' heel where Grace is concerned. Who was teasing me about acting crazy over Charlie?"

Brad smiled as he thought about Josh's complete infatuation with Emily's younger sister, Charlie Best. "Yes, but Charlie changed your entire personality. It's like you're a different guy, now."

He pressed his lips together until they whitened. "I wish you'd tell Grace to tell Charlie that."

"She still won't talk to you?"

"She still maintains we're too different and I'm only infatuated with her because she's a challenge."

"Are you sure she's wrong? No offense, but she's probably the first girl who hasn't fallen into your arms when she was given the opportunity."

A scowl spread over his face. "If I can't even convince you, how can I convince Charlie? I wish I could undo my past, but I can only change what I do from here on out."

"I'll admit so far the change has been fairly impressive. I just wonder if you'll keep it up if Charlie keeps resisting you."

His voice was bitter. "I guess you'll have to wait and see."

"Josh, I'm sorry. I shouldn't have said it that way. I'm really only worried you'll get hurt if this keeps up."

"It hurts already, but I'm committed. And you know if I commit, I stick with it to the end."

Brad thought *the end* might be rather painful for Josh, but he kept that idea to himself. "So was it clear or cloudy?" he asked, referring to the appearance of the spinal fluid Josh had drawn.

"Actually, it was clear. I've been thinking... Could the headache escalation be solely a result of the spinal tap?"

"I don't know—it was incredibly painful."

"But it's subsided now, and that's consistent with a spinal tap headache."

"True." He considered the idea. This diagnosis had a much better prognosis than SAH.

"And to be honest, your cognitive function seems perfectly normal right now, except perhaps where Grace is concerned." Josh winked at him.

"So go home and get some sleep. If the tap is positive, they can do an MRI without you."

He frowned. "I think I should stay until we get the results."

"Go home—you're making me nervous."

Josh stifled a yawn as he stood and stretched. "Okay, I think I'll go. But I'm coming back if there's a positive result on the lab."

"Hey Josh... I... Thank you." The lump in his throat felt gargantuan. "I owe you one."

"I hope you never get a chance to pay me back in the ER. But I'll let you buy me dinner if your brain doesn't turn to jelly."

Brad chuckled. "Thanks a lot."

*****

Olivia arrived at five a.m. with ample time to drop by Brad's room before her rotation at the hospital.

"Hey, we didn't get a phone call," she said when she saw his eyes were open. "So what does that mean? Are you still waiting for the results?"

Brad smiled. "No, it means the results were good—no xanthochromia in the samples."

"And what does that mean? Is this something I need to know for school?"

"Not for your RN, but you might as well learn it for when you're in med school. If the bleeding is from the brain instead of trauma from the lumbar puncture then the heme is degraded into bilirubin. And the bilirubin is detectable after twelve hours by spectrophotometry as xanthochromia, which is really just a big word for a yellow color in the cerebrospinal fluid. So... no xanthochromia means no subarachnoid hemorrhage."

She repeated the words, attempting to file the information in her brain for later retrieval. "What about the other symptoms? The headache and the confusion?"

"The initial confusion was from the concussion, and we think the headache came from exertion after the spinal tap."

"This stuff is so awesome! I'm gonna do emergency medicine for sure."

He chuckled. "You might change your mind during medical school."

"So if you're okay, when do you get to go home?"

"Well, this time I'm not leaving until Josh signs off on it. I think he might kill me if there's a repeat of yesterday."

"He's at home?"

"Yes, I talked him into getting some sleep."

"And Ben?"

He made a face. "I'm still mad at him, even though I absolved him yesterday when he tricked Kara Dickson into a confession."

"I'm glad you feel that way, because I have a great idea how we can get back at him for his tall tales."

"Really?" His eyes danced with glee. "If I need to do anything, I'm in. What's the plan?"

"You see, he has this broken tooth, and I have this friend who's a dentist..."

*****

Ben was glad he was already sitting down in the dental chair when the dentist walked into room—otherwise he might have fallen on the floor. She was drop-dead gorgeous. Long, straight sandy-blonde hair framed huge almond eyes—brown with caramel stars in the middle, and a dark brown perimeter. They were spectacular—he could swim in those eyes. She had smooth golden skin stretched over high cheekbones and a pert up-turned nose.

And then she smiled at him.

His heart fell into his stomach. Her plush lips spread to reveal perfect even white teeth. She was a dentist—of course she had beautiful teeth. What had he expected? Whatever he'd expected, it wasn't this. Why hadn't Olivia warned him about her? She'd said her friend was cute, not stunning. He didn't want this girl to look inside his mouth. How well had he brushed his teeth that morning? Was his breath okay? Would she know he hadn't been flossing?

She held out her hand. "Hi. I'm Dr. Williams. Shanna Williams."

He stared at the long delicate fingers stretched toward him. How could fingers be so attractive?

"Eh-hem," she cleared her throat.

"Oh, sorry." He took her hand in his. Sparks. There were definitely sparks. Did she feel them? Her grip was firm. He liked a strong grasp—he hated girls who gave dead-fish handshakes.

"Uhmm…"

He realized she was trying to free her hand from his clenched fingers. "Oh, sorry again." As her hand slipped from his, he felt a profound loss.

"So you're Olivia's friend, right? I've already seen the x-rays from your dentist in California. Let's take a look and see if this chipped tooth can be restored with a bonded filling or if you'll need a crown." She began to lean the dental chair back.

"Uhmm… You know, it's not that bad. Really, we don't need to fix it today."

"Are you nervous? You don't need to be afraid—I'm really quite painless."

"I'm not afraid, but I thought we might talk for a few minutes before we start."

"Well, I don't have a lot of extra time. Why don't I check the tooth, and we can talk while the anesthetic is working?"

Before he could protest again she had a mirror in his mouth.

"Hmmm… I think it's small enough a composite will do the job. I'll need to get you numb so I can remove the restoration adjacent to the chip."

Her eyes mesmerized him. He sank into their depths, noting shades of green he hadn't noticed at a distance. He stared at the smooth skin on her face, noting the cute wrinkle that appeared between her eyebrows as she concentrated.

"There you go. Now we'll just need to wait a few minutes for the anesthetic to take effect."

"You already gave me a shot?"

She smiled and nodded, returning the chair to a sitting position. "Yep, I'm painless. So tell me about yourself, Ben. What do you like to do? Do you have hobbies?"

His mind went blank. "I… uhmm… I like a lot of things. What do you like?"

"I love to read."

"Me too—I love to read." The lie slipped from his mouth without thought. "What kind of books do you like?"

"Everything really. I like romance, mysteries, thrillers. My favorite is probably young adult fantasy and dystopia."

"Me too—I love fantasy and dystopia."

"So what books have you read lately?"

He blinked, his heart racing. Why had he told her he liked to read? He hadn't read any books. The last book he could remember reading was *The Scarlet Letter* as a senior in high school. If she caught him in this lie, he was going to be wearing a scarlet letter.

"*Harry Potter*." He'd seen all the movies, so maybe he could fake it.

"Have you read all the books?"

"Yep, read 'em all."

"Did you like the books better than the movies?"

She was a reader. To her, the correct answer would always favor the books. "The books were better, but I thought the movies were well done."

"I loved the movies, but of course they couldn't get everything in. Did you realize they left Peeves out of the movies?"

"Right, I noticed that." Who or what was Peeves? He hoped she didn't ask him.

"And Oregon? He was such a good character in the books. Didn't you miss him in the movies?"

"That was the worst. I really missed that guy." He felt his mouth beginning to droop. Maybe he was numb enough to distract her from talking about books he hadn't read. "I think I'm numb now."

She raised one perfectly arched eyebrow. "Okay, I'll call my assistant."

In a matter of seconds his mouth was propped open in a manner that must be unattractive, and the assistant was holding his cheek back with the loud vacuum tube.

"You know, Ben." Shanna pushed a cotton roll next to his tooth and started the loud whining drill inside his mouth. "There wasn't a character called Oregon in *Harry Potter*."

His eyes grew large as he struggled to talk against a mouth full of fingers and instruments and cotton. "There wasn't?" came out as, "Aa-ya uh-eh?"

"Nope."

He heard a male voice behind him. "Sorry, Dr. Williams. I'm afraid my brother has a habit of telling little fibs."

Shanna said, "Ben, if you don't stop squirming, I might accidentally cut your tongue off."

Ben heard Olivia's voice in the background. "I think cutting off his tongue might be a bit too severe for a bit of storytelling. But perhaps if he hasn't learned his lesson, we might bring him back for that."

He could feel his cheeks turning red. If he survived this procedure he was going to kill those two. Worst of all, he'd blown his chances with Shanna. He studied her face, inches away, frowning in concentration. For this girl, he might have been willing to take up reading. Or at least listening to audiobooks.

"I'll read as many books as you want if you'll go out with me," came out as, "Ah ee eh eh-ee ook ah yoo ah eh yoo oe ou eh ee."

She smiled behind her facemask. "I might be willing to go out with you, even if you don't read any books. But you have to promise never to lie to me again."

What could he say to a woman with a drill in his mouth? "I ah-iss."

She chuckled as she put another scary-looking bit on her drill. "Okay, one date—just a trial." She asked her assistant, "Can you rinse that for me?"

Brad said, "Wait a minute... Did my brother just make a date with you after lying about his reading history?"

"I can't believe it," Olivia said, walking into the operatory with a decided scowl and her hands on her hips. "Shanna, you were supposed to torture him, not go out with him."

Shanna shrugged her shoulders. "Sorry. It's hard to be mad at him. He's just so cute with those sad green eyes and his mouth propped open, full of cotton."

"Eel ake ah-uh aw ow ake."

"No, it's not necessary to take cotton on our date. I'm sure you'll look fine without cotton in your mouth." Shanna's eyes crinkled in a smile.

Brad said, "But don't worry—his mouth will be open the whole time. And he'll probably have his foot in it."

*****

Kara wasn't nervous about the meeting. Curious would be a better way to describe her feelings. Steven Gherring, chair of the board of directors at Mercy General, had called the night before to invite her to meet him at his office. The thought occurred to her he might have caught wind of her failed attempt to manipulate Brad, but she dismissed the idea. Gherring had mentioned a phone call he'd received recently from her father, so he was probably fulfilling an obligation.

Her dad had a lot of influence and a long reach—she'd been admitted to the residency because he'd 'made a few phone calls'. Her grades and rank in medical school certainly hadn't warranted her acceptance in the elite program. But unlike her lackadaisical attitude in medical school, she'd worked diligently during her residency at Mercy General. She was confident in her intellect and her record. She didn't need Dr. Gates to satisfy her goals in life, but he would have been a very pleasant addition. Her mind replayed a clear image of the abdominal muscles she'd exposed the previous day. Yes, she would have enjoyed having Brad in her bed, possibly as a permanent partner. There were other eligible men, but it might be difficult to find someone with all the attributes Dr. Brad Gates had brought to the table.

As she exited the elevator and approached the receptionist, she put the unpleasant thought from her mind. She was in her element, interacting with one of her father's cronies. These men were always easy to manipulate, eager to please her father and flattered by the attention she doled out. She only waited for a few moments before the imposing carved wooden doors opened and Steven Gherring emerged from his sanctuary, wearing a benevolent smile. Impeccably dressed and incredibly handsome, the tall, fit man was as appealing in person as he appeared in the magazines.

"Come in Dr. Dickson—we've been expecting you."

She strolled across the marble floor in three-inch pumps to shake his outstretched hand. Her chosen shoes allowed her to look down on most men, but at six feet and three inches, Gherring still managed to maintain a height advantage. "We?" she asked, glancing curiously over his shoulder into his office. "Is someone else going to be at our meeting?"

He gestured for her to enter ahead of him. "Yes, Dr. Dickson. I'd like for you to meet my wife, Anne Best Gherring."

Her smile only faltered for an instant. A wife would be a bothersome addition, eliminating the benefit she usually gained from flirtation. But she knew how to interact with socialites as well, having played the game for some thirty years. Her eyes took in the attractive, willowy woman with thick brown hair and laughing brown eyes.

"Mrs. Gherring, I'm thrilled to finally meet you. I've only seen your picture in the media before, and I must say you're even more striking in person. I love that necklace! You must tell me where you got it."

Anne chuckled. "It came from the Target in Ft. Worth. But it's about ten years old, so I doubt you can still buy one."

Kara's intake of breath caused a coughing fit, which luckily disguised her outbreak of laughter. She remembered now Anne hadn't been married to Gherring all that long. She hadn't yet learned the rules of cultured behavior. She shot a sympathetic glance toward the billionaire, but was astounded at the adoring expression on his face as he regarded his wife.

One corner of his mouth lifted as he took in Kara's quizzical countenance. "Anne was a unique answer to my fifty-year dilemma. The only way to be certain a woman didn't love me for my fortune was to find one who isn't attracted to money. And I must say I've learned a lot from her about what's truly valuable in life."

She pasted an isn't-that-wonderful look on her face and hurried to change the subject to a more comfortable topic. "And so you're a friend of my father?"

"As a matter of fact, we're very old friends. I knew your father in law-school." She allowed him to guide her to a seating area. She noticed Anne kicked off her shoes to tuck her feet underneath her.

"I hope you don't mind me getting comfortable. I have to play the formal role all day, and I'm tired by the end of it."

Kara could only wonder how this woman managed to function in high society with such an obvious lack of polish. She managed a stiff nod.

Gherring said, "So Dr. Dickson…"

"Please, call me Kara."

His smile was unflappable. "So Kara, I spoke with your father this weekend. As you're probably aware, he called upon me three and a half years ago when you were seeking entrance into the emergency medicine residency at Mercy General."

"Yes, and let me say how grateful I am for the chance you gave me. I hope my record demonstrates I haven't wasted this valuable opportunity."

He continued as if she hadn't spoken. "When he first contacted me, he expressed a grave concern he'd failed you. He was afraid you had grown up to be…" He gazed at the ceiling. "How did he say it? Oh yes, he thought you might have grown up to be a 'spoiled, pretentious brat with no regard for the welfare of others.'"

Kara felt the blood rush to her face as he continued with a bland smile. "So since your time here is nearing an end, he was understandably concerned with the results of your time in the residency."

He paused is if to give her an opportunity to respond, but for once, she seemed to have lost the ability to speak. "So naturally, he wanted me to keep an eye on you. And before we spoke this weekend, I reviewed your record. On paper, you appeared to have excelled in every area, but close examination left me with some questions as to your actual moral motivation."

She felt the blood pounding in her face as she sputtered, "What do you mean? What close examination?"

"I spoke with your fellow residents and, of course, your attending, Dr. Branson." He paused, giving no further explanation, allowing time for his words to sink into the pit of her stomach. She wouldn't expect a glowing reference from any of her fellow residents, whom she regarded with a certain amount of disdain. And Dr. Branson's view of her would've been tarnished due to recent events.

As she opened her mouth to respond, he spoke again, his eyes wide and his face bright. "But then Dr. Branson shared your extraordinary news."

She stared at him for a moment before realizing her mouth was hanging open. She closed her lips while considering every possible bit of information that might qualify as extraordinary news.

"Of course, I'm referring to your application to work for Physicians Across Borders—such a wonderful organization. And this clearly indicates to me, and to your father, you could still become the selfless, noble physician and humanitarian he knew you could be."

Relief flowed through her veins like a drug. She relaxed as the tension left her body, exultant her bogus application to the philanthropic organization had been of benefit after all.

"Yes, it's such a great opportunity. I certainly hope I'll have a chance to work with them."

"Where were you hoping to go?" asked Anne. "It sounds exciting. But I have to admit, it also sounds dangerous and exhausting."

"I'd be happy with any place in Africa. I'm not afraid of rough conditions."

"I'm certain we can arrange for that to happen," said Gherring, with an enigmatic smile.

A spidery feeling crept up her spine. "Really? What do you mean?"

"Only that your father and I have both used our considerable influence to assure your acceptance to the program."

"But... But I haven't even completed the application yet." The blood in her veins felt as if it had been circulated through a freezer.

"No worries. Dr. Branson gave me your application, and we've expedited the process. We cut through all the red tape and went right to the top."

Her voice rose into shrill tones. "You had no right to do that! I hadn't decided for certain I wanted to complete the application. It was none of your business!"

He shrugged. "You can take it up with your father if you like. He said something about a trust fund that would be dependent upon your completion of a term with them."

Her mind churned. Surely she could talk her dad out of this insane idea. He wouldn't want her to pursue a term with the organization if he understood the dangers involved.

Gherring's smile disappeared as he leaned toward her. "I spoke with your father again last night. He was quite disturbed when he heard about your recent nefarious activities and attempted blackmail of Dr. Gates."

"Attempted blackmail? You've got to be kidding!"

His blue eyes were icy. She shivered, wondering how she'd ever thought she might be able to manipulate this man. "My legal advisors tell me the charge might not stick, but it would likely ruin your career. Understandably, many hospitals are reluctant to hire physicians who might attempt to run a scam such as the one you attempted, Dr. Dickson."

He stood and walked toward the door. "But make no mistake... If I hear you've changed your mind about serving with Physicians Across Borders, I won't hesitate to bring formal charges against you with the board."

He opened the heavy door and gestured toward the exit with his open hand. Kara glanced at Anne, hoping to find some support from the unsophisticated woman with the friendly face.

Anne smiled. "By the way, I just love your purse! You must tell me where you got it. Perhaps I can find a factory second somewhere."

Chapter Fourteen

GRACE WAS FEELING BLUE. She'd hardly seen Brad since they'd had their little define-the-relationship talk at the hospital, and they hadn't spent any time alone together. It wasn't anyone's fault—life had simply interfered. Ben had had his shoulder surgery the day after Brad had been released from the hospital, and her school had held an open house.

She felt her phone vibrate in her pocket, and her lips slipped into a smile. He'd been very prolific with his texts during the past few days, ending each one with *I live you!* By mutual, unspoken consent, neither one of them had spoken the other "L" word, instead using her accidental euphemism. She was still uncomfortable talking about love and marriage, but she admitted her feelings for Brad were stronger than any she'd experienced before. Fortunately, he wasn't pressuring her to commit any time soon. At least he hadn't so far.

It was Friday afternoon, and her first-graders were getting restless, knowing the weekend was fast approaching. She would have to delay reading Brad's text for a few more minutes until the bell rang to signal the end of the school day.

"Does anyone have special plans this weekend?" she asked. At least fifteen hands shot into the air. "Yes, Donovan?"

The round-faced boy with adorable dimples said, "We're going to my Gramp's house in the country. He has a fishing pond, and I always catch a bunch of fish."

Hands were waving at her, begging for their turns. "Thank you Donovan. Yes, Rita? What are your plans?"

"Uhmm... I forgot..." Tears began to swim in her eyes.

"I bet you can remember, Rita. Were you doing something with your parents? Or going somewhere? Or…"

"I remember. It's my Momma's birthday, and we're going to Coney Island!"

"That sounds fun, Rita. Yes, Horatio?"

His eyes were big as he pointed over her shoulder. "There's a man looking in the window!"

Every eye in the room riveted on Brad's smiling face at the window. Grace knew her face was flushed as she moved to open the door.

"What are you doing here?" she murmured.

"I brought you flowers." He grinned, whipping a bouquet from behind his back.

The room erupted in giggles and shouts. "Oooo!" "Ms. Marshall has a boyfriend!"

"I had to bring another set of flowers to pacify that crazy girl at the front. But she didn't get any candy." His other hand appeared holding out a huge bag of miniature Hershey bars. "There should be enough to share."

Cries erupted. "I want some! Me, me, me!"

Despite her protests, the children were soon surrounding them, pushing and shoving to receive a piece of candy.

"Wait, wait!" she shouted. "I will give you a piece of candy if you will promise me to take it home and ask your parents for permission before you eat it."

"There should be enough for everyone to have two."

Chaos ensued, but soon every child had two miniature candy bars, and they were obediently stashing them in their backpacks and preparing to go home, chatting with excitement.

Grace muttered, "I can't believe you stooped to coming to the school and bribing the children."

His smile was unrepentant. "Whatever. I was desperate to see you." He stood so close to her she had to crane her neck to look up at him. "You don't know how tempted I am to sweep you into my arms and kiss you senseless."

She felt her face flaming and hurried to change the subject. "How's Ben doing after his surgery? Is he hurting a lot?"

"He's Ben—he always lands on his feet. He's high on pain medication and loving being waited on hand and foot. Right now, he's telling all his old stories and jokes to Shanna Williams. And she laughs because she hasn't heard them all, like I have."

"Now who's that? The name sounds familiar."

"Olivia's dentist friend."

"Oh—that's right. Olivia told me all about that. She was ticked because Ben didn't learn any kind of lesson."

"He's such a lucky dog. It's always like that with him—he gets away with murder."

The bell rang, and all the children ran toward the door. Grace chuckled. First-graders ran everywhere when they were excited—walking was almost impossible.

But Horatio hung back to walk beside Grace and Brad. "Ms. Marshall, is that your boyfriend?" His lower lip pooched out and he kicked the floor as he walked.

"Yes, Horatio. This is my boyfriend, Dr. Gates."

His eyes widened, and he stared at Brad. "You're a doctor?"

"Yes, I work in the emergency room."

"Cool! Do you see lots of blood and stuff?"

"Lots of blood. And broken legs and arms, too."

"Wow! What's the grossest thing you saw today?"

Brad pursed his lips while contemplating his question. "I didn't see a lot of blood today, but one guy threw up and it almost hit me."

"Awesome!" He moved to walk next to Brad, grabbing his hand. "Will you tell my big brother, 'cuz he won't believe me."

Grace grinned. "I see how easily I'm replaced." She didn't have to worry about Horatio's misplaced affections anymore. He was in love with Brad.

*****

"What should I wear?" Grace held up two sweater choices for Hannah. "I've got an actual date with Brad tonight at six, and I'm kind of nervous."

"You can borrow my blue top with the scoop neck. That color makes your eyes look blue."

"I don't know. Do you think it may be too low cut?"

Hannah grabbed her hand to tug her up the stairs. "Come on. Let's try some things on."

"Wait." Claire bounded behind them. "I'll help with her makeup."

Olivia looked up from her study perch on the bed when the giggling trio tumbled into the room. "What's going on?"

"We're getting Grace ready for her date with Brad," said Hannah. "Do you have an opinion on what she should wear?"

In seconds she abandoned the book for Grace's closet. "You should wear these tight black jeans and these cute new boots with the four-inch platform heels. You haven't even worn 'em since you bought 'em."

"That's because I bought them on sale at the beginning of summer," said Grace. "But you don't even know where we're going on the date."

Olivia said, "I'm assuming it has something to do with sports, since it's you and Brad."

"You're right," Grace admitted. "It's the Rangers and the Islanders—it'll be so much fun."

"Now what sport is that?" asked Olivia.

"Olivia," Claire scolded. "How can you grow up in New York and not know the Rangers and the Islanders are hockey teams?"

Hannah said, "That's okay Olivia—I didn't know either. So it's ice hockey? Will it be cold? Hang on a minute, I'm gonna grab some tops from my closet. It's too bad you're such a shrimp—I've got some adorable jeans that would look great on you." She disappeared into the hallway.

"It doesn't matter where they're going," said Olivia. "She has to look good. This is like a first date—they're practically starting over again."

"Thanks a lot. I was already nervous," said Grace.

Claire patted her back. "Don't pay any attention to them. It's just a date with a guy you've spent lots of time with. It's not like you haven't kissed him since you got back together."

"Uhmm... Actually, we haven't kissed yet. We haven't really had an opportunity. And Brad's been nice, but he's acting... I don't know... I guess the best word to describe it is *cautious*."

Olivia grinned. "Like I said before, it's a first date. And we're going to make sure you look so good he won't be able to resist kissing you."

Grace felt heat radiating from her face. "I don't want to look too sexy or anything. That's how I started this whole mess."

Claire tilted her head. "What exactly did you do? You've never told us the truth."

"I don't want to say—you'll think I was crazy. And anyway that's all in the past."

"Come on. Fess up. You'll feel better, and we'll know how to dress you." Olivia started pulling clothes out of the closet and tossing them on the bed.

"Fess up about what?" asked Hannah, returning with an armful of tops.

"Evidently, Grace is going to tell us how she screwed everything up with Brad."

"No, I'm not."

Claire began to spread the tops out on the bed in an orderly fashion.

"Yes, you are," said Olivia, in a smooth, soothing tone. "Because, we still have a very interesting video of you when you first woke up after your biopsy. And so far we haven't posted it or shown it to Brad."

"You wouldn't!"

Hannah chuckled. "Olivia wouldn't, but I would."

"You little vixen! You'd better not!"

The sound of Hannah's tinkling laughter told Grace she was defeated. "Okay, fine. I'll tell you, but you have to promise not to judge me. And you have to hand over the video. And I'm pretty sure this blackmail breaks just about every Marshall Law."

*****

"Are you sure you'll be okay while I go out tonight? Josh won't be off duty until midnight, so you'll have to fend for yourself." Brad examined his brother, who was ensconced on the couch, surrounded by pillows, with a glass of water in one hand the remote control in the other.

"I think I'll be fine, thanks. This hydrocodone is great stuff. And Shanna said she might stop by later."

"Then I won't worry about you."

"Where are you going with Grace?"

"Rangers game tonight."

"Wow. So romantic." His sarcasm was all too apparent.

"Hey—she loves sports."

"I know, but isn't this your first date in months? Shouldn't you be doing something special? Something where you wouldn't be surrounded by thousands of other people the entire night?"

Brad felt a moment of uncertainty. Was it a bad idea to take Grace to an ice hockey game on their first date since getting back together? He hadn't really thought it through. He didn't want to blow it again.

"We'll grab a coffee together after the game."

"Do you have mints with you? You don't want to kiss her with coffee breath." Ben waggled his eyebrows.

"Shut up—I don't need your advice." Mental note... Buy some breath mints on the way to pick up Grace.

"And have you figured out how you're going to handle things so you don't scare her off again. You've done it twice already."

"That wasn't my fault. Grace freaked out a little because she wasn't ready for a serious commitment."

"And now she's ready?"

Brad felt himself perspiring despite the chill in the air. They hadn't really talked and cleared the air yet. He didn't know how she felt about their relationship. She'd admitted she loved him... Well, she'd admitted she *lived* him. But it meant the same thing, didn't it? They needed to have a serious talk. No wait—that was a bad idea. Maybe they should avoid talking about their relationship at all. Grace had been really happy until he'd brought up their future. Had anything really changed?

"Hey, little brother." Ben smirked at him. "Would you mind getting me a refill of water before you go out on your date and mess things up with Grace again?"

"I'm not going to mess things up with Grace." Brad snatched the glass from his hand and stomped into the kitchen.

"You should probably get going so you have time to stop and buy some breath mints."

It would be so satisfying to dump the glass of water on top of his brother's head.

*****

"Don't look at me like that." Grace cringed under her sisters' open-mouthed stares.

"What are we supposed to do?" asked Olivia. "How else can we look at you?"

"You promised you wouldn't judge me."

"We don't have to judge you," said Hannah. "You already know what you did was awful."

Claire said, "I don't get it. Why would you tease him and trick him into trying something with you? And then you broke up with him because he *didn't* try anything?"

"You totally missed the point. I needed to break up with him, and I thought it would hurt both of us less if I had a really good excuse, like if he tried to go past the lines."

"And tell us again, why did you think you needed to break up with him?" asked Hannah.

"I totally get that part. You've been avoiding serious commitments for years. You act all brave and self-assured around guys, but you're really a big chicken." Olivia's words hit home.

"It's not about being brave—it's about being smart. I knew it was a dumb idea to let myself get too attached to a guy before I'm ready. I want to be a principal. So after this year, I'll be taking classes at night to get my master's degree. Having a serious boyfriend would just complicate things."

"Are you leading him on? You're still not going to have a serious relationship, even after everything that's happened?" Claire's voice was as horrified as her expression.

Grace's stomach churned and she felt her eyes stinging. "I still don't know. I only know I love him, and I was miserable without him. And when I thought he might die, I felt like I would die with him."

"Stop upsetting her," Olivia told Claire. "She doesn't have to decide about the rest of her life tonight." She pulled Grace to her feet. "Come on, let's get you dressed before you really start crying and get your face all red and blotchy. You know you don't want to lose him, and that's all you need to know."

Hannah said, "I think you should wear my blue top. It looks cute on you, but it's not cut too low. You don't want to look like you're tempting him again."

"You'd better not let him slip through your fingers," said Claire. "There're not many guys who'd put up with everything he's gone through with you."

"Don't listen to Claire," said Olivia. "He's lucky to have you, even with rusty-colored straw hair."

Claire giggled at this, and the mood was lightened. Grace soon found herself clad in blue-jean tights tucked into ankle high boots. Hannah's blue shirt was declared the winner of the six she modeled. Each of the other tops had some fault—too short, too low, too bright, too high-schoolish, too matronly.

Claire stood back, surveying her sister with a critical eye. "Something's off. Don't you have some other boot you could wear? Some with a higher heel?"

"I do, but they're not very comfortable."

"Comfortable, shmomfortable! That doesn't matter. Beauty comes at a price." Claire dug into the bottom of Grace's closet. "Ah ha! These are perfect. And these boots will fit tighter around your ankle."

Grace groaned, "But they hurt my feet after I wear them for an hour."

"Let's see them on," said Olivia.

With the new ankle boots zipped onto her feet, Grace strutted across the floor.

Hannah said, "I have to admit, Grace, those are really cute. And they make your legs look really long and show off your runner's calves."

Grace's foot wobbled with her next step. "But I don't live up to my name when I wear these boots. I'm afraid I'll fall."

"You'll have to hang onto Brad's arm for balance." Olivia's eyebrows bobbed up and down.

"But what about my feet hurting?"

"It'll be worth it," said Claire. "What's a few blisters when your legs look that good?"

"If you put a Band-Aid on where it rubs your foot, it'll prevent a blister," said Olivia.

"You guys are like the Borg. *'Resistance is futile.'*" Her sisters stared back with blank faces. "You know... The Borg? They assimilate you, and the decisions are made by the collective?"

At their continued silent bewilderment, Grace exclaimed, waving her hands in dramatic fashion. "Where did I go wrong? How can all three of my little sisters be so clueless about Start Trek?"

"Oh, I know *Star Trek*," Hannah declared. "That cute guy with the amazing blue eyes was in it..."

"Chris Pine? Yeah, he's hot. He was in *Shadow Recruit*." Claire's expression was dreamy. "See Grace, we're not clueless."

"You only know the hot actors. I'm talking about classic sci-fi here. You have to know about *Star Trek* and the Borg. The Borg was like the greatest villain of all time."

"Who has time for that when there are so many books to read?" said Olivia. "I swear Grace, you should have been a boy, the way you like sports and sci-fi and all that stuff."

"I bet Brad is glad she's not a boy." Hannah stood back with her arms crossed to survey her work. "You look really cute, Grace."

Grace tugged on her cropped hair as she looked in the mirror. "I can only ever be *cute* with this boy-cut, not beautiful like Dr. Dickson."

Olivia said, "Oh Grace, that woman is awful. She's so ugly on the inside it doesn't matter how she looks on the outside."

"And let's face it, whatever guy you end up with needs to be prepared for accidents like this. You're kind of prone to mess-ups," said Claire.

"More like catastrophes." Hannah chuckled.

"I had plenty of help with this one." Grace pulled off her boots to place Band-Aids over the red spots on her little toes.

"Oh! I think I heard someone at the door. He's here!" exclaimed Olivia. "Hurry up! I'll go down and have him wait at the foot of the stairs. That way you can make a grand entrance coming down the stairs. You look great, Sis!" She kissed Grace on the cheek before scurrying out.

Grace stood up and wavered a bit on her platform boots. "These boots are like stilts. I'll have to hold onto the banister until I get to Brad, or I'll lose my balance."

"Yeah, and you're already kind of off-balance," teased Claire. "As demonstrated by that stunt you pulled on Brad several months ago."

"Don't worry. I'll never do anything like that again. In fact, I've decided we're only going to do light kissing. I'm going to be the epitome of self-control, so I'll never tempt him again."

Hannah exchanged a grin with Claire. "I'm thinking, 'Famous last words,' but I won't say it."

Chapter Fifteen

BRAD WIPED HIS PALMS ON HIS PANTS, praying his deodorant would hold up to his frayed nervous system. Why was he so anxious? It's not like it was his first date with Grace. In fact, he hadn't been this nervous on his first date with her. She'd thrown him for a loop over the last few months, and he'd lost his confidence with her. He tried to listen to Olivia, but her words flowed over his ears like a babbling brook.

Then he saw her. Standing at the top of the stairs like a vision. Her short hair only emphasized the size of her eyes, which were huge and round and locked with his. He felt a warm glow in his chest that spread throughout his entire body, simply from looking at her. One hand gripped the banister as she started down the stairs, her eyes dropping down to watch her feet. When she reached the second to last step, she paused, her gaze rising to lock with his once again. He saw her catch her breath and realized he'd been holding his.

He held out his hand to her, his fingers waiting... longing for her touch. She hesitated, only for a moment. Releasing the banister with her right hand, she switched her clutch to the right, so her left hand was free to grasp his. It felt right. It felt as though her hand belonged with his. Her wide hazel eyes crinkled as she smiled and stepped toward him.

She fell into his arms. Literally. He laughed as he caught her, easily supporting her weight and lifting her upright. But his chuckles ceased when he saw the pain on her face.

"What happened? Are you okay?"

"I turned my ankle." She took a step. "Ow! I can't believe it! These stupid boots!"

She hobbled to a nearby chair and sat down, wincing as she removed the boot. Brad knelt in front of her with Connie and the three sisters ogling over his shoulder. "Let me see." He pressed on her ankle and foot and manipulated her ankle.

"Ow! Dang it! This is so stupid. I'll be fine if I lean on you a little. I just need to walk it out."

"No, you've sprained it for sure. We'd better not go."

He saw tears welling in her eyes. "I don't want to miss the game. I promise it's feeling better already." She attempted to stuff her foot back into the boot.

"Don't be silly, Grace. At least you can wear a flat shoe." He pulled the boot from her grasp and handed it to Olivia.

"I'll be right back." She lunged up the stairs, returning with a pair of flat boots.

He supervised her as she changed shoes, cataloging the reaction on her face as she attempted to hide her pain. He knew the plan to walk and take the subway would have to be scrapped. After forcing her to swallow some ibuprofen, he rigged an icepack with a Ziploc bag.

She rejected the ice, standing to move toward the door, putting weight on her foot despite her white-faced strain. He hurried to support her, but she pushed her way out the front door with grim determination.

"Wait Grace." He followed quickly, shutting the door behind them.

"I'm fine. I really want to go."

He grinned. "Okay. I got that, already. But I have a plan."

"What?"

He could read the suspicion on her face. Before she could react, he scooped her, squealing, into his arms. She giggled, locking her hands behind his neck. It was all he could do not to pull her against him and kiss her senseless. His heart pounded in his chest, even though he was hardly exerting himself to carry her the half block to the main street.

He set her feet down and hailed a cab. By the time they arrived at Madison Square Gardens, she was grinning, her sprained ankle forgotten in the excitement. And the grin never left her face throughout the entire two-and-a-half-hour game, in which the Rangers scored the winning goal in the last two minutes. She was on her feet much of the time, and he was almost convinced her injury was quite minor. But when he noticed her limping as they exited, he forced her to sit and allow him to inspect her ankle. He discovered a pronounced swelling and berated himself for agreeing to take her to the game after the injury.

"I need to take you straight home—this ankle looks bad."

Her crushed expression broke his heart. "I don't want to go home yet. We haven't even had time to... to talk or anything. Not since... you know... since everything happened... And we haven't... you know... I missed you and..."

He wanted to be alone with her, too. But he didn't want to talk—he wanted to kiss her. He gave in without further protest, attempting to hide a smug expression stemming from her obvious desire for the same thing he wanted.

"What if we went to the top of the Rock? There won't be many people up there at this time of night. No, I know... Let's go to Central Park. Have you ever been on a carriage ride? I know it's kind of touristy, but since you can't walk..."

"I've lived here all my life and never taken a carriage ride in Central Park. It sounds fun."

He knelt with his back to her. "Climb on—I'll give you a piggyback ride."

Carrying her outside toward the taxi, his nerves were hotwired, firing on all circuits, from the contact of her soft form as she clung to his back. What he really wanted was to get her alone—really alone. He wanted to kiss her lips, her neck, and so much more. But he knew that could never happen. He had to be certain they never had too much privacy, so he didn't tempt his frazzled willpower.

*****

The carriage ride was as romantic as Grace had always imagined. Brad chatted about Ben's surgery and recovery as his arm slid around the back of the cushion over her shoulder, his hand rubbing lightly on her arm in a seemingly idle fashion. She didn't notice when he stopped talking. She was only aware of his hand as it slid up her arm and across her shoulder to caress her neck, sending millions of tiny sparks along millions of tiny nerve endings. He leaned in toward her lifting her chin with his fingertips, while continuing his fiery assault on the skin of her neck. Her eyes closed of their own accord, and she held her breath, waiting for the touch of his lips against hers. And then she heard something strange—a wet, plopping sound. A pungent smell accosted her nose.

"Oh, good grief! That's awful! Did the horse just..."

Brad laughed. "Are you sure that wasn't you, and you're not just blaming the poor horse?"

Her punch landed on his rock-hard bicep. "Ow!" she exclaimed, shaking her hand.

"What do you mean, 'Ow'? You're the one who hit me."

"But you deserved it. And anyway, your arm hurt my hand." She flashed him a crooked smile as she rubbed her knuckles.

He grasped her fingers and lifted the reddened knuckles to his lips. "Let me kiss it and make it feel better."

She almost swooned at the combined sight and sensation of his lips as they pressed gently against her hand, causing a warm current to flow up her arm. As if he knew the heat had traveled that direction, he began to move his lips across her hand and wrist, flipping it to kiss a slow sweep up the inside of her forearm, Gomez-style. His lips seared an icy-hot trail on her skin until she squirmed in her seat. By the time he reached her shoulder, her muscles had melted, resulting in her boneless collapse against the carriage seat.

As her head fell back in surrender to her overwhelmed senses, he accepted the opportunity as an invitation. Her breathing was short and shallow, anticipating, reveling in the feeling of his lips nibbling on her neck. But when he reached the soft hollow under her jaw, she saw bursts of light behind her eyelids, and a moan almost escaped her lips.

His low chuckle reverberated against her neck. He whispered, his breath hot against her skin. "Shhh! Not so loud."

Had her moan been audible? How embarrassing. Her face burned, and she stiffened, opening her eyes to determine if the carriage driver had overheard.

"I made a noise? Was it really loud?"

His fingers stroked along the line of her jaw, causing her eyes to flutter closed. "Don't worry—he's not paying any attention." His voice was soothing and hypnotic, as were his fingers. She couldn't move, even if she'd had the desire. He returned his lips to her skin, back to the moan-making spot on her neck, and she felt goose bumps rising on her leg. Who knew there was a connection between those nerves?

As he moved his mouth under her chin and over the ridge of her jaw, closer and closer to her lips, she found herself holding her breath until she felt light-headed. Impatient with his teasing, she found the strength to stretch her hands behind his neck and pull his mouth against hers. Still, he held back, warring against her, only affording her the lightest brush of his lips.

"Brad! Please!" The words slipped out before she realized she'd spoken.

"Please what?" His eyelids closed halfway, and he flashed an impish grin.

Her furious glare didn't seem to faze him. He maintained his resistance, grazing his lips over her mouth, sending lightning bolts through her system with each slight contact. Her heart was thundering in her ears, drowning out the sounds of the city.

"Please... Please kiss me."

"Hmmm... I'm not sure that's a good idea." He released her and leaned away, sitting back and crossing his leg, while tapping his finger against the side of his head. She stared at him, dazed and confused.

"What do you mean? Of course it's a good idea. You don't want to kiss me?"

"Oh, I want to. Believe me, I want to. But I'm not certain I should."

"Why not?"

"Because it seems to me every time I kiss you, you end up running away from me."

She sputtered, "That's not true."

"Isn't it?" He crossed his arms.

Maybe it was true, but she didn't have to admit it. "So you're never going to kiss me again?"

"As much as I hate to do this, I think we need to talk first. I want to be certain we've addressed all your concerns up front, because I can't handle having you leave me again."

"But I don't have any concerns now."

In the glow of the lamplight she could see one of his eyebrows shoot up. "Really? If nothing bothers you, then talking about us shouldn't be a problem."

"Look, can't we just kiss and enjoy each other's company the way we used to? The way we did before any of this ever happened?"

"No, something has to change. We have to be different than your other relationships or you'll eventually discard me like you did all the other guys."

Her breaths came faster, and she felt her vision narrowing. He wanted to talk about the future. He wanted a commitment, and she wasn't ready.

"Grace?" He was peering into her face, his brows knit with concern. His voice sounded far away. "Grace? What's wrong, baby?"

"I can't... I can't..."

"Grace!" He held her in his arms, leaning her back across his lap, plying her face with kisses. "Don't you pass out on me!"

He planted a forceful kiss on her lips, and the world that had faded came plummeting back. Her eyes opened wide, and her heart thudded in her chest. He deepened the kiss, and shock waves shot throughout her system. She didn't ever remember feeling this in all the times he'd kissed her before. Her nerve endings were raw. She was painfully aware of every place his body contacted hers, even through her thick sweater. He played her senses like an instrument; his talented mouth made her entire being hum with pleasure.

She tried to maintain contact as he withdrew his lips. But he ended the kiss and sat up straight with a pained expression. "I shouldn't have done that. We still need to talk."

She attempted to snuggle against his chest. "But I liked it. Why do we have to talk and spoil everything?"

He responded by propping her back into a sitting position beside him. "I have to know you won't make another unilateral decision to end our relationship."

"But I'm not ready to make a commitment." Her squeaky voice sounded almost as distressed as she felt inside.

"I'm not asking for a commitment. All I'm asking is you promise to talk to me."

"About what?"

"About everything. I want to know what you're thinking. I want to know what you're worried about. I want to know what you like and dislike. And if you think you've discovered a reason we shouldn't be together, I want you to tell me. Don't you think that's fair?"

She didn't respond. Her mind was racing as she considered his demand.

"What are you thinking? What's making you hesitate?"

"It's the what-ifs. What if you ask for more? What if I change my mind? What if you change your mind? What if you meet someone prettier and smarter? What if—"

"Whoa!" he chuckled. "How do you not have a massive headache? Is there always that much stuff going on in your head? Do you worry all the time?"

"It's not funny. Don't you see all the things that could go wrong? Someone is bound to get hurt."

"But I'm willing to take the risk. Anyway, it couldn't hurt any worse than it did when you broke up with me. I couldn't sleep. I wasn't hungry. I was awful to my friends."

"You're right. I was pretty miserable, too. Even my sisters didn't like me."

"And I'm not going to meet someone prettier and smarter."

"But Dr. Dickson—"

"Kara isn't prettier or smarter than you, Grace. I promise I was never attracted to her."

She bit her lips to hide the pleased smile that sprang to her face at his words. Even though she wasn't really jealous of Kara, she couldn't help feeling insecure in comparison to the tall, striking doctor. She could tell by the fervor of his answer he meant what he said. Still, she was nervous about the idea of a future commitment. "But I can't forget you said the M-word, and I'm not ready for that."

His moan was so loud that the carriage driver looked back over his shoulder. "Look Grace, I'm sorry. The M-word slipped out of my mouth, but I won't say it again. In fact, when you decide you're ready to discuss it, you'll have to bring it up yourself."

"But I'm planning to get my master's in education, and that'll take a couple of years."

"I promise not to push you, but I don't promise not to tempt you." One corner of his mouth twitched into a crooked grin, and he lifted her hand, turning it over to kiss her wrist, sending tremors down her spine.

"But that's another thing. I can't control myself with you. I don't think I can stop you when I need to." Even as she spoke the words, she made no effort to withdraw her hand from his ministrations.

"I know." He moved his lips a bit further up the soft skin of her arm.

"But I don't want to go too far. I mean, I want to, but I don't want to—"

"I know, but I can stop." He kissed a little higher up.

"But I'm the girl—I'm supposed to be the one who puts the brakes on."

"Says who?" He lifted his head away, frowning.

"Everybody knows that's the girl's job, and I've always done it before."

"But that was before you met a man who drove you wild beyond the extent of your willpower." His smug expression was too much for her.

"Exactly! And you're proud of yourself for it. But when we slip and go past the line, I'll be devastated."

"We won't slip—I'll be responsible. Not that it's easy for me, but I can handle it. For one thing, I'll make sure we don't have too much privacy. After all, you test my willpower, too."

"But how do I know I can trust you?"

His smile dissolved, and his eyes narrowed. "I would hope I proved myself to you when you came on to me in the apartment with that low-cut blouse and short skirt."

She felt a rush of blood to her face and neck—she'd hoped he'd forgotten the details of that particular escapade. She turned her face away.

"I'm sorry, Brad. I really am."

His hands gripped her shoulders, pulling her into his arms. "No, I'm sorry I mentioned it. Look, I'm prepared to prove myself to you every day."

He rubbed his hands on her back, and she automatically melted in his tender embrace. She wrapped her hands around him, snuggling in his warmth. It felt so right—like she belonged there.

"Eh-hem!" The carriage driver cleared his throat in a loud voice. "We're back."

Grace blushed, knowing he'd caught them in a hug. How had she managed to forget his presence?

Brad pulled some money out of his pocket, and handed it to the man, who smiled and tipped his hat. Then he climbed down and turned his back to Grace.

"Hop on—your chariot awaits."

She crawled onto his back, and wrapped her arms around his neck, trying not to choke him. "Hey, where are we going?"

He carried her with ease up the path back into Central Park. "I'm not ready to go home. We haven't finished talking yet."

"But I don't want to talk anymore."

"I promise to make it worth your while." His voice carried a lilt of amusement.

"How?"

"Well, after I've kissed you enough to make up for the months we lost… No, that would take all night. After I've kissed you enough to make up for one of the weeks we lost together, I'll take you for dessert at Ellen's Stardust Diner."

"Can I get a burger and a chocolate shake?"

She felt his laugh rumble in his back. "Sure. But I don't know how you stay so little with that appetite."

She laid her head against him, relishing the feel of his warm muscles flexing, until he stopped at a secluded park bench.

"I thought we'd pretty much covered all the topics. What else are you going to make me talk about?" She knew she sounded petulant, but she couldn't help it.

"I want to know the inside rules."

"What inside rules?"

"The ones that if I break them, you'll ditch me. For instance, now I know I'm not supposed to mention marriage unless I'm talking about someone else's marriage, like Spencer and Emily. What else?"

"There aren't any rules."

"Sure there are—you and your sisters know them. I bet I could guess one or two of them. Like, I bet if I ever hit you, you'd ditch me, and your brother would kill me."

"Well, that's obvious."

"Right, so I want to know the less obvious ones, like the one about the M-word. What about the L-word? Am I still supposed to avoid that one?"

"I don't know. I've told everyone else that I... that I... you know... I *live* you, but I'm scared to say it to you."

"Then you don't have to say it until you're ready."

The tight feeling in her chest eased a bit. Maybe talking wasn't so bad.

"And just so we're totally clear, do you really want to move out of New York City or not?"

"I only wanted you to move because I thought you were working yourself to death. I still think we might need to move some day, and I'd be perfectly willing to go."

He shook his head. "I can't tell you everything that's going on, but suffice it to say I'm happy where I am. But explain this to me. How is it you can worry about our future together and where we might live, but you can't talk about the possibility we might *have* a future together?"

"Because those are two totally different things, of course. And by the way, I can see you rolling your eyes around, even though it's dark. Didn't your mother ever tell you they might get stuck up there?"

"But you'd be willing to move away from your family so we could be together if it was best for me and my career?"

She firmed her lips and nodded once. "I absolutely would."

"And if we moved away from here together, would we be... uhmm... the M-word?"

Grace felt a rock drop into her stomach. "I don't want to talk about it."

Brad stared at her with his mouth open. "Really? So we can talk about moving away together, but we can't talk about getting hitched?"

"Maybe we could say *hitched*, if we were talking about some theoretical occurrence in the far, far future."

"You know you're crazy, right?"

"It's possible. After all, you're crazy, and I *live* you."

Before she realized what was happening she was high up in the air, squealing, as he held her by the waist, twirling in circles. He began to yell. "I'm crazy! And I'm in love with you! Grace Marshall! I *love* you! Hey everybody! I love this girl!" His shouts attracted the attention of a nearby group of young people who began to whistle, whoop, and applaud. He stopped spinning and wrapped his arms around her, allowing her to slide down against him until their faces were level.

"Grace Marshall—you crazy girl. I *love* you. And I'm going to kiss you over and over again. And I'm not going to stop until you tell me you love me back."

When his lips met hers, the world exploded in her head. She was aware of nothing but the man who held her in his arms... the man who held her heart in his hands.

And he kept his word.

From the Author

Thanks for reading *Best Foot Forward*. If you enjoyed this escape from reality, I hope you will take a moment to leave a review. If you do, I will love you forever. I might even name my first child after you. (Although she might be angry when we have to do the whole name-change thing at the age of twenty-seven.)

Best Foot Forward has been through several professional edits for content and format. However, we are not infallible. You might catch a spelling error or other mistake and, if you do, I would really appreciate it if you let me know. You can contact me at tamiedearenauthor@gmail.com.

Sign up for new release announcements and monthly gift card giveaways at *http://TamieDearen.com/Newsletters*

Follow on Facebook: Tamie Dearen Author

Follow on Twitter: @TamieDearen

Made in the USA
Columbia, SC
21 December 2017